HOT STORM

Hostile Operations Team - Strike Team 2

LYNN RAYE HARRIS

The Hostile Operations Team® and Lynn Raye Harris® are
trademarks of H.O.T. Publishing, LLC.

Printed in the United States of America

First Printing, 2021

For rights inquires, visit www.LynnRayeHarris.com

HOT Storm
Copyright © 2021 by Lynn Raye Harris
Cover Design Copyright © 2021 Croco Designs

ISBN: 978-1-941002-66-7

Prologue

THE FIRST THING MALCOLM McCOY THOUGHT WHEN
the bullet hit was that he'd had better days. The
second was that if he had to die, at least he was
protecting his teammate. Bonus points for saving his
teammate's woman from grief since she wouldn't have
to be devastated when a chaplain showed up at her
door to tell her the man she loved was dead.

No, the chaplain would show up at Mal's parents'
house in Galveston instead. It was his mom who'd be
devastated at the news of his death in a war zone, not
Haylee. His dad too, but Dad would hold it together
while Mom sobbed.

"Mal, you fucking idiot," Dean "Wolf" Garner
growled in his ear. "What'd you go and do that for?"

Cade "Saint" Rodgers was there too, his face a
blur as he bent over Mal's legs and worked to stop the
bleeding.

"Couldn't... let... you... get hit. Promised

Haylee," Mal forced out between clenched teeth. Motherfucker but his leg hurt.

"It would have hit the vest, you stupid fuck," Wolf said roughly. "You've got no business promising my fiancée anything. She knows what we do is dangerous."

"Couldn't. Be. Sure." Mal panted as the pain expanded in a hot ripple through his body. "About… the vest… I mean." He tried to get a look at his leg, but Wolf pushed him down again. Around them, the gunfire continued. The rest of the team was pressing on, pushing the enemy back while Saint and Wolf took care of him.

It'd be a hell of a thing to die out here in the high Afghan mountains after as many missions as he'd been on to precisely this place. Afghanistan's Hindu Kush was a thing of beauty. Too bad tourists couldn't have a look anytime soon.

"I was fine," Wolf said. "Holding my own. Until you broke cover and launched yourself at me."

"Take it easy," Saint said. "You can argue about this later when we're back at camp and blowing off steam with a few beers."

"How bad?" Mal gritted out.

"Missed the artery, but you're gonna need some reconstructive surgery, I imagine. Tore through ligaments and probably nicked the bone. You're a lucky fucker, Mal."

Mal tried to grin. "Don't feel lucky."

Cade injected him with pain killers. "This'll help.

Wolf, call back to HQ and get us some air support and a ride. It's time to get out of here. I think we've made our point."

The fighting had raged for three days, but Strike Team 2 had steadily driven this particular pocket of tangos higher into the mountains while picking off several of their fighters. The end of the mission had been near—and then that one guy split off from the rest and circled around. He'd been aiming at Wolf when Mal saw him and drew his attention. It'd been enough to save Wolf's ass, no matter what the grumpy bastard thought.

"Copy," Wolf said. "One air taxi coming right up."

Mal lay back on the dirt and stared up at the sky. It was turning pink and purple with the fading sunlight. If not for the gunfire, the place would actually be peaceful. He didn't want to see Haylee Jamison's face against that backdrop but he couldn't help it. He saw her everywhere. The harder he tried not to look, the worse it got.

They'd rescued Haylee from a Guatemalan jungle a few months ago, and though Mal had thought she was beautiful and intriguing then, it'd been his teammate who'd captured her attention. Haylee had eyes for no one but Wolf from the very start.

And good for Wolf, dammit. He deserved Haylee. They deserved each other. And Mal, well, he was on the outside. Where he intended to stay. Nobody said a man couldn't fall in love with another man's woman.

You could, but you damned sure couldn't do anything about it. And when a terrorist had a bead on your buddy, you didn't think about whether or not his woman could be yours if the bullet found a home. You definitely didn't think that.

You did everything you could to be the one who took that bullet instead.

He'd taken the bullet meant for Wolf. But that still didn't ease the guilt he felt every waking minute of his life. Nothing could. Nothing except a bullet whose aim was true.

Chapter One

Scarlett Reed swiped butter on her toast and poured a cup of coffee. It was just before seven but she didn't need to be to work until eight. Fortunately, she lived close to the private hospital where she worked as a physical therapist assistant.

"Hey."

Scarlett looked up as her roommate entered the kitchen. Justine Ziskowski was a nurse at the facility. She was also Scarlett's savior. When Scarlett had arrived in town a couple of months ago and needed a place to live, Justine had come through despite not really knowing anything about her.

"Morning," Scarlett said. "I hope I didn't wake you."

Justine worked the night shift at the hospital. She was usually home by five and in bed by six. "No," Justine said, grabbing a cup and pouring coffee. "I was up. Moving to day shift next week, so staying up a little longer to try and shift my sleep cycle."

"Really? That's great!"

Justine shrugged as she wrapped both hands around the mug and gave a slight frown. "Yeah, pretty great."

Scarlett didn't like the nagging feeling taking up residence in her belly. Then again, she was always jumpy these days. She had reason to be. "Is something wrong? You don't sound happy about it."

Justine reached for her hand and wrapped her fingers around Scarlett's. Scarlett didn't resist even though the contact still shocked her sometimes. But Justine was one of those warm, effusive people who acted as if they'd known you for years instead of only months. "I don't know how to say this, so I'll just say it. Neil asked me to marry him."

Scarlett blinked. Then she laughed and threw her arms around the other woman in a spontaneous hug. "Congratulations! This is perfect!"

Justine laughed too. "I know, right? We've only been dating forever, and I thought he was determined to stay single. I'm still in shock."

"He realized what's important."

Neil was a doctor at the hospital, and an ambitious one at that. But sometimes people realized what was truly important in their lives. It'd been known to happen. Not in Scarlett's life, because she couldn't do anything normally, but in other people's.

"I think so." She sighed, and Scarlett's belly twisted again. "I can't keep this place. I'm going to sell it."

Scarlett's joy popped like a balloon. "Oh."

"I'm so sorry, hon. I know you haven't been here long, but it won't be for a while yet. I just wanted you to know so you could start looking. Unless you want to buy it?"

Scarlett shook her head sadly. "I'm afraid I won't qualify for a loan just yet. It's too soon after the bankruptcy. But thank you for asking."

"Aw, sweetie. I'm so sorry you had to go through that. It won't stay on your record forever, though. My mom and dad bankrupted when I was a kid, and they have better credit than anybody these days."

Scarlett forced a smile. "I know it'll get better. Thank you for saying so."

Her stomach had taken up residence in her toes. She hadn't gone through a bankruptcy, but it was easier to say that than the truth. When she'd left Florida, a new identity was the quickest way to leave the past behind. But new identities were sorely lacking in credit and job histories. If not for Dr. Jessica Saunders, Scarlett wouldn't even have a job in a hospital now. But Dr. Saunders had gone above and beyond to help Scarlett out when she'd needed to leave, and she would always be grateful.

"I'm not kicking you out or anything," Justine said. "There's a wedding to plan, and I've got to get some things done around here before I put it on the market. It'll be a month or so before I can even have a realtor out," she mused.

"Plenty of time," Scarlett said cheerfully, though she didn't feel cheerful at all. In this market, Justine's house would go fast. Whether or not she got anything done first.

Scarlett felt wrung out. Apprehensive. Almost as if there was someone watching her and pulling strings to upend her life yet again. Those last few months in Florida had been hard. She hadn't known what was going on, or why she'd had such a run of bad luck. She'd hadn't known why her car got flat tires repeatedly, why her mail went missing, why her friends stopped asking her to go out with them, or why things kept going missing in her house. She'd thought she was crazy at one point.

But she hadn't been. It was *him*. The man who'd been stalking her, obsessing over her. Pretending to be a normal guy when he was anything but. It had taken her so long to see the signs. So damned long.

The only person who'd believed her was Dr. Saunders. Even when Joshua came to her work and threatened to make her disappear if she persisted in breaking off their relationship, nobody else had believed her. Josh was too good, too smooth. He knew how to play the game, and he played it well. As an Air Force special operator, he'd been trained to do so.

Scarlett downed her coffee and ate her toast,

though it sat like a knot inside her. Justine chattered about the wedding and possible honeymoon destinations until Scarlett had to leave for work.

"Have a good day," Justine said. "And don't worry about finding a new place. I'll help you, and I know that Neil will too. It'll all work out."

Scarlett smiled, but she didn't feel it inside. "I know you will. I'll be fine. But I'm going to miss you, that's all."

Justine gave her arm a squeeze. "I'm not going anywhere, hon. We'll still see each other at work, plus you are of course coming to the wedding! You have to be a bridesmaid."

Scarlett swallowed the lump in her throat. She knew Justine meant it. She was just that kind of person. Everyone she met was a friend. "I'd be honored. Really."

After saying goodbye to Justine, Scarlett picked up her purse and gym bag and went to her car. It was an old Kia Sportage that she'd gotten cheap, but it was reliable. She'd had a new car in Florida, a too-expensive European import that she'd been so proud to buy, even if the payments had been astronomical. She'd loved that car. The last time she'd seen it, it'd been submerged in a lake and she'd been shivering on the bank, wrapped in a blanket as police lights painted the darkness in neon blue.

Scarlett shivered as she put the Kia in reverse. That part of her life was over. Josh didn't know where she was, and he wasn't going to find out. She'd made sure of that. But sometimes, like now, she felt a chill skate over her spine—and she feared that no matter how far she ran, it would never be enough.

Chapter Two

MAL WAS GRUMPY. NO DOUBT ABOUT IT. HE SNAPPED at the nurse, then apologized for the outburst. He complained about the food, though there was nothing wrong with it. And when Wolf and Haylee showed up to visit, he wanted to pull the covers over his head until they went away.

He didn't, of course.

Haylee was beautiful, as always. Her dark hair was pulled into a knot at the base of her neck today, and she wore a cream linen suit that set off the golden tones of her skin to perfection. Wolf gazed at her with lovestruck eyes. Mal felt his scowl deepen. Not because of Wolf, but because he didn't want to give anything away by looking at her in the same way.

Why in the fuck did he have to fall for a woman he couldn't have? A woman who belonged to his buddy? Lusting after her was a betrayal.

But he couldn't stop himself.

His heart tapped hard in his chest and his ears pounded with the blood that beat there as he worked to keep his expression neutral. No lovestruck eyes.

No. Lovestruck. Eyes.

Haylee reached for his hand, and his entire body melted as her warmth flowed into him.

"I can't believe you did that, Mal," she said. "But thank you for trying to protect Dean for me."

Wolf groaned. "Haylee. Baby. I was wearing body armor. I'd have been fine."

Mal had been wearing armor too, but he didn't point that out. Didn't matter when bullets hit extremities.

Haylee's hand stayed wrapped around his. He tried to concentrate on the feel of her skin, the softness of it. She threw a look at her fiancé. "Maybe so, but Mal didn't wait to find out, did he? I'm grateful he cared enough to try."

Wolf sighed. "I am too. But now I owe him."

"You don't owe me," Mal croaked out. Haylee squeezed his hand, and he thought he might die of delight. If he didn't die of embarrassment first. He was lying in a hospital bed, bandages on his leg, and he probably looked like three-day old shit.

"We owe you dinner at least," Haylee said. "As soon as you feel better."

"Okay," he said awkwardly. Why couldn't he sort himself out when Haylee was around? At least it'd be nice to sound cool and not like a blithering fool when she was near.

"When are they letting you out of here?" Wolf asked.

"Not sure. They're moving me to the rehab facility today. I've got to start PT." If he were anyone besides a HOT operator, he'd have been sent home yesterday. But he was what he was, and Riverstone was here to take care of him as if he were the president of the United States. He'd spend time at the rehab facility, then once he could get around on his own, he'd be released. He'd have to return for regular physical therapy, but at least he'd be in his own house.

He couldn't wait for that.

"How long will you be on leave?" Haylee asked in that sweet voice that haunted his dreams.

"Not sure. A few weeks convalescence. I'll be back at work as soon as I can though."

Wolf nodded. "You'll be at a desk for a while. Probably ops center."

Mal hated the idea of sitting at a desk while his team went on missions, but it could always be worse. He could be dead. If he was dead, he wouldn't get to enjoy Haylee's hand on his.

The door opened and a nurse walked in. Mal nearly groaned when Haylee pulled her hand away. She placed it in Wolf's. Mal was green with envy. He also despised himself for it.

"Hi. I'm sorry to interrupt, but I wanted to introduce myself. I'm Scarlett. I'll be working with you on your PT."

"We should go," Haylee said softly.

Mal wanted to protest, but Wolf was already standing up. "Yeah, we'll get out of your hair for now."

Haylee leaned down and pressed a kiss to his cheek. Mal closed his eyes and breathed in her scent. Vanilla and something flowery. Damn.

"Don't overdo it, Mal," she said. "We'll come back and visit again."

"I won't," he said gruffly.

Once they were gone, Mal closed his eyes tight. It wasn't until he heard movement that he realized someone was still there. *Scarlett.*

He opened his eyes. Scarlett was standing over him now, her long blonde hair held back in a neat ponytail. She had blue eyes and pale skin. She was tall, about five eight or so, and slender. Too slender in his opinion. Haylee was curves and lushness. This woman was a stick in comparison. Not that he cared.

"Are you in pain? I can check and see if it's time for another dose of meds."

"No. I'm fine."

Scarlett frowned. "Okay. You don't look fine though. It's best to stay ahead of the pain, especially as we begin therapy. I'll be pushing you to use your leg again, and your muscles are going to protest."

"I'm fine. It's not pain."

She shrugged. "All right." She put her hand on his leg, checking the bandages. Her touch was soft and cool. Not burning like Haylee's hand had been. But it was soothing somehow. "I'll be removing this bandage when we start. You'll be able to keep it uncovered, but no getting it wet until the staples come out."

"Makes it hard to shower."

"We can improvise something for you. Plastic wrap, or a plastic bag taped around the leg. You're not going to be able to get up or down on your own for a couple of days, so you'll need help in the shower. But we can get it done."

Great, now he had to have someone help him shower. Better than living in his own stink though.

"When am I moving to rehab?"

"Sometime this afternoon. We'll start your therapy right away."

Mal blinked. "Really? I can't even get up and down on my own and I have to start PT?"

Scarlett nodded. "I know it seems crazy, but the doctor likes you to get those muscles moving as soon as possible. All they'll do is grow weaker if we don't work them. Don't worry, we'll start easy enough."

"I don't need easy," he growled. "I'm a warrior. I've endured worse."

She arched an eyebrow. "It's not about your endurance. It's about what your muscles and ligaments can handle. You just had surgery to repair shattered tissue and tendons. There are screws in your body, and healing takes time. Therapy takes time too. This isn't a quick fix situation, Mr. McCoy."

He jolted at her use of mister instead of sergeant, but there was no rank on his file in this place. There wouldn't be. "Call me Mal."

"Okay, Mal. But you get my point, right? Slow and steady wins the race. We'll increase the load as therapy progresses."

He could feel the scowl on his face. "Whatever you say, ma'am."

Her eyebrow stayed arched. "Oooh, way to patronize me."

Mal snorted a laugh. He didn't want to react, but he couldn't help it. Not a single nurse or doctor had clapped back at him the way Scarlett just had. He'd been grumpy since he'd awakened in the hospital, and he'd apologized for it when it was particularly bad, but nobody ever sassed him back. They just kept doing their jobs as if he wasn't even there. Well, okay, they knew he was there, but they didn't react to his temper.

Until now. He took another good look at her. She was pretty in a girl-next-door way, but not drop-dead gorgeous. And sassy. He liked sassy. Kept things interesting.

"Sorry," he said. "I'm kind of annoyed with the whole thing, to be honest. One minute I was doing my job and the next I was on the ground, hurting like a motherfucker—sorry. Didn't mean to swear."

She shrugged. "I don't mind. I expect you to swear at me quite a lot over the coming days, truth be told. I said we'd start easy, and we will, but I intend to push you to your limits too. You won't like me much some days."

"You can't be as tough as the instructors I had when I decided to try out for Special Ops."

He thought she stiffened a little.

"I guess we'll see, won't we?" She said it with a smile, but he had a weird feeling that she'd flipped a switch inside. Like what he'd gotten so far wasn't what he'd get from now on. She'd be calmly professional. No more clapping back at him when he irritated her.

"I guess so."

She took a step backward. "I need to get going. I'll see you in rehab later today."

"Can't wait," he deadpanned.

After she was gone, he lay back and stared up at the ceiling, trying to remember every single moment of Haylee's hand on his. But he kept mixing it up with Scarlett's hand on his leg.

The pain meds eventually kicked in and he drifted off to sleep. He hoped he'd dream of something pleasant. Instead, he dreamt of being shot—only this time it was in the heart.

Chapter Three

SCARLETT WAS WAITING WHEN MAL ENTERED THE
room on crutches. He was a big man, tall and
muscled, but not overly huge. He was, as he'd said, a
warrior. She'd been fine with that—*was* fine with that
—right up until the minute he'd said he'd tried out for
Special Ops. Memories of Josh had come flooding
back then. He'd bragged to her about his training.
About how many ways he knew to kill a person. She
hadn't taken it as a threat back then, when she'd been
starting his physical therapy, but she knew differently
now.

So, *so* differently.

She'd been rattled at the reminder of Josh and
she'd had to get out of Mal's room. Once she could
breathe again, she'd told herself how stupid she was
being. She'd worked with a lot of military personnel,
and only one of them had ever been a psychopath.
Besides, though Mal was going to be the first military

man she'd worked with since arriving at Riverstone, he wasn't going to be the last. She had to buck up and get used to it.

Mal was angry and in pain, but that didn't make him a psychopath. Not that she intended to get close enough to find out. That'd been her mistake with Josh. She'd let him charm her, and she'd finally agreed to go out with him. Big mistake.

She wasn't making that mistake ever again. Maybe she should have asked Dr. Saunders to help her find a position in a facility that wasn't affiliated with the military in any way, but the truth was she liked working with veterans and active-duty personnel. She felt like she was helping do her part in a small way. Making sure she honored her mom's sacrifice every day. She'd only been a kid when her mom deployed to Iraq. And when she hasn't come home again, well, Scarlett and her dad had fallen apart. Dad had done the best he could and they'd managed to figure it out, though he was gone now too. Plowed his damned motorcycle into an embankment taking a curve too fast when Scarlett was still in college.

"Let me help you onto this chair," Scarlett said briskly, shoving away memories of her parents and thoughts of her psycho stalker.

"I can do it," Mal grumbled, maneuvering himself to hover over the chair. He still had the crutches under his arms and he couldn't quite figure out how to lower himself. Mostly because the muscles in his quad were still asleep and he wasn't going to have any control over them yet. The nerve block he'd been given was a good one, that's for sure. He was still feeling the remnants of it two days after surgery.

Scarlett stood with arms crossed and waited for reality to settle in. Mal only frowned harder as he shifted his weight to the right leg. Then he dropped the crutches and grasped the chair arms with strong hands. Scarlett's heart lodged in her throat the second he dropped the crutches, but he didn't have any trouble holding himself up on those arms.

Arms that strained and popped with hard muscle. He had a tattoo on one. An eagle in black and white that held a flag. There were other parts to it as well, but that was what she could see beneath the hem of his sleeve.

Slowly, he lowered himself onto the chair. Scarlett helped move his leg until it was in front of him, then stood back with hands on hips as he settled in and grinned up at her.

He had a disarming grin. A dimple in one cheek made him seem almost boyish, though he was anything but a boy.

"Told you," he said smugly.

"Yeah, yeah, you told me. But I had to help move your leg."

"Not for long if I've got anything to say about it."

"You probably do," she said with a smile. "The patient's willingness to do the work goes a long way in recovery. But don't push it too hard or you'll find yourself three steps backwards from where you started, okay?"

"Pushing hard is what I do. Can't survive otherwise."

"I know, but this isn't battle, okay? Trust me. Do what I tell you and you'll be back on your feet in no time."

"You like being bossy, don't you?"

He said it with a grin, so she didn't take offense. "It's one of the perks of the job." She reached for the stretchy cloth bandage wrapped around his thigh and knee. "I'm going to take this off now. Let's see what's going on under there."

She knew what was going on. He'd taken a bullet through his left thigh, right above the knee, and it'd damaged tendons on its way through. He also had a bone injury, though fortunately not a bad one. Still, bones were painful when they were hacked into.

"Guess I won't be dancing at Buddy's next week," he said when she finished unwrapping the leg. A long incision ran down the front of his thigh. He stared at it with a frown.

"No, probably not," she said, feeling badly for him. He looked a bit stunned at the extent of the damage, and then he looked determined.

"I'm not letting this stop me," he said with a hard note in his voice.

"I hope you let it stop you from dancing next week," she said lightly, trying to bring some humor into the situation. "You don't want to look like a dork on the dance floor, right?"

His eyes met hers. Her heart skipped a tiny beat. *What the hell?*

"Dork? What are you, six?" He didn't say it angrily though. That was good.

"What would you call it then?"

"Maybe I'd look like that *Dancing with the Stars* guy. Derek Hough, right? You ever think of that?"

Scarlett couldn't help but snort a laugh. "Derek Hough? Not even with a perfectly healthy leg, mister."

He shook his head as if sorely disappointed in her. "Man, not even five minutes in your company, and you're dissing me hardcore. I need a new therapist. Stat."

Scarlett wrapped up the bandage and tossed it onto a counter. "Sorry, but you're stuck with me. We drew straws over who had to take you. I lost."

His eyes widened.

"Kidding, Mal. We don't draw straws and I'm thrilled to work with you. Why don't you show me how far you can lift your leg."

She could see him concentrating. The leg didn't move. He kept trying, then huffed out a breath and glared at nothing in particular. "That's not what I expected."

"I know, but we need a benchmark. You'll get there, I promise." She gripped his leg carefully. "Now let's start with some simple mobility exercises. After that, we'll do ice and stim—that's like a tens unit where I'll apply electrical stimulation to the muscles. I'll have you back to your room in no time so you can watch *Dancing with the Stars* on repeat all day."

He groaned. "Geez, Scarlett. Way to hit a guy when he's down."

She helped him extend the leg as much as possible, then helped him lower it again. "I get the feeling nothing keeps you down for long."

"Not if I can help it."

"You'll be pleased to know you're in control on this one, then. You've had damage, and the muscles will take time to heal, but there's no reason you can't expect a full recovery."

He grimaced as she moved his leg. "I'm not going to be real patient with this process. Just thought you should know."

"Trust me, I know. I've been doing this long enough."

He watched her manipulate his leg. "How long?"

"I graduated with my PTA degree six years ago, and I've been working in the field since." She felt that little pang of regret she always felt that she hadn't been able to go to school for longer and become a physical therapist instead of an assistant, but the work was rewarding and she enjoyed it.

"How long did that take?"

"It's a community college degree. I'm a therapy assistant, and I work under the supervision of a physical therapist to provide care."

"The PT is the guy who came to see me earlier, right?"

"Yeah, that's him. He'll work with you too, but most of the exercising and measuring will be me. He'll evaluate your progress and make changes though."

"Huh. Well, don't tell him, but I'm glad I got you instead of him."

Scarlett blinked. "Really? Why?"

"You're prettier to look at."

She could feel the heat in her cheeks. And the pounding of her heart as she thought of how things had begun with Josh. A little banter, a little flattery. She'd enjoyed the attention at first. Was this guy flirting with her too? And what was she going to do about it?

"Shit," he said a moment later. "That was inappropriate. I'm sorry."

"Um. Yeah, maybe a little. But thank you. For saying I'm pretty and for apologizing for it."

He shook his head ruefully. "I'm an idiot. I didn't mean anything by it. Believe me, I'm not trying to pick you up or anything."

"It's okay," she said, though now she was getting hung up on the fact he so vehemently said he wasn't trying to pick her up. Like maybe she was pretty, but not pretty enough?

Ugh, stop that. You don't want him to flirt. You don't want to flirt back. You don't want another special ops guy. You don't want another guy at all. Not for a long, long time.

"Believe it or not, I was raised with manners. Sometimes they fail me."

She met his gaze. Green eyes stared earnestly back at her. She wasn't getting any alarm bells from this guy, though she also didn't trust her judgement anymore. Still, he seemed sincere. And it didn't hurt her to proceed as if he was. She wasn't going to go out with him even if he did decide to try.

"Where are you from?" she asked, moving the conversation onward.

"Galveston, Texas."

"I've never been there. What's it like?"

"Flat. But the weather's beautiful and we're on the Gulf, so lots of fishing and water sports. And great food."

"Sounds nice."

"It is. My mom and dad are still there. Still live in the house I grew up in." He looked at his leg and frowned. "I need to call them."

"You haven't told them you were hurt yet?"

He shook his head. "Didn't want them to worry."

She couldn't say anything about that since it wasn't her call to make. But if she had parents still living, she felt like she'd tell them everything. Maybe, if her parents were still alive, she'd have never fallen for Josh's slick charm. She knew she couldn't really say that, but it was nice to think if she still had a daddy, he'd have been there to protect her.

"What about you?" he asked. "Where are you from?"

Scarlett's heart thumped. "Florida."

"Just Florida?" he asked when she didn't say anything else.

"Fort Walton Beach."

He nodded. "That's near Eglin Air Force Base. There's a special operations unit there."

She really needed to learn how to lie better. She should have said Miami. But what if he knew Miami like the back of his hand? No, the truth was always better. Or some of it anyway. "Have you ever been there?"

He grunted as she moved his leg. "No."

"I worked with military from that unit." She didn't usually talk about her time at the hospital in Florida to anyone, but the words had popped out before she'd realized what she was saying. Too late to call them back now.

"How'd you end up here?" he asked.

She manipulated his leg carefully, not meeting his questioning gaze. "I decided it was time for a change. Better opportunities at this hospital."

"Riverstone is pretty amazing. It's my first stay. Hopefully my last."

She stood and reached for the e-stim equipment. "Yeah, better not make a habit of this."

He snorted. "Don't intend to. Is that all you got today? We're done?"

She hooked up the leads to his leg. "Unless you'd like to sign up for the 5K we're running later this afternoon? I'm sure I can find a team spirit T-shirt for you."

"Nah, I'll pass. But thanks anyway." He grinned at her and her heart flipped. Why did he have to be so damned beautiful? Josh had been attractive, but not like this guy. This one was almost too good-looking.

Really, Scarlett? Is that even possible?

"Let me know if you change your mind."

"Pretty sure I won't."

She turned on the current and let the electricity work his muscles. "I'll come back and check on you in a few minutes."

"I'll be here," he said wryly. "Got nowhere else to go."

Chapter Four

"You've come far in a week," Scarlett said as Mal lifted his leg so she could measure the degree of movement.

He was ridiculously pleased with her praise. He'd been working hard to improve his range of motion. Doing all the exercises he was given and trying not to push it too far. He wanted to push it, but Scarlett had impressed upon him the dangers of straining the muscles too much. If he overdid it, he risked setting back his progress by weeks. Not something he wanted to do.

"I want to be able to go home," he told her. Though, oddly enough, he thought he'd miss seeing her every day. When he was home again, he'd come in for PT three times a week.

She smiled at him. She had a nice smile. It was a little cautious, but it was there. "I think that'll happen sooner rather than later. You just keep doing what I tell you."

"Yes ma'am."

She laughed. "You're learning. Quite a difference from the man who growled at me a week ago."

He lifted his leg and did the exercises she'd given him while she watched. "I'm grumpy, not stupid."

"Brawn and brains. Nice combo."

"Careful or I'll think you're flirting with me," he said, grunting as he completed the exercise. He looked up in time to see her pale. Alarm flared in his brain. "Hey, it was a joke. I'm not planning to report you for harassment or anything. Honest."

She turned away to fiddle with the big elastic bands she had him use sometimes, refolding them even though they weren't messed up. "I know you're kidding. I'm not worried."

"Hey." She didn't turn around. "Scarlett, please look at me."

She spun with a smile on her face. Another cautious one. "What? We're cool, Mal. It's fine."

"I'm not trying to upset you. It was a joke, and I guess a bad one. I know you aren't flirting with me, and I'm not flirting with you. I'm, uh, kind of hung up on someone, so you don't have to worry about me."

Her eyebrows lifted. "Really? A woman?"

He blinked. "Of course a woman. I'm not gay."

"Not that there's anything wrong with being gay," she said coolly. Testing him.

"I didn't say there was! One of my best friends from high school came out a few years ago. Shocked the hell out of me since I never had a clue, but he's still like a brother to me. I mean I don't get it or anything, but I damn sure support him."

She nodded. "Good. I'd hate for you to be the kind of asshole who thinks they have a right to tell other people how to live and who to love."

"I'm not. And how did we get to my opinion about gay people when I'm trying to tell you I'm not flirting with you?"

"We just did. So tell me about this woman."

His heart thumped. "Not much to say. She's not interested in me."

Scarlett's mouth dropped open. "You're kidding."

"I'm not. Are you mocking me?"

"No, definitely not." She scratched behind her ear. Her cheeks seemed to redden a little. "It's just that, well, you have to know you aren't unattractive. I mean some of the nurses have been…." She cleared her throat. "Well, let's just say that you attract attention. And speculation."

"It's complicated," he said. "But she's not interested and she's not going to be." He didn't add that he was in this hospital because he'd thrown himself in the line of fire to protect the man she loved. He wasn't noble or anything and he didn't deserve praise. Far from it.

"Maybe she'll change her mind. It can happen."

"It could. I don't think that'd be a good thing in this situation though."

She studied him carefully. "I'm not going to pretend to know what you mean, but I'm sorry it's that difficult for you, Mal. What I know of you, I think you're probably a really good guy and I'm sorry she isn't able to see that for whatever reason."

"She's in love with someone else." It hurt to say the words, and it rocked that core of guilt in his belly too. He hadn't ever said it aloud to anyone. Why now, why Scarlett, he didn't know. But it was a relief in a way. He'd feel the self-loathing and regret later.

"Oh my." She put her hand on his shoulder. It was small and firm. Warm today instead of cool. "I'm really, really sorry. I don't know what else to say."

"There's nothing. It is what it is, and I'm used to it."

She pulled her hand back and leaned against the counter to face him. "Is it wrong of me to hope you stop being hung up on her then?"

He grinned ruefully. "No. It's something I've wished for a while, but it doesn't seem to happen."

"Yet. There's always hope. You might meet someone even more fabulous."

"Maybe. I hope so."

Her chin jutted out stubbornly, as if she'd made a decision. "I know that must have been difficult to tell me. I'll tell you something in return. I'm not flirting with you because I had a bad experience. With a military guy like you. When I'm ready to put myself out there again, it won't be with anyone in the military."

That was information he hadn't expected. And it made the way she looked at him sometimes make sense. Like he was a barking dog on a tether and she was afraid he'd snap the lead and bite her.

"I get that," he said carefully. "How about we make a truce then? Make this easier for both of us."

"I'm listening."

"We can be ourselves with each other. No worrying about flirting, or not flirting, or what the other person means by something they said. Since I expect my PT will be of some duration, it'd be nice to make the decision to be friends now. It'll make everything better, don't you think?"

She seemed to think about it. "I can get onboard with that. But Mal, when I say I had a bad experience, it was bad. I don't trust people. That's not personal, okay, so don't take it that way."

He wondered what had happened to her, but even if he asked, he knew she wasn't going to tell him. Wasn't his business anyway. If she wanted to tell him at some point, she would. "Understood. But if we're going to be friends, I hope you know you can count on me and my buddies to have your back. If you have any trouble from your bad experience—if he bothers you at all—we'll be there."

She studied the floor for a moment. "That's nice of you to say. But you really don't know me. What if I'm the crazy one and he's just a normal guy?"

He liked how straightforward she was. How she cut through the bullshit and got to the point. Scarlett wasn't dumb, and she didn't pretend to be. "Is he a normal guy?"

"No, he really isn't. Personally I'd call him a monster, but he's very charming. And there were plenty of people who thought I was the crazy one. Just so you know."

"Consider me warned. Can you tell me what he does in the military?"

She hesitated for a long moment. "Special Forces. He went on missions in Iraq and Afghanistan, and other places he said he couldn't tell me. A lot like you, I imagine. But he's history and I don't want to talk about him anymore, okay?"

Mal didn't like the note of fear in her voice, but he put both hands up in surrender. Now wasn't the time to press her on it. "Gotcha, friend. No more discussions about our lousy luck with the opposite sex."

She grinned, and he liked the way her face changed in that moment. Scarlett was really pretty when she didn't look worried or scared. "Agreed. Now how about we take some measurements and get the stim treatment on your leg?"

———

SCARLETT WAS SITTING on the patio with a glass of iced tea and a book when Justine walked out the kitchen door and flopped into the chair beside her.

"Dang, my internal clock isn't quite used to day shift yet."

Scarlett arched an eyebrow. "Maybe a glass of wine when you get home isn't the best way to help you adjust."

Justine took a swig of white wine and arched an eyebrow in return. "Thanks, momma, but I need this after the day I had."

Scarlett laughed. "Sorry you had a rough one."

"Eh, it happens. That's why I need wine." Justine reached for the box of almond flour crackers Scarlett had taken outside to snack on. "These aren't that diet crap you like, are they?"

"What diet crap?"

Justine sniffed a cracker. "Multi-grain. With seeds and no cheddar cheese flavor anywhere to be found."

Scarlett shook her head. Justine had a thing for junk food. Scarlett liked junk too, but she tried not to eat too much of it. Besides, having the multi-grain crackers now meant she could have fries when she really wanted them. "They're good. Try one."

The other woman popped one in her mouth and chewed. "Not bad. It'd be better with some ranch flavoring though."

Scarlett laughed. "Not everything needs ranch or cheddar."

"Says you," Justine said, chewing another cracker. "Neil and I are having nothing but ranch and cheddar at the wedding."

"Even the cake?"

"Especially the cake."

The two of them laughed, and then Justine took another sip of wine. "I talked to a real estate agent today."

Scarlett's heart fell. "Oh yeah? What did he say?"

"She said this market is hot right now and I shouldn't wait too long to sell."

"Then you shouldn't."

"I feel badly about it though. You've only been here a couple of months, and when you arrived I had no notion I'd be getting married or selling this house. I thought of keeping it and renting it out, but Neil is going to sell his condo and we're going to buy a bigger house for the two of us. We have to sell to afford the down payment."

Scarlett loved that Justine cared about displacing her, but there really wasn't a choice. Scarlett was mature enough to accept that fact. "It's okay, Justine. Really. I've been asking around at work, but maybe it's time I started looking at listings."

"I'll write you a letter of recommendation if it'll help. So will Neil."

"I appreciate it." Passing a credit check to get an apartment on her own was impossible, but big complexes and management companies weren't the only game in town. A letter would help, along with a hefty deposit probably, with an individual landlord. Not that she could really afford hefty, but she could afford healthy.

"Neil's bestie from college is moving to DC. We're

going out for drinks sometime next week. Care to come?"

Scarlett's nerves prickled. "Define drinks."

Justine laughed. "Alcoholic beverages. Or not. Your choice. I'm not judging."

"I meant define it as in who will be there."

Justine took a casual drink of her wine. "Neil and me. Ricky. You. Anyone else I invite between now and then."

"And do you intend to invite anyone else, or are you trying to set me up with Ricky?"

"Would that be so bad?"

Scarlett squirmed inside. "I'm not ready for dating. I had a bad breakup before I moved here."

"All the more reason to get back on the horse." Justine grabbed her hand. "Come on, it'll be very public, and we won't call it a date or anything. Just four adults having drinks. If you don't like him, you can leave."

Scarlett wanted to say no. But Justine had been so helpful and kind since Scarlett had arrived in Maryland, and she felt guilty at the thought of refusing. It was a group setting. Drinks. She could do that much. Then she'd get the heck out of there.

"I'll go. But it's not a date, and I'm driving my own car."

"That's great! Neil will be so pleased. He thought you and Ricky might like each other." She put a finger to her lips. "But it's not a date. No dating."

"Nope."

Justine leaned in. "This isn't about the big hunky guy you've got in rehab, is it?"

Scarlett blinked. She had more than one patient in rehab that she worked with, but there was only one who fit that description. "Mal? No, we're just friends."

"Just friends. With a guy who looks like that." Justine shook her head. "*Gurrrl*. It must have been a bad breakup if you aren't going for that tasty morsel."

Mal was seriously pretty to look at, but even if she was interested, he wasn't available. Hung up on a woman who was in love with someone else. Damned shame. Not that she was telling Justine that. It'd be like airing a commercial during the Super Bowl. Everyone would know.

"I'm done with men. Hell, I might even switch to the other team and give that a go for a while," she said wryly.

Justine snorted. "Life would be easier, wouldn't it? But when you like dick, you have to put up with the rest of the man to get it."

"I'm on a dick moratorium. I can do without for a while."

"Sounds like hell," Justine said with a laugh.

Scarlett laughed too, but she didn't tell Justine there were worse hells than swearing off men for the foreseeable future. Much, much worse.

Chapter Five

EVERY DAY WAS BETTER. MAL WAS WORKING HARD AND improving quickly. He could walk without crutches now, but his leg ached when he pushed it too much. Scarlett wanted him to use a cane. He protested, but when the aching got too bad, he did what she said. He always did what she said eventually.

She was waiting for him when he hobbled into the room where they did their workouts. Lately, he'd been getting a little twinge of delight each time he saw her. He didn't know why, but maybe it was how easy they got along together. Since their talk a week ago, there'd been no more awkward moments. No fear in her eyes, no jokes gone amiss. She smiled when she saw him, and they ribbed each other good-naturedly when the occasion rose.

It was the kind of easy relationship he had with his teammates in a way, though not quite as close or intense. He'd die for those guys and they'd die for him. Fortunately, he and Scarlett weren't living in that kind of environment where life or death hung on split-second choices.

Scarlett was leaning against the counter, legs crossed at the ankles, looking at the smart phone in her hand. Her long blond hair was pulled back in a neat ponytail as always. One end hung over her shoulder, spilling hair over her breast. Her features were delicate, almost elfin. She had pale skin and long lashes, a small, upturned nose, and elegant hands that kneaded his muscles in heavenly ways.

She smiled at him, and he smiled back. "How's it going, Hopalong?" she asked.

"Ha, ha," he deadpanned, taking his seat so she could do the measurements for his range of movement. "Hopping less all the time."

"Told you that would happen."

"You did. Doc says I can head home this week if things keep going well." He hadn't expected to spend two weeks in the hospital, but that's what happened when you were a precision military machine in need of repair. They kept you close and made sure you were progressing well. HOT had too much invested in him to let him go home too soon and fuck it all up.

Scarlett nodded. "I don't see why not. You can get up and down on your own now. That's huge. Though you're going to be out of commission for a while, you can convalesce at home instead of here. I know that'll make you happier."

"It will. Though I gotta admit, I like having

someone cook every meal for me. When I go home, it's back to takeout and cooking for myself."

"You can cook?"

"My mom made me learn when she taught my sister. I protested like hell, but she didn't care. When I told her I didn't need to cook because I was going to get a wife who would do it all for me, she lost her shit. I learned to cook, sew on a button, and write thank you notes. Mom wasn't playing. My sister found the whole thing hilarious."

Scarlett laughed. He liked the sound of her laugh. Soft and tinkly. Delicate like she was.

"I think I like your mom. What's your specialty then?"

"Like most men, I prefer to grill or smoke. But I can fix anything with a recipe. It's just reading and paying attention."

"I don't cook," Scarlett said. "Never learned."

Mal blinked. "Really?"

She nodded. "My mom was a nurse, and my dad was a mechanic. They worked long hours, so they brought home a lot of takeout—or one of them threw something together when they had time. I don't think either of them thought to teach me, and I never asked."

He noticed she said *was* in reference to her parents, but he didn't ask her about it. He went with something less personal. "Do you want to learn now?"

"I don't know. I mean I'm good with microwaving things, and there's a lot of stuff you can eat that doesn't need cooking. I eat cheese and crackers for dinner a lot of times. I can make toast, so that's an easy breakfast. I get by."

"If you can read, you can cook. I could show you sometime if you want."

Where had that come from? Mal couldn't quite believe the words had come from his mouth. Scarlett tilted her head from side to side as if she were thinking about it.

"Maybe. But first I have to find a new place to live, so I think that's going to be taking up my time for a while."

"What's wrong with where you live now?"

Scarlett grabbed one of the stretchy bands and handed it to him. He knew what to do so he stood and looped it around his foot.

"I'm rooming with one of the nurses here and she's selling the house to get married. I can't afford to buy it, so I have to move."

"Where are you looking?"

Her gaze dropped. "Close to work if possible. I'm trying to find a small apartment by myself or a house to share with someone, but so far there's nothing."

He didn't ask why she didn't go to one of the bigger complexes and rent. There were always apartments available, but he didn't know her financial situation. Maybe she couldn't afford to rent in a big complex. Maybe she needed a roommate.

Or maybe she just needed something different.

"I have a garage apartment at my place," he said.

This time he wasn't surprised by the words coming out of his mouth. He knew enough about Scarlett to know he wouldn't mind her renting the space over his garage. "It's in need of some cleaning and repair, but the building is sound and the space is safe. I was planning to rent it out after I repainted and cleaned, but it's good to go if you don't mind a studio setup."

Scarlett's expression was one of surprise. And maybe hope. "Are you serious?"

"C'mon, Scar, do you really think I'd make up a garage apartment just to tease you?"

She flushed. "No, of course not. But I've been thinking it was impossible to find what I wanted, and here you are, offering up a place that sounds perfect. I'm kind of astounded."

"If you think an old studio over a garage sounds perfect, then you might need to up your standards."

"Nah, my standards are fine. But are you sure you want to rent it out?"

"Very sure. When my organization moved here, I wanted a place of my own instead of sharing with friends. I bought an old farmhouse on a couple of acres. It's not the most modern space in the world, but it gives me stuff to do when I'm not working."

She looked apprehensive. "I don't know. I mean we don't really know each other…"

"No, not really. But we've gotten along well for the past couple of weeks, right? And I can get my teammates to vouch for me if you're worried I'm going to turn into a jerk or something."

"Are you insulted that the possibility has occurred to me?"

Was he? No. Whatever she'd been through, it'd obviously been bad if it'd made her so wary of men. But it was also safe to be wary as a woman. "Nope. I have a sister, remember? I realize that men don't have to be as cautious as women, and that we don't think about things like holding our keys as weapons when we walk to our cars in deserted parking lots. It's a different world for women. I'd never be insulted over your caution."

"Wow."

"Wow?"

"I don't think a man has ever said that much to me about women's everyday fears."

"A lot of men don't stop to think about it." He hesitated, thinking about what to say. But he needed her to know he understood. He sensed it was important to her. "My sister was attacked a few years ago. She wasn't raped because someone happened onto them before the guy got that far, but it was close. I've never forgotten her fear or how long it took her to venture out again."

Scarlett's expression changed to one of concern. "Oh no, I'm so sorry. She's okay now, though, right?"

"I think so. She doesn't talk about it, but she's got a boyfriend she's serious with now. He's helped her a lot too." Mal took his phone from the table where he'd set it when he walked in and opened the pictures.

Then he turned it toward Scarlett. "This is her. And here are my parents."

Scarlett took the phone and swiped between the photos. "You two look a lot alike."

"We're twins."

Her smile was instant. "Really? That's so cool. No wonder you look so much alike."

"She was born first and she never lets me forget it," he said affectionately. He'd been in training when Mel had been attacked. He'd wanted to race home and take care of the guy, but that wasn't a practical option. The justice system had worked, but only because the guy had committed a string of rapes that'd gone unsolved until a bystander saw him attacking Mel and intervened. If not for that, he'd have probably gotten away with another one.

Scarlett handed his phone back. "Is your place far?"

"Farther than you might like. About twenty-five miles south of here. I'm kind of in the country."

"Hmm. How much are you asking?"

"How much can you pay?"

"Mal. I'm not a charity. And I still haven't decided if it's a good idea, so don't go easy on me."

He snorted. "Don't go easy on you and make it irresistible?"

"Something like that."

"Okay, well after I get it fixed up, I figure I could get about six-fifty for it since I'm not close to anything and it's tiny. But if that's more than you want to pay, I can take less. Especially since I can't paint it right now."

"You're making this difficult."

"I know. But come look at it after I get discharged. If you haven't found anything by the time your roommate puts her house on the market, it's yours. Bring a friend if you want, or I'll have my buddies come and bring their wives and fiancées. Whatever it takes to make you feel safe."

Her face scrunched up. Then her expression cleared. "Okay, I'll come look at it. Thank you for offering. I really appreciate it."

"Don't thank me yet," he said. "You may jump in your car and take off the instant you see the work it'll take to clean it up. If you don't, we'll decide on a fair rent then."

She held out her hand. Mal took it, enjoying the soft feel of her skin against his. He wasn't quite prepared for the tiny spark that flickered inside him though. That was interesting.

"Deal," she said.

"Deal," he replied.

Chapter Six

SCARLETT DIDN'T TAKE ANYONE WITH HER TO MAL'S place when she went to see it a few days days later. She thought about it, but her gut told her it wasn't necessary. She wasn't afraid of him assaulting her. Her particular fear had nothing to do with that. No, she was more afraid of insidious abuse. The kind that made you question your own sanity as you asked yourself whether or not what you thought was happening was really happening.

Still, when she arrived at the white farmhouse set on two acres, Mal was sitting on the front porch with a woman. Scarlett realized it was Haylee, the woman who'd come to visit with one of Mal's teammates a few times. Haylee came down the stairs, smiling as Scarlett got out of her car.

"Welcome, Scarlett. I was just visiting Mal and he said you were on the way. I thought I'd hang out and say hi."

Scarlett took the hand the other woman offered and gave it a squeeze. Then she glanced at Mal, who was slowly making his way toward them. She didn't know if he'd asked Haylee to be here on purpose, but she suspected he had. Yet another reason to like him.

Haylee's phone rang as Mal reached them. "I have to take this," she said. "Sorry. Be right back."

"Sure, take your time," Scarlett said.

"Hey, Scar. How'd that date go last night?" Mal asked when Haylee stepped away.

Scarlett rolled her eyes. "It wasn't a date. It was drinks."

"Yeah, but your friend set you up."

Scarlett was beginning to regret telling Mal about that. But yesterday, when she'd known she had to go for drinks that night, she'd been jumpy about it. Mal had stopped by for his therapy and given her the good news that he'd been released. She'd panicked at the thought of him not being there every day when she made her rounds, and she'd let it show. She still didn't know why she'd felt that way, but she'd been just rattled enough to blurt out her evening plans instead of telling him she was going to miss seeing him. It didn't even make sense to miss him since he still had to come in for therapy three times a week.

"She did, but I made it clear it wasn't a date. And I took my own car, like I told you."

"Wise," Mal said. "I assume there weren't any sparks?"

"No. No sparks. He was nice enough, but definitely not my type. I stayed longer than I should have, but I managed to get out before they went to another bar for dancing."

And discovered a big scratch keyed down the side of her car. She'd stood in the parking lot looking at the other cars, but hers was the only one with a scratch that she could see. She'd gotten inside with a sick feeling rolling in her belly. Not entirely because of the scratch, but also because it had happened to *her* car. It made her think of those dark days with Josh manipulating her reality. But it couldn't be him. If Josh had found her, he'd do a lot worse than put a scratch on her car.

Mal looked thoughtful. "What's your type then?"

Scarlett resisted blurting out that he was. Until Josh had wrecked her life, she'd have said that her type ran to big, strong, protectors. Which meant that Ricky should have been perfect since he was none of those things, but he hadn't been. Too soft, too nerdy, too interested in spreadsheets. And too into himself if the way he'd talked was any indication. Everything had been about him, which was too much like Josh for comfort.

"Not sure I have one these days," she said. "I'm currently on dating hiatus."

"I see."

Haylee finished her call and returned with a smile. "Want me to take her up there, gimpy?" she asked Mal.

Mal's mouth twisted. "Ha, ha. You're a comedian. Between you and Scar, I'm going to have a complex about my leg."

Haylee bumped his arm playfully. "Sure you are. Now give me the keys and I'll take her up. You shouldn't be climbing those stairs."

"I have stairs in my house, Haylee."

"I know that, genius. That's why you don't need to climb any that you don't have to. Scarlett, help me out here."

Scarlett was watching Mal's face when Haylee turned to her. There was something there. Something that wasn't exasperation or stubbornness. It was a softness. A longing. He hid it quickly, but not before Scarlett saw it.

Well, shit.

Haylee was the woman he was hung up on, as he'd put it. And she was in love with his teammate. Poor Mal. In that moment, Scarlett knew she could trust him. He really wasn't interested in her. It was both a relief and a disappointment. Not that she was interested in him, but it'd be nice for once if a decent, handsome guy liked her. Maybe she'd be brave enough to try again if so.

Scarlett looked at the other woman. She was gorgeous, with dark hair and sparkling dark eyes, and she was lucky enough to be in love with—and loved by—the kind of Special Ops warrior who would protect her with his life rather than hurt a hair on her head. *Two* of them actually, though she didn't know it. Envy rolled through Scarlett, along with a big dose of self-pity.

"We can manage," Scarlett said brightly, pushing the self-pity down. "You go sit on the porch and Haylee and I will look at the apartment. Another week and you'll be able to climb those stairs, but let's not push it."

"Fine," Mal grumbled.

He thrust the keys at Scarlett rather than Haylee. She told herself not to read anything into the gesture, but it pleased her nonetheless.

"Take your time. I'll just be here on the porch, bored and lonely."

Haylee rolled her eyes. "You have a cell phone. Go look at Facebook or something."

Scarlett and Haylee walked around the house toward the back. The garage was behind the house in a cluster of trees. Scarlett stopped, taking it all in. The building was white, like the house, and there was a set of stairs on one side that led to a balcony where she could put a small table and two chairs. The greenery was lush and shady. She could picture flower boxes hanging from the balcony.

"It's pretty, right?" Haylee said.

"It is. I hope the inside is half as pretty."

"I've never been inside. Guess we'll find out together."

They climbed up the stairs—fortunately not

rickety—and Scarlett inserted the key. The lock was smooth, as if someone had oiled it recently. Mal had been up there, darn him. He really needed to be careful.

Scarlett pushed open the door and walked into the room. It was a studio, like he'd said. It was a little dark inside, probably from all the trees overhead, but the windows at one end were big and let in a lot of light. Some lamps would help with the dark corners.

"It's not too bad," Haylee said from behind her, flipping on the light switch.

Scarlett glanced at her. "No, not at all. It needs a good cleaning, but the space is nice."

"Hardwood floors need refinished probably."

"A good cleaning and waxing would help until then."

"For sure. Nice kitchen, really. And the sink is beneath a window, which I always like."

"Me too." The cabinets were white. Scarlett pulled one open. It was wood, not laminate, and the hardware was original. The sink was porcelain, and the window had the original wavy glass. Scarlett twisted the lock and tried to lift the window, but it didn't budge. "Been painted shut over the years. A knife and some elbow grease will fix that."

Probably all the windows had been painted shut, but she'd dealt with that before in one of the houses she'd lived in with her daddy. She'd helped him so she knew how it was done.

They explored the rest of the space. It wasn't big, but she could see where to put a bed, where to have a living area and dining table. Things she didn't have, but she had a little money saved to buy some stuff if she hit up the thrift stores and vintage shops. The bathroom was on one side of the studio and took up the entire length of the building. There was a clawfoot tub with a handheld shower fixture that she'd need to figure out, a sink with a good-sized counter, a toilet, and a big closet for storage.

Aside from being farther from work than she liked, it was perfect. And the price was definitely right. She paid Justine seven-fifty to live in her house, but Justine's place was much closer to everything. This was going to be a little bit of a drive, but Scarlett didn't mind so long as her car held up. Plus there was something peaceful about the setting with all the trees. Looking out the windows, she almost felt like she was in a treehouse.

"So, what do you think?" Haylee asked, walking up beside her and looking at the view. "Too much work or what?"

"Nah, I think I like it. It's a little far from the rehab facility, but that's what podcasts are for, right? Besides, it's quiet out here, and I like that."

"Doesn't get much quieter. I think it'll be good for Mal to have someone around right now anyway."

Scarlett turned to her. "Why do you say that?"

Haylee shrugged. "He's not very talkative about what happened, but I think sacrificing himself to save

Dean took a mental toll as well. Not that he'd ever say so to me."

Scarlett could only gape at the other woman as she put two and two together. Dean was Haylee's fiancé and Mal's teammate. And Mal had taken a bullet for him. The man who was marrying the woman he loved.

Daaaamn.

Her heart went out to him as she thought about what he must be feeling. The guilt and pain. The longing.

"You say sacrificing himself. What happened?"

"They won't really talk about the details—can't talk about it—but they were on a mission when an enemy combatant took aim at Dean." Her voice caught on his name. She swallowed hard. "Sorry, still not used to it sometimes. The danger, I mean. All of it. Even though I met Dean when his team rescued me from a Guatemalan jungle—that's a story for another time though."

She sniffed and Scarlett put a hand on her shoulder and squeezed.

"I know better. I really do. I'm just so emotional lately." Haylee drew in a deep breath before continuing. "Mal saw what was happening and put himself between Dean and the shot. You know the rest."

Not entirely, but she knew Haylee was talking about Mal's leg. Scarlett wanted to know the rest of it, though. What had been going through Mal's head when he'd tried to save his teammate. How he'd gotten out of the combat zone, and what he felt now.

"I don't know him well," Scarlett said carefully. "But he seems fine in rehab. Honestly. He jokes with me, jokes with the nurses, and he's curious about many things. He asks me about myself, my training, where I'm from. I know that's not a lot, but it's a normal interest in stuff. I'm no psychiatrist, of course, but I think that's a good sign."

Haylee nodded. "I think so too. I just feel so guilty. I mean I know it's not my fault. Dean keeps telling me it's the way they're trained and all that, but I can't help thinking if Mal hadn't intervened, Dean might not have come home."

"I don't think he'd want you to feel guilty."

"No, probably not. I know you aren't going to take this apartment with the idea of being Mal's caregiver or therapist or anything, but I'll feel better knowing you're here. Knowing there's a friendly face nearby if he needs anything."

Scarlett thought maybe Haylee was making Mal a lot more helpless and feeble than he really was, but she wasn't going to correct the woman. If it made her feel better that Scarlett was there, then so be it. Not that she expected it would make a difference at all. Mal wasn't depressed. He just wanted what he couldn't have. What Haylee took for the mental toll of the mission and its outcome was most likely Mal repressing his feelings for her.

Poor Mal.

"Like I said, I don't know him well, but if he's going to be my landlord, I guess I'll see him a lot more than just at appointments. Maybe he'll come borrow a cup of sugar or something."

She said it jokingly, but Haylee nodded. "Yes, that's true… Are you single, Scarlett?"

Scarlett felt herself closing in. She forced a smile. "Terminally so, I'm afraid. The last one was no picnic, so I'm done for the next decade or so."

"I'm sorry. But I understand. Been there, done that. Then I got lucky and met Dean. It happens when you least expect it sometimes."

Scarlett didn't think Haylee had quite been to the same place that she had with a guy, but most women hadn't. Thank heavens.

"That's what I hear. Still, I'm not looking."

"Gotcha. So, should we go tell Mal the news? Or do you want to look around some more?"

Scarlett threw another glance out the window. She loved the trees and the green field behind it. So pretty. It helped with any hesitation she felt over the distance, or the fact she'd be only steps from a military warrior's house. But Mal wasn't Josh. He wasn't going to turn into an obsessive, controlling dickhead when she least expected it. Hell, the man had thrown himself in front of a bullet for a teammate—at least partly because of the woman standing beside her now. That wasn't the act of a psycho.

Maybe, finally, things were going her way. For the first time in months, she felt happy with her decision.

Happy with what the future could bring. Josh was a bad memory. He wasn't going to find her ever again. She might never relax fully, but she could learn to enjoy each moment.

"I'm good. Let's go."

Chapter Seven

"You can stop clutching the armrest," Mal said, throwing a glance at his passenger. "It isn't that bad."

Scarlett let go and sniffed. "Sorry. I'm just used to driving myself—and you did run a yellow light."

"It'd just turned yellow."

"But it was still yellow."

"Yellow lights are merely suggestions."

"A suggestion to stop so you don't get creamed when it turns red."

"Relax, Scar. We're fine. I'll stop at the next one if it makes you feel better."

"I'm just ribbing you, Mal. Though you did kind of floor it when the light turned."

They were in Mal's truck, headed for a thrift shop where Scarlett had bought a couch that folded out into a bed. She'd been at the garage apartment every day for a week, cleaning and moving some of her things in. He'd offered to help, but she'd declined. Until now.

She needed help picking up a couch, and she wasn't fitting it into her little SUV. When he'd asked her earlier when she was moving in, she'd said as soon as she got her bed into the apartment. Then she'd told him she was going to rent a truck from Home Depot so she could pick it up. He'd told her that was ridiculous when he had a truck and could help her.

She'd been reluctant, but she'd finally agreed when he'd pointed out that his help was free. Better than renting a truck from a home improvement store.

"Yeah, well, we've got a couch to pick up, don't we?"

She laughed softly. "Thanks again for offering to help. I really appreciate it."

"That's what friends are for."

"I know. I'm just not used to it. I've only been in the area for three months now. I don't know many people."

"You have friends at the hospital."

"Some, yes. They work long hours, though, so I couldn't ask any of them."

"I feel like you aren't an asker anyway."

"Why do you say that?"

He made the turn into the thrift shop parking lot and found a spot near the door. "Not sure. You just seem very… *enclosed* is the word I'm looking for. Like you don't want to bother anyone."

"It's called introversion."

"I know what an introvert is. I'm not one."

"I can tell," she said with a smile. "You've been up to talk to me every day."

"Not just talk. I helped with some of the cleaning."

"You did. Thanks again."

"You don't have to thank me. I should be cleaning the place. It's my responsibility as a landlord to make it nice."

"We had that discussion when you insisted on renting it to me at a ridiculously low price, remember?"

When Scarlett and Haylee had returned to the house that day last week, Haylee had said her good-byes and left him and Scarlett to discuss arrangements. He'd asked Haylee to be there when Scarlett arrived because he didn't want her to feel uncomfortable being alone with him. He didn't know what her ex had done to her, but he knew it'd made her wary of men. He'd like to find the guy and put some fear into the bastard, truth be told.

"It's not worth more than three-hundred right now. If I gut it and renovate, different story."

"First of all, I don't believe you. Even if you're out in the country, it's still within commuting distance to DC. And secondly, no need to gut it. It's charming."

"Charming. That's one word," he said, opening his door and stepping out onto the pavement. Maybe it was worth more, but he didn't feel right charging her more when she was going to have to do a lot of work herself. It didn't sit right with him. Plus, he didn't need the money. He had enough with his military pay.

Scarlett walked around the truck to join him. "Don't tell me you didn't fall for some of that yourself when you bought the place. Your house isn't exactly a testament to modern architecture. It has plenty of old charm."

"And plenty of work to be done, too."

"Why did you buy it then?"

He opened the door for her and she went inside the building, turning to wait for his answer inside the cool foyer.

"I needed something to do with my time when I wasn't working. Plus, I grew up in an old house that always needed work. Living in something modern wouldn't feel right."

"I get that. We moved around a bit, but my favorite house was an old farmhouse with a barn and a well that you could still drop a bucket into. We were only there for a couple of years, but it was the most fun I think I had as a kid."

"And now you're having fun scrubbing floors and windows and vacuuming up spider webs, huh?"

"You know it," she said with a grin.

"Come on, Scar," he said, reaching around her to pull open the next door. "Let's get your couch. Then we can grab some lunch on the way home. I'm starved."

———

IT WAS JUST A COUCH. And lunch. But Scarlett found herself surprised from one moment to the next that this was even happening. She hadn't intended to say yes to Mal's offer of help. She'd meant to go to the Home Depot and rent that truck, racing to the thrift shop to get the couch loaded and home again before an hour was up. Justine had said she and Neil would help on their next day off, so that's what Scarlett had been planning for. She hadn't asked, like she'd told Mal, but Justine had offered. Scarlett just wasn't sure when that day would come.

But then Mal asked her when she was moving in. She'd explained about the couch—and he'd said they should go get it right then. She'd meant to say no. And then he'd pointed out the expense of the truck. She wasn't an idiot, and math was one of her strong suits. The money she'd save on the truck would enable her to buy that cute little end table she'd been eying, provided it was still there.

Plus having the couch would mean she could stay the night in her own place instead of shuffling back and forth to Justine's. Now that Scarlett had found a place, Justine was having contractors in to do some work before listing the house. The noise and dust were an annoyance Scarlett wanted to leave behind as soon as possible.

Scarlett walked up to the cash register to let someone know she was there for the couch. The woman behind the counter looked up, her eyes straying over Scarlett's shoulder. She straightened suddenly, thrusting her boobs out, and smiled.

"Hi. Can I help you?"

"Scarlett Reed. I'm here for the sleeper sofa. I paid for it two days ago."

The woman blinked at Mal, then dropped her gaze to Scarlett for a moment. Her expression wasn't nearly as welcoming as it had been. "Sleeper sofa. Right. Give me a sec."

She disappeared into the back room, but not before throwing a look over her shoulder at Mal. Scarlett shook her head when the door closed.

"You're lethal, Mal."

He shrugged. "Not trying to be. Can't fight Mother Nature, though."

"Modest too."

"That's me, Scar. Modest to a fault."

"How's your leg holding up?"

"It's angry with me, but that's okay. My therapist says I have to exercise it."

"Your therapist also thinks you need to be careful and not push it too far. I believe she told you that as well."

"She did, but between you and me, I think she's overprotective of me."

Scarlett snorted. "Really? Why would she do that?"

He leaned on the counter, his gaze sparkling as he raked it over her face. God, he was attractive. Dark hair, mossy green eyes, a chiseled jaw, and muscles that had muscles. Lean muscles, not crazy, overly veiny ones. His lips were firm, full, and kissable.

Kissable? Where the hell had that come from?

"Because she's my friend. She likes me."

Scarlett's heart beat far too fast for a conversation between friends. The disappointment throbbing in her brain because he'd called her a friend shouldn't be there, but it was.

"She thinks you're okay."

"Just okay?"

"Really nice. And a little dumb too. Renting your apartment to someone for a ridiculously low amount of money when you could get more. That's not bright."

"Not as dumb as you'd think, though. I didn't lift a finger to improve anything and now I'm getting money for what was just an empty space."

"Not as dumb as you pretend then. Hmm."

He barked a laugh. "You're fun, Scar. I really like having you around."

She flushed with pleasure. "Happy to be of service."

"You know, when I woke up in that hospital a month ago, I didn't know what they were going to tell me about my leg. I didn't know the extent of the damage, or if I'd even have a leg. I admit I was feeling kind of lost when the doc told me it was going to take time and I'd be out of work for a while, but meeting you has been the highlight of the whole thing."

The flush grew warmer. Scarlett balled up her fist and socked him playfully in the arm. "Don't even try and make me cry. It won't work."

He tweaked her nose and she rocked back, surprised but also flustered by his touch.

"I'm not trying. I just want you to know that I like you. Being with you is easy, and I don't say that to many people. No reply necessary, so don't wrack your brain trying to think of an appropriate response."

"Okay, I won't. But thanks. I'm taking everything you said as a compliment, so don't ruin it for me with a joke."

His grin did things to her insides. "Not planning to."

The woman returned from the back room, smiling stupidly at Mal. "If you go around to the loading dock, they'll have the couch waiting for you. Is there anything else I can help you with?"

Scarlett rolled her eyes. The other woman didn't see because she was too busy smiling at Mal. He was smiling back, and Scarlett could see that the brain light had gone off in the woman's head. She was operating on hormones and desire at this point.

"I'm going to grab a couple of other things. I'll be back in a few minutes," she said to Mal. "You can stay here if you want."

"Nope," he said. "Going with you."

They walked away from the counter, and Scarlett threw him a side-eye. "You turn them stupid. It's amazing."

"What?"

"That girl. She could be a PhD in nuclear physics and you'd still knock every thought out of her head simply by looking at her."

Mal laughed. "You're giving me too much credit. I'd say you're pretty damned smart, and I don't turn you stupid, do I?"

"Not possible," she sniffed. "I'm immune."

"I'm wounded."

"I know. It's how we met."

He laughed again. "Jesus, Scar. You're so full of sass. Sometimes I think…"

"Think what?" she asked when he didn't continue the thought.

"Nothing important. What else are you getting in this place?"

She put her hand on the round end table, thankful it was still there. It'd been marked down, too. Only twenty-five-dollars today. "This, and maybe a couple of pictures. I still want to know what you were thinking, though."

He sighed as he hefted the table in one arm. It was light or she would have yelled at him for it. He didn't need to overtax his leg. He'd only been home for a few days, and it was just a month out from his surgery. Plenty of healing left to do.

"No, you really don't," he said.

She faced him, stubbornly unwilling to continue. She shouldn't care what he'd been thinking, but she did. She couldn't help it. "Maybe I do. I get to be the judge of what I want to know and what I don't."

"Yeah, but once you know, you can't un-know."

"Mal."

"All right, Scar. Don't say I didn't warn you." He leaned toward her just enough that his voice was only for her. Her skin tingled at his proximity, her breath feeling heavier in her chest.

Then he said the words. "Sometimes I think I want to kiss you."

Chapter Eight

WIDE BLUE EYES BLINKED UP AT HIM. MAL CURSED himself for having told her. She looked like a rabbit caught in a bright light. Too scared to move but too afraid not to.

"I told you that you didn't want to hear it," he said softly, regretting that he'd ruined the easiness between them with that admittance. It didn't change his feelings for Haylee, but lately Scarlett was taking up a lot of the real estate in his head. Probably because he saw her all the time. And he was about to see her even more now that she was moving into the apartment.

"It's a surprise, I admit. I thought you were in love with someone."

"It's a surprise to me too. And I am. But that doesn't mean I'm not human. I still want companionship."

"Sex, you mean."

Damn, he liked the way that word sounded on her lips. Yet he told himself this was dangerous territory. Scarlett trusted him and he didn't want to break that trust. Still, he nodded. "Yeah. But don't worry, I told you it was a fleeting thought. I'm not going to do anything to endanger our friendship."

"Or your three-hundred bucks a month."

And there it was, that shot of desire for her that stunned him every time. When she clapped back at him the way she did, he wanted to taste the sass on her tongue. It was uncanny.

"Right. Three-hundred bucks will buy me a lot of ammo." He made an exaggerated face. "Wait, no it won't. These days it'll get me a couple of big boxes of rounds for my personal weapons. But not chasing you off when I've come to like having you around is good enough for me. Doesn't mean the stray thought about kissing you won't pass through my head though."

More than a stray thought, he expected, since he was thinking about it right now. Maybe he should feel badly that he was thinking of her that way instead of Haylee, but damn, it was nice not to be tortured with thoughts of his buddy's woman for a change. He actually went to sleep at night without Haylee being the last thing on his mind. He should thank Scarlett for that, not chase her off with his occasional fantasies about kissing her.

"So long as it's just a thought," she said. But her eyes were dilated and her breathing seemed a little quicker than before. Interesting.

He made an X over his heart. "Cross my heart, Scar. I'll never kiss you unless you ask me to. Promise."

"And I'm never asking, so that's that. You better start thinking about something else."

"Oh, I'm sure my mind will conjure up all kinds of thoughts if left to its own devices." He didn't intend to let his words sound full of innuendo, but there was no controlling what came out of his mouth apparently. Scarlett was fun, and he loved to tease her. It was one of the highlights of his days lately.

"I don't want to know what you're thinking. If I ask again, tell me to buzz off."

"Buzz off," he repeated with a laugh. "Okay, I will."

"What's wrong with buzz off?" She blinked adorably at him.

"It's so polite. It sounds like something my grandma would say."

"Then tell me to piss off. How's that?"

He chuckled. "I would never be impolite to you, Scar." He hefted the table. "What else you getting? I'm hungry."

"I just need to look at the pictures."

She led him over to a wall where several pictures were hanging. There were also stacks against the wall. It all looked pretty crappy to him, but then she started digging. When she pulled out two matted and framed prints of flowers in vases, she looked up happily. "See? You never know what you can find."

"Looks like flowers to me."

"Yes, but these are prints of paintings. I'll just do a little update on the frames, and they'll go nicely in my home."

"What kind of update?"

"Paint, probably. Though you can get rub-on wax that changes the color too."

She kept digging, selecting four more pictures of various sizes. All were of flowers.

"I'm sensing a theme here," he said as she grabbed a nearby cart and stacked the frames in it.

"It's easier to make a room look put together if you stick with a few basic ideas. Besides, the studio is too small to mix it up too much. Okay then, I think I'm good. Let me pay for this and we can go get the couch."

"And eat," he said. "Don't forget that."

"As if you'd let me forget."

They went back to the counter and Scarlett paid for her items. Apparently, the thrift store was having a sale today because she got twenty-five percent off everything. Her entire bill was less than forty dollars, which seemed to make her giddy. Mal stacked the frames in the backseat of his truck, then they drove around to the loading dock. He got out to supervise the loading of a green velvet-looking couch, though Scarlett gave him a hard look when he tried to help the guys shift it in the bed. He put both hands up in surrender and let them finish. They tied it down, he thanked them, and then he drove carefully out of the parking lot.

Scarlett let him choose where they had lunch, so he took her to an out of the way restaurant on the water. They sat at a table on the deck with a view of the Chesapeake Bay and ate crab cake sandwiches and fries. A soft breeze blew in off the water, ruffling their hair. Scarlett was still wearing her ponytail—he'd never seen her without it—but a few stray strands had come free and blew across her face from time to time. She shoved them back impatiently, long fingers tucking them behind her ears until the next breeze freed them again.

"This is really nice," she said, gazing at the deep blue water and the sailboats in the distance. "I wouldn't have found this place on my own."

"You would have eventually. Took me more than a year."

"Maybe so," she said, dragging a fry through ketchup before popping it in her mouth. He'd wondered what she'd be like when she ate, if she'd order a salad and water, but Scarlett hadn't even blinked. She'd ordered the crab cake sandwich and the fries, and he'd bet she'd order dessert when she finished the fries. "I don't tend to venture out much. I know I should but I get tunnel vision with work and daily life, and I don't explore."

"Except for thrift shops."

She laughed. "I do have a thing for thrift shops. People get rid of nice stuff, and you can pick up good things cheaply. I paid a hundred bucks for that couch. I mean it's not the prettiest thing in the world, but it'll work and it's solid. I'll fix it up so it looks nice."

"Don't tell me you're going to reupholster it."

She laughed. "I don't have a clue how to do that. I mean I'll use throw blankets and pillows. That kind of thing."

"You're resourceful."

"I learned it as a kid." She dragged another fry through ketchup, only this time she seemed to be playing with it. Deciding what to say, probably. "My mom died when I was eight. I told you before she was a nurse, but she was actually an Army nurse. Deployed to Iraq. One day she went out in a convoy, and there was an IED by the road…" She swallowed. "Well, she didn't come home again."

"I'm sorry," he said, both surprised and saddened by her revelation. Too many stories like that one. He hated it for her, and for all the grieving families who'd lost loved ones in a war zone. "That had to be tough for you."

"It was. My dad was a great dad, but he was kind of hopeless about some things. He was depressed for a while. Lost his job. We moved a lot, and he always found work, but then he'd quit or get fired. I learned to hit the thrift stores and cruise neighborhoods looking for other people's cast offs that they put on the curb as trash. I watched a lot of DIY television and YouTube videos, and I fixed stuff up. Sold some of it too."

That didn't surprise him. The more he knew her, the more Scarlett struck him as a survivor.

"How'd you end up as a physical therapist assistant?" he asked, stealing one of her fries.

She swatted his hand. "Well, since Mom was a nurse, I knew I wanted to do something in medicine. For the stability, and because of her. To honor her. I researched what I could do. I almost settled on dental tech, but being a PTA sounded more satisfying. I didn't want to stare into people's mouths all day. So I applied to the community college, got a couple of scholarships, and worked my way through by waitressing and junking."

"What about your dad? Is he still in Florida?"

She shook her head, her eyes looking even sadder. "He died almost seven years ago. Motorcycle accident."

"Damn," Mal said. It was an impulse to reach for her hand. She didn't pull away, and he didn't let go, though the electricity sparking through him was a bit of a shock. He wanted to turn her hand over and skim his fingertips over her palm, up her wrist. He wisely didn't. Instead, he gave her a soft squeeze. "That's crappy, Scar. I'm sorry."

She shrugged, but she didn't try to disentangle her fingers from his. "That's life, right? Shit happens and then you die. Best you can do is keep moving forward."

"That's what I try to do."

She sniffed and pulled her hand away. He didn't

reach for it again, but he found himself strangely disappointed. "Enough about me. Tell me about you."

He wasn't done asking questions, but fair was fair. He really wanted to know about the asshat ex-boyfriend, but she'd already shared so much with him. He figured she wouldn't want to share more at this point. Not until he did some talking of his own.

"I already told you the basics. Mom and Dad and Mel are in Galveston. You know what I do and where I live. What more is there?"

Scarlett rolled her eyes. "Only everything, Mal. Your sister is named Mel? Short for Melanie, I assume?"

"Yep. Malcolm and Melanie. The only twins in our grade growing up."

She grinned. "Did your mom dress you alike?"

"When we were little, yeah. But that shit stopped when I started pitching fits about it in first grade. I got teased and I wasn't having it."

"And she was born first. You said that before, I remember."

"Yep. Three minutes before and she never lets me forget it either. Calls me little bro and shit, which is ridiculous since I outweigh her by at least a hundred pounds."

"I like her already. What's she do?"

"Mel was a teacher, but she's decided she wants to be a police officer like our dad. She's in training now."

"Service to community and country runs in the family."

"Yeah. Mom is a dispatcher. It's how she met my dad."

"Why didn't you go into the family business?"

"I planned on it, but first I wanted to do four years in the military. Four turned into eight, and I'm still here."

"You like your job then."

"I do."

"Even if you get shot doing it."

"I could get shot being a police officer. Not much difference." There was a lot of difference since he often got dropped into active war zones. His dad had never been shot in thirty years on the force. Thank God. Now if Mel could do the same, life would be great.

"If you say so." She didn't look convinced.

"Hey, you want dessert?"

"Is that water blue?" she said, nodding toward the bay.

"Sure is. Next question—you want it here, or you want to go get ice cream at a deli I know?"

"Is it as good as this place?"

"Nowhere better for ice cream."

"I'm sold."

He waved at the waitress for the check, then handed her cash when she brought it over. "I'll buy this and you can get the ice cream."

Scarlett frowned. "You don't have to buy my

lunch, Mal. I should buy yours since you're helping me out."

"I know I don't have to, but I want to. Consider it a thanks for all the work you've done to help me get back on my feet. Literally on my feet."

"You did that yourself by following instructions."

"Come on, you know you had to threaten me with fire to get me to do it. Plus you had to put up with my grumpy ass when I first hobbled into your room."

"You were pretty grumpy," Scarlett said. "Still are sometimes." She was looking at him with an arched eyebrow and an *uh-huh, take that* expression on her face.

He beamed at her. "But you like me anyway."

"You kind of grew on me. Like a fungus."

He laughed as he stood and held out a hand for her. "Come on, Scar. Let's go eat ice cream and then I'll text my buddies so we can get your couch inside. Before you know it, all your dreams of living within spitting distance of me will come true."

Chapter Nine

When they arrived back at Mal's place, there were four hulking men sitting on the front porch. They watched Mal drive up but didn't move from their positions. Mal rolled the window down as Scarlett tried not to stare. These were the guys he'd said he was calling. She recognized a couple of them from the hospital when they'd come to visit him, but the only one whose name she remembered was Dean. He was Haylee's fiancé.

"What are y'all doing loitering on my porch, amigos? Viper and Ghost work you too hard today?"

"Just waiting for you to get here, bro," one man said. " 'Bout to take a nap it's been so long."

"Scarlett wanted ice cream," Mal said. "Can't refuse a lady."

Scarlett wanted to sock him. "You suggested it," she practically screeched. "Don't blame me."

They'd gone to a deli in a cute little town with an

old square and sat at a picnic table beneath a tree, eating ice cream and talking about random stuff. She'd enjoyed herself. The whole afternoon had been enjoyable, in fact. Mal was easy to be with, and he didn't give her any bad vibes at all. There had been that moment when he'd said he sometimes thought about kissing her, though.

Her entire body had flushed hot. She'd even imagined what it would feel like to have him kiss her. The idea hadn't terrified her, though. It'd excited her.

But then she'd remembered the way he'd looked at Haylee and reality crashed down on her like a bucket of bricks. If he was thinking of kissing her, it was only because he was looking for a diversion from his feelings for a woman he couldn't have. Even if Scarlett had been inclined to let him kiss her in the first place, which she wasn't dammit, that would have stopped her cold.

Mal drove over to the garage and parked in front of it. The guys came down the steps and followed, arraying themselves around the back end of the truck when they arrived. Two of them looked at her curiously.

"How's it going, Scarlett?" Dean asked. "This guy giving you any trouble?"

"It's going well," she said, "especially with you guys being so nice as to help get my couch upstairs."

"Not a problem," he replied.

"As for Mal," she continued. "He's unpredictable as hell."

Mal said, "Hey!" at the same time the others laughed.

"Yep, that's Mal. I'm Cade," a tall handsome man said, sticking out his hand. "We met briefly at the hospital, but you might have forgotten. This is Noah Cross and Ryder Hanson. I don't think you've met them yet."

"I remember you," Scarlett said, shaking his hand before saying hi to the other two. They were all big, all muscular, all lethal. She knew they were a Special Ops team. That knowledge should have her quaking in her shoes, but strangely it didn't. Still, any one of them could be as controlling and unpredictable as Josh. In truth, any man could be. But a nerdy man like Ricky was a lot less scary than one like Josh, which is what all these men were.

Warriors. Men who killed because it was the job.

"You sure you want to live here with Mal so close?" Ryder asked.

"Hey," Mal said again. "Scarlett likes me. Stop trying to sew doubt in her mind."

Scarlett laughed. It was clear these guys were ribbing each other, and that they enjoyed it. She knew Mal wasn't doing his job right now, so it was nice to see that his team was still there for him. Or, in this case, for her. Because he'd asked them to be.

"I do like him," she said. "But he can be a grouch sometimes. He does do all his exercises though, even when he's pissy about it."

"I'm only pissy because I'm not fully healed yet. Nobody told me it was going to take this much time."

"Everything takes time," Scarlett said. "You aren't a machine."

"All right, all right," Mal said, waving his hands around like he was shooing a fly. "Let's get Scarlett's couch upstairs so she can sleep here tonight and nag me every day from now on to be careful not to stress my leg."

"I don't nag," Scarlett said primly. "My job is to tell you what reality is. If you can't accept it, it's on you."

"Seems like nagging to me. That look you gave me at the thrift shop when I was trying to help those guys? Pure nag."

"No, that was me telling you without words that you'd better not injure yourself on my watch. Especially while doing me a favor."

"Nagging me like a pack mule."

"I think you mean flogging."

"Flogging. Nagging. Whatever."

The men were watching them with interest, four sets of eyes bouncing between them like they were at a tennis match. Scarlett felt herself coloring. "Are we going to keep arguing or are you going to let these guys get the couch upstairs so they can go home?"

"Not stopping them, Scar. You were arguing with me."

She wanted to bean him. "I am *not* arguing with you. You're arguing with me!"

Cade snorted. "All right, boys, let's get this furniture moved while Mal and Scarlett sort it out."

They got the couch off the truck and up the stairs in less time than it had taken the guys at the thrift shop to load it. They also got the pictures and end table and took it all in one trip. Scarlett trudged up the stairs to supervise the placement of the couch and table, then stood back to assess the space. Excitement bubbled inside her at the idea of all she could do to make the place her own. Already, she could breathe easier than she had for the past three months in Justine's house. Not that Justine wasn't an angel, but living in someone else's house as a roommate wasn't Scarlett's idea of home for herself. You were always thinking about someone else's needs, their preferences, and when they owned the property, you were careful not to get too comfortable.

"Is that good?" Cade asked. "Or do you want us to shift it?"

Scarlett let her gaze slide to the men. Five of them, including Mal who'd clearly followed them upstairs, all standing in her space and waiting for her to tell them whether or not she wanted her couch moved an inch to the left. It was sweet in a way.

"That's perfect. Thank you again. I'm very grateful."

Noah slung an arm around Mal's neck. "We're grateful to you for taking care of our boy here. We need him back as soon as possible."

"I'm working on it," Mal said.

"He is," Scarlett replied, feeling charitable toward him again now that he wasn't talking in circles about nagging and arguments. "He's making incredible progress."

"Thanks, Scar. I appreciate that."

"It's true," she said, not missing the looks the guys were giving her. Looks that speculated she was more than just Mal's tenant and physical therapist. She started to say something to the effect of they were just friends, but that would only confirm what these guys were thinking. Anyway, if that's what they thought then they were going to get a surprise when they finally realized nothing was going on.

"Why don't you bring Scarlett to Buddy's Friday night?" Dean said.

Scarlett blinked, but Mal was already answering. "Hey, that's a good idea. Want to come, Scar?"

"I don't know what Buddy's is."

"It's a bar, but not a bad bar. A sports bar where we hang out. Eat, drink, play pool. That kind of thing."

"I don't know…"

"Brooke and Bliss will be there," Cade said. "And maybe Eva, though Jake isn't sure they can make it. What about Haylee?"

"Yeah, Haylee's coming," Dean said.

Scarlett must have looked confused because Mal explained. "You already know Haylee. Brooke is Saint's fiancée and Bliss is Hacker's ex-wife and current fiancée."

Ex-wife and current fiancée. That was a story if ever there was one.

"Saint and Hacker?"

"Sorry. Cade is Saint. Sky Kelley is Hacker, but you haven't met him yet. The women will be there, so you can talk to them instead of hanging with us guys. Make some new friends."

Scarlett wasn't sure what to say, but the men were watching her expectantly. On the one hand, she wanted to hole up inside her new apartment. On the other, she liked that Mal's friends wanted to include her in their gathering. She reasoned that she was his friend too, so it wouldn't be all that odd for her to go. Even if the guys thought there was more going on between her and Mal, there wasn't.

"I, um…"

"C'mon, Scar. You need to have some fun sometime," Mal prodded. "Like today."

She had been working a lot, and she'd been stressing over finding a place to stay and then finding furniture once she rented Mal's place. An evening out with a bunch of people was preferable to drinks with Justine, Neil, and Ricky. She'd survived that, but she hadn't enjoyed it. And maybe she wouldn't enjoy this either, but there was only one way to find out. "Okay, sure. Thanks for inviting me."

"Great," Mal said. "She's coming. Hey, you aren't a pool shark are you?"

"Um, no. Is that a bad thing?"

Dean was laughing. "No, it's not. Haylee is, and so

is Remy Marchand. He's on a different team, but he hangs out there too. They fleece unsuspecting newcomers sometimes."

"But now you aren't unsuspecting," Mal said.

"Haylee wouldn't fleece Scarlett," Dean replied. "She likes her."

Scarlett didn't know what to say to that.

"Remy would. Hey, you guys want a beer or something?" Mal asked.

"Sounds great," Cade said. The others agreed.

"Come to the house. Scar, you want to come too?"

She looked at the five faces staring back at her. Overwhelm was her primary emotion at the moment. "No, thanks. I'm full from lunch and ice cream. I'll just stay here and put stuff away."

Not that she had a lot of stuff, plus she needed to go back to Justine's and grab the remainder of her clothes and toiletries since she hadn't thought she'd have the couch today.

"Text me if you need anything," Mal said. "Doesn't matter what time of day or night."

"Thank you, I will. And thanks again for all the help. I'll buy you guys a drink Friday."

"You don't have to," Dean said. "We're happy to help. You're Mal's friend, so that makes you our friend too."

She felt like he meant it. It touched her more than she could say.

The guys filtered out, the sound of their footsteps echoing down the stairs, their voices lifting in laughter and conversation as they went. It was quiet when they were gone. She usually liked quiet, but right now it felt empty and lonely rather than comforting.

Scarlett picked up one of the framed pictures she'd found and carried it around the room, holding it up in various spots to see where it should go. But her mind kept straying to the moment Mal had leaned toward her, all hulking, handsome male, and told her he sometimes thought about kissing her.

She really shouldn't feel a thrill chasing down her spine at the memory. But she did.

Chapter Ten

THE KNOCK ON HER DOOR WAS UNEXPECTED. Scarlett was in the bathroom, putting the finishing touches on her hair and makeup, when it came. Her heart careened into her ribs, but she told herself to calm down. Josh hadn't tracked her here. Yes, she'd panicked a little bit when her car was keyed, but nothing had happened since. It hadn't been him. She didn't see how it could be. She'd changed her name, her hair, left everything behind when she'd fled. She still had her driver's license in her name since she hadn't legally changed it. The only person in Maryland who knew her real identity was Dr. Stacey Puckett, the administrator at Riverstone. Puckett knew because Dr. Saunders had needed to tell the truth if she was going to help Scarlett find a new position.

Whoever was out there right now wasn't Josh. In fact, there was really only one person it could be.

Which meant she was going to kill him for climbing the stairs instead of texting her.

Scarlett marched from the bathroom and across the room, vowing to make curtains for the door sooner rather than later as she met the gaze of the man grinning back at her. Mal was unrepentant as she yanked open the door. His gaze traveled down her body and back up. He whistled. She thought she should be annoyed, but she wasn't. She was pleased, darn her.

"Man, Scar, you clean up nice."

She looked down at the white cropped jeans and sandals she was wearing, the green flowy top that matched his eyes now that she thought of it, and back up at him. "I'm always clean when you see me."

"Yeah, but your hair is usually in a ponytail. I was beginning to think that's the only way you wore it."

She felt her face heating. She'd left her hair loose, curling the strands so they formed big waves when she ran her fingers through the curls. She probably should have cut her hair when she'd left her old life, but she'd settled for dying it blond instead. She'd just touched up her roots last night, in fact.

"I wear ponytails because it's easier at work. Why are you here and why did you walk up those stairs?"

"I thought we could ride together. No sense taking two cars. And I walked because I don't quit."

"It's not quitting to give your leg a rest," she said, knowing it was like talking to a brick wall. "Are you asking me for a ride?"

"Actually, I was asking if you wanted to ride with me."

"Thank you, but I like driving myself. Means I can leave when I want to."

He shrugged. "Then I'll ride with you. I don't much care when we leave."

She could only stare at him. He pushed past her and into the apartment, turning around in the space. "Whoa, you've done some work."

She shut the door behind her. "A little. I could do more if I hadn't agreed to go out to a bar tonight."

It'd been a busy week at work and she'd been tired every night when she'd gotten home.

He gave her a look. "You don't want to go? I can cancel for us. I'll stay here and help you hang the rest of your pictures. We can watch television—wait, you don't have a television. Why not?"

Scarlett sighed. "No, don't cancel. Your friends were nice enough to invite me, and I said I'd go. And I don't have a television because I have a laptop. They've got this cool thing called streaming these days, but I need to get internet first."

"You can use mine," he said. "Unless you're doing something illegal."

"First of all, I most certainly am not. Second, I'm not going to piggyback off your internet."

"It's not a problem. I've got good service to the house, and Hacker set me up with an amazing mesh router system. It reaches out here, which you had to have noticed when you checked your phone."

"I noticed. But that doesn't mean the signal is strong."

"It is. Give me your phone and I'll put the password in."

He held out his hand. She stared at it, unsure what to do or say. A million thoughts went through her head, mostly centered around Josh and how he'd insinuated himself into her life in so many small ways. He'd taken it over before she'd realized it. She'd vowed to never let that happen again.

Mal's hand dropped. "I'm sorry, Scar."

She jerked her head up, meeting his gaze. "W-what?"

He shoved his hands in his pockets. His expression was serious. "Based on the look on your face, I think I crossed a line there. I'm sorry."

Wow. "I, uh…" She smoothed the edges of her top, gathering her thoughts. "It's not your fault. I accept your apology."

"Care to talk about it?"

She shook her head. "I know not every man is the same as my ex, but he was very controlling."

Way not to talk about it, Scarlett.

"That's not cool. I'm not that way, Scarlett. Really. I was trying to be a friend, but doing it badly."

She sighed. "Not badly. It's my issue."

"Yeah, but we're friends, and I respect your issue. If you want to use my Wi-Fi, I'll write down the password. And if you want to get your own connection out here because you don't want me seeing what you do, then I understand that too."

"I'm not doing anything I need to hide," she said, aware that was an ironic statement to make when she was in fact hiding who she really was. Which meant being on his internet was probably better than having her own. She'd have to use her name with the service provider, and that was just one more thread leading to her whereabouts.

All she did was watch TV shows and YouTube videos. She wasn't worried about Mal seeing what she was doing. She didn't bank online, and she had no credit cards.

"I wasn't suggesting you did. But it's presumptuous of me to assume you want to use my connection instead of getting your own. That's what I meant. You're entitled to your privacy."

We don't have any secrets, do we, Erin? There's no need for secrets between us.

Scarlett shivered at the memory of Josh's insidious voice, suggesting and manipulating her into giving him more and more control. She'd fallen for it because she'd had no one else. Her dad had moved them around too much for her to be very good at building lasting friendships, so all her friends were work friends. Fun people to be around and go to clubs with, but not the kind of people who'd known you for your whole life and could tell you when you were making a huge mistake.

"I don't mind using your Wi-Fi," she said. "I don't do a lot online anyway."

"Okay, good. I'll write the password down, but be sure to chew it up and swallow it once you're done."

He was grinning at her again, and her anxiety levels notched down. "You must think I'm crazy," she said softly.

"Nope, not at all. I asked if you were the crazy one. You assured me you weren't. That's good enough for me."

He was trying to make light again, and she appreciated it, but she also felt badly for letting the past color the present. "You're pretty trusting."

She didn't mean to keep pushing, and yet she couldn't help it. She was used to going it alone, so the sooner she found out that Mal didn't really want to be friends with her, the better.

"Not at all," he told her. "Cop's kid, remember? And a soldier with a pretty tough job to do. I know when someone is up to no good. Whatever secrets you're keeping, they aren't threatening to anyone but you."

"What makes you think I'm keeping secrets?" she asked, stunned at his perception.

"Aren't we all?"

She thought of his secret, the one he'd clearly not told any of his teammates. She didn't kid herself that she was the only one who knew, but she suspected she was the only one in his immediate circle that had guessed *who*.

"I suppose we are," she said softly. "You ready to go? I'll be the designated driver, in case you want to get a little rowdy."

He gave her a sad smile. "I appreciate that, and I'll take you up on it if you don't want to ride in my truck, but I don't drink much when I'm out with the guys and their women."

She understood why.

———

MAL FOLDED himself into Scarlett's Kia and gave her directions for Buddy's Bar & Grill. Truthfully, he was surprised she'd let him ride with her after he'd barged into her space and bossed her about the internet. Something about Scarlett made him feel protective, though. He wasn't sure what it was, or why, but he often found himself wanting to know what she was doing and if she was feeling safe. He'd gone up to her place with intentions to offer her a ride, but he'd found himself digging into her life before it was over.

Way to go, genius.

"Wow," Scarlett said as she turned into the parking lot at Buddy's. "This place is hopping."

"Yeah, it's pretty popular. Great wings and burgers, several pool tables and arcade machines, and good prices. Can't beat it."

Scarlett parked but she didn't shut off the engine. Her hands were wrapped around the steering wheel, her knuckles white.

"You okay?"

She turned her head. Her blue eyes hit him somewhere at gut level. What the heck was that all about? She really was pretty though. Her long hair looked silky as it framed her face in a cloud of waves. She'd put on lipstick and mascara, something she didn't wear when she was working. The effect was a little shocking, really. He was used to his no-nonsense physical therapist with her ponytail and unremarkable features, but this was Scarlett as she really was when her time was her own.

"Honestly, I'm a little nervous."

He liked that she trusted him enough to admit that. "Can I ask why?"

"I don't go out much anymore, and I'm not used to the crowds and noise."

"You went on that drinks date where your friend tried to set you up."

"I did, and I was nervous then too."

"So how did you get past it?"

"I just marched inside and pretended. Then I left."

"Do you want to leave? We don't have to go in."

She shook her head. "Honestly, I let you ride with me because I kind of thought I might ghost you tonight when it came down to it. I'd get here and then turn around and go home."

He reached for her hand, covering it where it sat on the wheel. Her skin was cold. "Scar, you don't have to go inside. We can go home."

She studied where his hand lay on top of hers. She didn't pull away, though. "I promised to buy the guys a drink for helping me."

"They'll understand."

She drew herself up, shook her head as if gathering her courage. "Nope, I'm going in."

"Okay, but when you're done, let me know. We'll leave. I won't ask questions and you don't need a reason."

"Thank you."

"Just don't leave me stranded, Scar. I'll have to tack the Uber fee onto your rent."

She blinked at him. He grinned.

"Oh jeez, I thought you were serious."

"I'd really rather you didn't ditch me, but I'll get a ride from one of the guys if you do. And I won't bring you bagels in the morning like I'd planned."

"You're going to bring me bagels?"

"I thought it'd be a nice gesture. Welcome to the neighborhood kind of thing. I'd have done it sooner, but you were gone early every morning."

She was laughing now. It made his heart happy.

"There is no neighborhood. It's you and me on two acres in the middle of nowhere."

"Not quite the middle of nowhere."

"Okay, not quite." She sucked in a breath. "I'm ready now. Let's go in."

They got out of the car and she came around to his side. He waited for her to change her mind, but she started walking toward the door. People had spilled out onto the front porch Buddy had recently added, beers in hand, talking loudly as music pumped from the jukebox inside.

"Mal," someone yelled.

"Hey," Mal yelled back as a man strode off the porch toward him. "Haven't seen you in a while, Shade."

Corey "Shade" Vance from the HOT SEAL Team grinned ear to ear. "You know, off saving the world and shit. Heard you took a hit, man."

"A little one."

Scarlett coughed. Shade let his gaze stray to her, which Mal knew he'd been wanting to do from the start. "Hey, I'm Corey."

"Scarlett."

Shade took her hand and kissed it. Mal pulled him away. "Enough. Scar doesn't need you pawing at her."

"I'm not pawing at her. I'm saying hello."

"Yeah, well, you've said it then. Back off and let her breathe."

"I can breathe, Mal," she said.

Mal put an arm casually on her shoulders. "This is my good friend Scarlett Reed. She's also my physical therapist. We aren't dating because we're pals, but she's not dating anyone. Swore off men, didn't you, Scar?"

He could feel the shudder roll through her. He wondered if it was revulsion or laughter. A quick look at her face indicated the latter. "That's right. Swore them off after the last one."

"Damned shame," Shade said.

"This is Corey Vance," Mal told her. "His call sign is Shade, so we tend to call him that. Just so you don't get confused."

"Everybody has two names. How could I possibly get confused?"

She was looking up at him with a sarcastic arch to her eyebrow. He had a strong compulsion to kiss her.

Nope. Not ruining this.

"You'll get used to it. We answer to either name."

"But your name really is Mal. Or am I missing something?"

Shade snorted. "You aren't missing anything. We all get saddled with names our teammates give us, but this one gets plain old Mal. Personally, I think they should have called him Doc—or Bones."

"Doc or Bones?"

"You know, Doc McCoy on *Star Trek*. Also called Bones McCoy."

"Yeah, but they didn't," Mal said, really thankful nobody'd named him Bones. "Piss off, Shade."

Shade laughed and put an arm around Mal's neck, hugging him tight. "Glad you didn't bite the big one out there, buddy. Later, Scarlett. If you want to dance, I'm your man. Keep it in mind."

"I will. Thanks."

Shade sauntered away and they walked up onto

the porch before easing inside. "Sorry about that," Mal said in her ear so she could hear him.

"It's fine. I'm an introvert, not a head case. So why *Mal?* Why didn't you get something else?"

"I'm just a Mal. They tried, but it was what stuck. Probably because of *Firefly.* Captain Mal Reynolds," he added in case she didn't know the show.

"I've seen it. And I'm still mad there's only one season."

"You and the rest of the world," he said. "Hey, there's the gang. You ready for this?"

"Ready as I'll ever be."

"Remember, no taking off without me."

Her frown was exaggerated. "If I have a sudden urge to leave, I'll get your attention."

"How?"

"How?"

"Yeah, how do you plan to do it?"

"I'll tap you on the shoulder and say, hey, let's go. What else do you expect?"

"That'll work," he said. "Even if it's boring. You could do something more fun—like make a duck face at me."

She shook her head. "You're silly."

"Made you laugh though."

He liked it when she laughed. Liked that it erased the lines of worry and fear that seemed to haunt her. Mal looped his arm through hers and led her toward his people.

Chapter Eleven

After Mal introduced her around, Haylee took Scarlett's hand and led her over to the women's table.

"They're just going to tell tall tales and make fart jokes all night," Haylee said. "Come on over here for the adult conversation."

Haylee did the introductions and then they settled in to talk. Scarlett was a little apprehensive, because she always was in crowds, but the women made her feel welcome. There was no cattiness, no sizing her up with disapproval.

Brooke was sweet as pie, which made sense because she ran a bakery. Computer expert Bliss was cool and elegant, but had a warm Southern accent that emerged from time to time. Eva was the most interesting of all. She was tattooed in gray and black, and every bit of it was amazing. On her, it looked suave and beautiful. She was a tattoo artist, of course, and she was with the big guy wearing a Harley T-shirt. Naturally, Bliss was with Hacker. And Brooke was with Cade, who Scarlett gathered from conversation was the leader of the team.

"How's our Mal doing?" Brooke asked. "Is he behaving himself and doing all his exercises?"

Scarlett sipped her iced tea. "He does all his exercises. He sometimes does more than he should, but I think he's getting the hang of it. He's doing remarkably well for someone who went through what he did."

The women exchanged a look. Scarlett recognized it for the fear it was. What if it was their man?

"I'm so glad," Brooke said. "Mal's such a good guy."

"He is," Scarlett agreed.

"You've moved to his place," Bliss said.

"To an apartment over his garage. My roommate needs to sell her house because she's getting married. Mal offered, I accepted. It's a great little place. Just what I need."

"It's cozy," Haylee said. "And I bet it'll be even cozier when you're finished decorating it. Mal said you bought some things," she added when Scarlett threw her a confused look. "Pictures and stuff at the thrift store. I love thrifting."

"You do?"

Haylee was a journalist and seemed so put together that Scarlett couldn't picture her sorting through bins at Goodwill.

"Hell yes. Who doesn't love getting a bargain?" Haylee threw a look at Bliss. "Maybe not you."

Bliss laughed. "How do you know?"

"You're wearing a silk shirt to a bar, and that purse is Hermès if it's anything."

"A lot you know. It's an Hermès dupe. Got it on Amazon."

"You're kidding."

"Nope." She hooked the bag off her chair and thrust it at Haylee. "Take a look. You'll see the differences up close."

Haylee examined the bag and handed it back. "Fine, but that's still a silk shirt."

Bliss ran her fingers down the perfectly pressed blue silk and shrugged. "I like luxury, what can I say?"

They passed the next half hour like that, talking about all kinds of topics, eating loaded nachos off a plate in the center of the table, and laughing like friends who'd known each other forever. Scarlett liked it, even if she felt like an observer rather than a participant. Not because they didn't try to include her, but because she didn't have a lot to add.

"Where's the restroom?" she asked after their waitress came by to refill glasses with tea, soda, and water.

"Past the pool tables and down that hall," Eva said. "I'll go with you."

The pool tables were packed with players. One of them was laughing with a couple of others, but when Scarlett and Eva walked by, he tracked their progress.

"Do you know him?" Scarlett asked.

"Can't say that I do. But people sometimes stare. The tattoos."

"I think they're beautiful," Scarlett said, then felt awkward for blurting it out.

Eva smiled. "Thanks. I do too, but they are definitely not for everyone. Hell, I may regret it when I'm eighty, but maybe not. Maybe they'll hide all the wrinkles and disguise any sagging."

They entered the restroom and did their business, then headed back toward the table. Eva got waylaid by someone who wanted to ask her about her tattoos. Scarlett didn't linger because she didn't want to seem like she was eavesdropping. The room had grown more crowded in the time since she and Mal had walked in. She searched for him in the crowd, finally spotting him with his team, sitting on a stool and laughing at something one of the guys was saying. She could study him from afar and not feel self-conscious about it. There was no one to see her, no one to question.

She'd had fun so far tonight, and she owed that to him. He made it easy to be around him. His friends made it easy too. She liked them. These women weren't as flighty and spontaneous as Justine, and the men weren't as stuffy as Neil. She liked Justine and Neil though. They'd been good to her, that minor glitch with Ricky the accountant notwithstanding.

"You look familiar," someone said.

Scarlett spun toward the voice. It was the man

who'd been watching her and Eva earlier. He was holding a pool cue and studying her curiously. He wasn't much taller than she was, but he was lean and muscled—like so many of these military types—with sandy hair cropped close and brown eyes that narrowed as he watched her.

"Do you say that to all the ladies?" she quipped.

"No, I mean it. I've seen you before."

Scarlett's heart thumped. "I work at a hospital. Maybe you came in for treatment."

"Haven't been to the hospital lately." He snapped his fingers. "Florida. You look like a girl I met down there."

She hoped her skin didn't look as white as it felt with the blood draining from her head. She put a hand out to steady herself on a bar height table. "Sorry, I…"

"She had red hair, but you could be her sister."

Scarlett forced a laugh. "You know what they say —we all have a twin somewhere."

"Yeah, probably right. Still, I thought I'd ask. You never know."

"No, I guess you don't. Are you new around here?" Not that she wanted to keep talking to him, but she needed to know.

"Been here six months. I was at Eglin before that. Special Forces Detachment there."

Ice formed in her veins. He'd been in Josh's unit. She didn't recall ever meeting him, but that didn't mean he didn't know Josh. And he'd clearly recognized her from somewhere.

Her stomach churned with acid. "Oh, cool. Hey, I have to get back to my friends."

He gave her a suggestive look as he took a step closer. "They can wait, can't they? We could go somewhere, talk a bit."

Scarlett took a step back. "Uh, they could if I were looking, but I'm not. I have a boyfriend."

He held up both hands. "My bad. Just thought you looked familiar."

"It happens," she said, trying to make her voice light in spite of the panic threatening to take over.

She turned on her heel and hurried back to the table where the women sat. Brooke frowned at her. "You feeling okay, Scarlett?"

Scarlett slugged back some tea, her fingers shaky where they grabbed the straw. "Um, I think I'm getting a headache. All the noise. Also, it's been a stressful week with the move. I think maybe I should get back home and get some sleep."

"Totally understandable."

She gathered her purse and slung it over her shoulder. A glance at Mal told her he was still having a great time with his friends. He'd said not to leave without him, but was it really fair to interrupt him? She was on the verge of asking the women if someone could give him a ride home when his head lifted and his gaze met hers. She tried to smile, tried to gloss over the fact she was a nervous wreck inside, but it must not have worked because he said something to his friends and then jerked his head toward the door. She nodded and said her goodbyes to the women before making her way over to where Mal waited.

"You want to leave, don't you?"

She clutched the leather strap of her purse. "I'm tired, Mal. You don't need to go with me. I'll just head back and get some sleep. No need for you to stop having fun because of me."

"I told you I'd go when you wanted to, and that's what I'm doing." He put a hand against the small of her back and steered her outside. She was so rattled she didn't say a word, even when his hand stayed there until they reached her Kia. He took the keys from her, unlocked the vehicle, and walked her to the passenger door. "You rest. I'll drive."

"I can drive."

"Scarlett. You don't have to do everything yourself, you know. You're tired, I'm not. I'll drive. I drank soda and water tonight. No alcohol."

She wasn't someone who let others take care of her. She didn't want to get used to it because as soon as you did, people left you—but she nodded for once and got inside the small SUV. She clipped her seatbelt while Mal walked around and settled behind the wheel.

She turned to look at the building as he reversed. The guy who'd said he recognized her was standing outside on the porch, watching her.

Or maybe he wasn't watching her. He lit a

cigarette and took a drag, and someone else stood there talking to him, waving his hands around as if to illustrate a point.

Stop being paranoid, Scarlett.

But how couldn't she be? He'd recognized her, and he'd come from Eglin. Had he known Josh? Or had they simply met at some point? She couldn't place him, which worried her. He could have been at one of the events Josh took her to, or he could have passed through the hospital. There was no way of knowing, and she wasn't about to go back and quiz him on it.

The farther she got from Buddy's, the better. In fact, maybe she should grab her clothes and boogie out of town entirely.

Except how was she going to do that? Dr. Saunders had used her connections with Dr. Puckett to get Scarlett a job where no one else had to know her real name. If she left this place, she wouldn't get another job in medicine. She'd be waiting tables and doing odd jobs, trying to cobble together a living while always keeping one eye over her shoulder.

It wasn't an existence she wanted.

"You okay?"

Scarlett swung around to look at Mal. He shot her a glance, eyes filled with worry, then looked at the darkened road again.

"I'm fine," she lied. "Why?"

"You seem spooked. Did something happen tonight?"

"What would happen? I had a great time hanging out with the ladies, but I just kind of reached my upper limit of what I could take. I don't like crowds."

"I saw a guy talking to you. Did he say something inappropriate? Should I go back there and kick his ass?"

Oh, shit.

"No, he didn't say anything wrong." She wrapped her arms around herself and squeezed. She was cold. Any second she'd start to shiver. Mal wasn't going to miss that, and then what? "It's no big deal, but he thought he recognized me. He was stationed at Eglin Air Force Base, and that's the area where I came from. I was afraid he might know my ex."

Mal seemed to process this information. "Your ex doesn't know where you are."

"No. It was a bad situation, like I said. I left everything behind and moved here. The last thing I want is for him to find me."

———

MAL KNEW he needed to tread carefully here, but it was obvious Scarlett was distressed. He wanted to know what her ex had done, and he wanted a name. He wanted to make sure the motherfucker never bothered Scarlett again, but he knew that trying to insinuate himself into the situation, even to protect her, wasn't going to go over well with independent-minded Scarlett. She wasn't used to counting on anyone, and that bugged him. He wanted her to know she could count on him.

Hell, he'd counted on her for the past few weeks. Counted on her to help him get mobile again, to help him heal and make it back to fighting form. Without her, he might have pushed too hard too fast. Not that another therapist wouldn't have told him the same things she had, but he found himself listening to her whereas he might not have listened to someone else.

Perverse but true.

"Do you think he's actively looking for you," Mal asked.

She hugged herself, her fingers digging into her arms. "I think he probably is, yes. He doesn't like losing, and while I'm positive he doesn't care about me, he cares very much about winning. I left, and that means he lost. If he could find me and make me come back, he'd win."

"Make you come back? How could he possibly do that?"

"I'm not sure I want to talk about this."

Frustration hammered him. "I know it's none of my business, but I want to help. You said he was a warrior, like me. But I can promise you he's not. Not really. Where I work only takes the best of the best, which means I'm more skilled than he is. If you need protecting, I've got your back. So does my team."

"I appreciate that, but there's nothing for you to do. I made a mistake going tonight. I should have realized that military guys congregate all over that place, and that it was possible someone who knew my ex would end up assigned here. I wasn't thinking."

Mal gripped the wheel as frustration rolled over him. "Not sure you're thinking now, Scar. It didn't have to be Buddy's. It could be Walmart, or hell, the hospital. The military is surprisingly small in some ways. You always run into someone you knew ten years ago at a different assignment when you're halfway around the world. Do you plan to spend the rest of your life hiding from this guy?"

She didn't say anything for a long moment. "If I have to, yes."

"Will you tell me what he did to you that's made you so scared?"

"I said I didn't want to talk about it."

"And I heard you. But dammit, Scar, I'm your friend. If I can help you, I will."

She blew out an explosive breath. "He took over my life, Mal. He cut me off from everyone, gaslighted me, and stalked me when I tried to break it off. Moving away was my only recourse. Happy?"

Anger boiled in his belly. "No, I'm not happy. I'm fucking pissed. *For you.* If he shows up looking for you, I won't let him get to you."

"You're still healing. How are you going to stop him?"

"I'm not helpless, Scarlett. Not even close."

She reached over and put a hand on his bicep. Her skin was cold. "Thank you for caring, but it's not your problem."

It was his problem. That's what she didn't understand. Hell, he wasn't sure he understood it himself. But Scarlett had come to mean something to him. He liked her. She'd been with him on a fairly rough journey and he wasn't going to forget that. He wasn't the kind of guy who abandoned his friends.

"I want you to tell me if he contacts you and makes you feel scared in any way. I won't get involved, but I want to know. I want to be ready in case you tell me you need me to step up for you."

She didn't look at him, turning her head to gaze out the side window instead. "Okay, I can do that."

Deep down, he knew she was lying.

Chapter Twelve

HALF AN HOUR AFTER GETTING HOME AND MAKING sure Scarlett was settled upstairs in her studio, Mal took off again. He'd considered staying where he was so he could watch for any trouble, but he reasoned that nothing was happening tonight. It was the first time she'd run into someone who she thought might know her ex, which had rattled her badly, but that didn't mean her ex was waiting in the shadows for Mal to drive off so he could approach. No one had followed them home, and there was no actual paper-work trail from Scarlett to Mal. He'd rented her the place without a contract or formal agreement, and the utilities were in his name.

They'd had that discussion about the internet, but then she'd said she wanted to use his Wi-Fi, so that's what they were doing. There was simply nothing to trace if her ex was hunting for her through public records. Unless she was posting pictures on Facebook and tagging herself, which he doubted. A quick search for Scarlett Reed revealed a handful of profiles, but none with photos of her. He'd have to ask her if she was on Facebook. Make some excuse about wanting to friend her. His profile was locked down tight and mostly there for his parents and sister, as well as a handful of high school friends from back home, but he'd make an exception for Scarlett.

Mal pulled into the parking lot at Buddy's and strode inside to find his team. They were laughing uproariously about something, but the instant they saw him, seven faces sobered.

"What's up?" Saint asked casually.

"Need to talk to Hacker," Mal said.

Hack put down his drink. "Here? Somewhere more quiet?"

"My truck."

"Think we'd all better come," Wolf said. "If that's okay."

"It is, but not sure you can help just yet."

"Let me get Brooke to watch the table for us," Saint said.

"I need to look around for a sec," Mal replied. "Be right back."

Saint frowned. "Okay. Need help?"

"Nope, I got it." Mal strolled through the bar and pool room, looking for the man who'd stopped Scarlett. When he didn't spot him, he returned to the guys and they went outside to his truck. After scoping out the area, they gathered around the driver's door which Mal had opened so he could sit down. His leg was aching pretty badly tonight, truth be told. He hated it, and yet he had to believe Scarlett when she told him it would get better.

"What's the problem?" Hacker asked when everyone moved in close enough not to let their voices carry in the night.

"It's Scarlett," Mal said. He filled them in about the guy from the bar, and what she'd said about her ex.

Ryder—call sign Muffin, poor guy—whistled low. "Damn, that's some shit."

"Yeah, and she's not telling me all of it. I'm certain of that."

"You want me to do some research," Hacker said. "Check into her background, see if I can find who this guy is. Where he is."

"Exactly. She's scared, and I don't like it. Maybe I'm reading it all wrong, because Scarlett is pretty private, but she seemed genuinely spooked tonight. She didn't like that someone thought he knew her. Hell, I half expect to return home to find her packing up her car."

He'd considered it before he left, but decided even if she was packing up, she wouldn't drive off until morning. She'd want to go to the hospital to pick up her things there, plus she'd want to smooth the way with management if at all possible. At least he hoped he was reading her right when it came to that.

Mostly, he hoped she wasn't contemplating fleeing.

He wasn't sure how to talk her out of it if she was, but he'd have to think of something. He didn't want her to go. He didn't want to go to his therapy appointments and see someone else instead of her, and he didn't want the damned apartment over his garage to stay empty for another few months.

"I'll get Bliss to help. She can do the more questionable stuff, if there is any," Hacker said. "She's tapped into those networks more than I am."

Bliss Bennett was a talented computer hacker in her own right. She'd been married to Hacker once, and would be again even though they didn't seem in any hurry to make it official. Mal was never quite sure how that relationship worked, but it didn't matter. Bliss was one of them now, working for HOT on a contract-for-hire basis. She could get her fingers dirty when they couldn't—if it came down to it.

"Thanks, man. I appreciate it."

"The guy who talked to her tonight was playing pool, and he was at the special forces detachment at Eglin before this," Saint said. "We should be able to narrow it down."

Wolf was standing with crossed arms. "If he's a new HOT recruit, we can narrow it down a lot faster."

"He could be," Saint said. "But I didn't see any faces I didn't recognize hanging out with any of the HOT people who were here. Doesn't mean I saw everyone, though."

"I'll get a list of new recruits," Hacker said. "And

find out if any came from Eglin, or been stationed there within the last year or two."

Mal was aware he was going behind Scarlett's back, and that she wouldn't like it if she found out, but dammit, sometimes you had to do what you had to do to protect a friend. By the time his team was done, they'd know her ex-boyfriend's name, his duty assignment, his missions, his shoe size, and whether he liked vanilla or chocolate. Mal would explain it to her later if he had to, meaning if she figured out what he was doing, but right now he had to do this. For her.

They made plans to start checking into Scarlett's background. Though it was only nine-thirty when they finished talking, Mal decided to return home instead of hanging out. It wasn't until he was halfway home again that he realized he hadn't thought of Haylee for hours.

———

SCARLETT HADN'T GOTTEN a curtain for the door yet, but she dug out a sheet she'd picked up at the thrift shop and fashioned something. The rest of the windows were uncovered, but they were all on the second floor and didn't have stairs leading up to them.

There were trees, though. Josh would climb a tree in a second.

"Stop it," she muttered as she checked the window locks. Most of the windows were still painted shut anyway. Maybe she'd leave them that way. It was harder than hell to get them open when they were painted shut, and there'd be a lot of racket if anyone tried to break all the panes so they could get through.

Scarlett huddled on the couch and fired up her laptop. She couldn't help but shoot paranoid glances at the windows and the darkness beyond, but everything was quiet outside. She reasoned with herself that Josh wasn't out there. Whoever that guy had been tonight, even if he called Josh immediately and told him that he'd seen her, Josh didn't have wings and he wasn't going to magically appear.

Scarlett navigated to Facebook and logged in. She'd started a new profile for one reason only. To keep tabs on Josh. She couldn't see what he only shared with friends, but he was enough of an attention-seeker that he put up a lot of public posts. It'd surprised her that he did that at first, but she was no longer surprised. It was part of his persona to appear as a caring, involved guy.

He'd shared a Go Fund Me post where someone needed money to pay for repairs to their elderly mother's home before the city kicked her out for being unable to bring it up to code after an inspection revealed violations. He'd included a heartfelt plea of his own. Scarlett seethed. He didn't care about the woman or her plight. He did care about the comments on his post, though.

"Josh, you're such a good guy."

"Thanks for sharing. Going to donate."

"You're an amazing person. You always try to help others."

And Josh's answer: *"Just doing my part. The world would be a better place if we helped each other more often."*

Scarlett scrolled, looking for evidence that Josh was still in Florida, but none of his posts featured photos or check-ins. She was tempted to log in under her real name in order to see the Friends Only posts, but she was pretty sure Josh had her password and was monitoring for logins from other locations. Too dangerous to try, so she navigated away from his profile. When she checked her notifications, she had one that said she'd been tagged in a photo. She clicked and a photo of her and Ricky came up.

"Justine!" she growled. She'd asked Justine not to post the photo she'd snapped when Scarlett had been caught unaware. Ricky had slipped his arm over the back of her chair and Scarlett was turning to look at him when Justine snapped the pic. Justine had laughed when Scarlett said something. *"It's just for us, darling."*

But there it was. Scarlett's heart thumped as she removed the tag. She hadn't posted any photos of herself since she'd left Florida. Scarlett Reed had a blood red rose for a profile photo. Scarlett Reed posted vague things about living each day the best you could or finding joy in simple things. She had enough of a profile not to seem suspicious to social media loving co-workers and acquaintances, but that was it. Maybe she should have shut it all down, but she felt better being able to check Josh's profile anonymously.

She probably should have logged into her old

profile immediately after the accident and deleted it entirely, but she'd been paranoid about Josh tracking her so she'd kept putting it off. And now it was impossible. A look at her old life revealed nothing new on her timeline. Coworkers posted things there, but they went unanswered.

"Miss you, Erin. Hope you're well. Update us when you can."

Scarlett's eyes filled with tears. It seemed a lifetime ago, though it was only three months. Dr. Saunders would have told her coworkers she'd been transferred, and they all believed she'd left without saying goodbye. She hated that. She'd liked the people she'd worked with, though she'd stopped doing things with them months before she'd left town when Josh had managed to cut her off from everyone. She hadn't even realized it at first. That's how good he was.

Scarlett logged out and went over to YouTube where she surfed through home decor videos. They soothed her so much, especially one lady with a soft voice who got things from thrift stores and gave them makeovers before putting them into her decor.

When Scarlett's phone buzzed with a text sometime later, she jerked. It took her a moment to realize it was after midnight and she'd been dozing with the computer on the small trunk in front of the couch. She'd curled up to watch and apparently she'd fallen asleep because she didn't remember this particular video.

She pressed stop and picked up her phone, her heart still racing. It was Mal.

I see light coming from up there. You okay?

Scarlett yawned and shifted as she lay back on the couch. It wasn't as comfortable as it would be if she'd folded it out, but she hadn't expected to sleep either. *I was asleep. You woke me up.*

Mal: *Sorry. But there's a variable light, like you're watching television.*

Scarlett: *I don't have a television, remember? It's my computer. I was watching videos, but I fell asleep.*

Mal: *Lucky you.*

Scarlett frowned. *Are you in pain?*

Mal: *It hurts a bit tonight. Nothing I can't handle.*

Scarlett: *Except you can't sleep because of it. Did you take a pain pill?*

Mal: *I don't like relying on those things.*

Scarlett shook her head. Damned stubborn man. *I understand, but taking a pill when you need it isn't a failure. You have to stay ahead of the pain, or you'll have nights like this one more often than you care to.*

Mal: *You're just full of joy, aren't you?*

Scarlett: *I'm keeping it real. You aren't Superman. You have to use the tools you have to get past this.*

Mal: *Maybe I could come up and talk to you for a while. That would take my mind off it.*

Scarlett: *You aren't coming up these stairs. Besides, we are talking. Or texting anyway. I'll call you if that helps.*

Mal: *It's not the same. I want to see you while I talk to you.*

She thought about it for a moment. But the truth was, she wanted to talk to someone too. She wanted to see his face. She trusted Mal. More importantly, she felt safe with him. It was an odd thing to admit to herself, but it was true. Mal was safe.

Scarlett: *I'll come over there. Meet me at the back door.*

Chapter Thirteen

MAL STOOD ON THE BACK PORCH, WATCHING Scarlett as she descended the stairs. She stopped once, as if listening for something, then hurried the rest of the way down. In the distance, lightning painted the night sky. It wasn't close, and it wasn't a zigzag bolt, but rather a flash of light that illuminated billowing thunderheads. It also illuminated Scarlett as she stepped onto the grass and trotted over to the screen door. He pushed it open for her and she came up the steps and onto the porch.

"Thanks."

"You're welcome."

She was close, her slender body emanating heat and a sweet scent that he recognized as flowers. Not a specific flower, just flowery. He wanted to put his nose against her skin and breathe it in, but that would send her bolting back out into the night.

"Do you want to come in, or do you prefer to sit out here?"

"What do you prefer?" she asked.

"Honestly, these chairs aren't the best for sitting in for long periods. I need to get better ones."

"Then we should go inside."

He held the door for her and she walked into the kitchen in front of him. "Do you want me to turn on the lights?" he asked when he'd followed her inside. She was standing in the middle of the kitchen, her features illuminated by the nightlight burning near the sink.

He had automatic nightlights throughout the house so he didn't have to turn on lights at night when he wandered. Not that he wasn't accustomed to dark spaces, but why not have dim lights illuminating the way when he could?

"I can see. I think a light would be too bright right now, don't you?"

"Agreed. Why did you stop for a second back there? Forget something?"

She turned wide eyes on him. "You were watching me?"

"Well, yeah. I wanted to make sure you were okay."

She wrapped her arms around herself. "It was nothing."

"Sure?"

"Yes. Okay, you might think I'm crazy, but I felt

like I was being watched for a moment. Now I know why. It was you."

He held up his hands. "I don't think it's crazy at all. I always trust my gut. You learn to do that when your life is on the line. Mine has saved me more than once."

"And saved Dean too," she said softly.

"Yeah." He pulled in a breath. "Want anything to drink? A snack? A pizza?"

She laughed. "Thanks, but I'm good."

He found himself enjoying the sound. Nothing about Scarlett was overstated. She wasn't in your face stunning, but she was unforgettable once you knew her. He'd been relieved when he got home and her car was still in the drive. She wasn't piling things into it and there hadn't been frantic movement in the apartment. He'd watched for a while, but the only motion had been the flickering light of her laptop.

He'd tried to sleep but it hadn't worked. When he looked out the window again, there was still light coming from her windows. He'd texted on impulse, but he wasn't sorry for it.

"You sure? Pizza works at any time of night."

"I'm good, Mal. But thank you."

"All right. I'm going to have a beer if that doesn't bother you."

"I'm not bothered by it. But thanks for asking."

He grabbed a beer from the fridge and twisted off the top, then led her to the sitting room at the rear of the house with the picture window that looked over a field. From there, they could see the brewing storm as the lights flashed inside the clouds.

Scarlett sat on one end of the couch. He hesitated, then chose a chair at the opposite end so she didn't think he was trying to get too close to her. She'd agreed to come, and that indicated a certain level of trust, but he wasn't going to do anything to make her second-guess his intentions.

"You feeling better now?" he asked.

"I'm fine. What about you? Did you take that pill?"

"In the past five minutes? No."

"Mal."

He knew what she was saying, but he hated the way painkillers made him feel. Plus he was used to working through pain. HOT warriors didn't pop a pill when conditions were hard and they were pushing to the edge of endurance. That's not how it worked.

Still, his leg ached tonight, probably because he'd put a lot of pressure on himself to work it this week. He wanted to be back at work, not hobbling on a cane when he couldn't walk on his own any longer.

"I know," he said. "But it's too late anyway."

"What do you mean it's too late?"

"You always say to stay ahead of the pain. I'm not ahead of it, I'm behind it. So why chase it with drugs? I took Tylenol."

She sighed. "Okay. That's something, I guess. The doctor wouldn't give you the serious stuff if she didn't intend for you to use it when needed, you know."

"I know." He sipped his beer. "But the fewer I take, the better. If it's really bad, I'll take one. Promise."

"What's really bad for you?"

He shrugged. "I'll let you know."

"What did you want to talk about?"

"Anything. Everything."

She laughed. "That's pretty broad."

"Yeah, but if I'd said I wanted to talk about you, you'd stiffen up and leave."

He could see the wary expression on her face. "Why would you want to talk about me?"

"Because you interest me. And because you're afraid of something, and I don't like it."

"Everyone's afraid of something."

"I know. But not all fears are the same, are they?"

She shook her head. Then she said something that threw him so hard he didn't know how to recover. "How long have you been in love with Haylee?"

He blinked, his mouth falling slightly open as pain rolled over him. It wasn't the same pain as usual though. It was different somehow. Not as sharp or lasting. More like a regret than an active wound.

"You don't have to answer that," she said when he didn't respond. "I shouldn't have said anything."

He took a slug of beer. "No, you have every right considering how hard I've bugged you about your ex." He set the beer down, looked at his hands. "Shit. You must think I'm a complete asshole. Wolf is my friend."

"I don't think that at all. It's clear you feel rotten about it."

"Jesus, all this time I've had to keep it in. And here you are asking me about it. How did you guess?"

He'd always been careful, but clearly he hadn't been careful enough. He prayed she was the only one to see it, though.

"It was the way you looked at her that day I came to view the apartment. And I honestly wouldn't have guessed if you hadn't told me you were hung up on someone who was in love with someone else. It all made sense then."

He leaned back against the chair and gazed up at the ceiling. "I've never touched Haylee. We've never dated. She's always been with Wolf since I've known her. But you know how they say love hits you like a lightning bolt and you just know?"

"I've never experienced it, but yes."

"I was watching her play pool one day and it happened. Boom. My heart felt like it'd been zapped and I couldn't stop thinking about her. The harder I tried, the worse it got." The words hurt, but not as much as he'd expected. He'd never said them aloud to anyone. Never been able to. Who would he have told?

"I'm sorry, Mal."

Guilt sliced into him. "That's it? No words about what a terrible friend I am? No questions about if I'm sure it's love or have I tried dating someone else to get over it?"

"First of all, I wouldn't say any of that to you.

Second of all—and I'm sorry to say this but I'm going to anyway—I don't think the lightning bolt means anything. It was one moment in time. It doesn't predict your entire future."

"You don't believe in love slapping you in the face when you least expect it?"

She shook her head. "Not really. But you do, so that's what matters. You looked at Haylee one day, a woman you'd presumably known for some amount of time but never viewed romantically, and boom, lightning. Now you're in love with your friend's girl and you feel like shit about it."

He wanted to protest, and yet he couldn't. He'd found Haylee attractive from the first because what man wouldn't? But the way Scarlett put it, it sounded ridiculous. Like he had no control over his own emotions and he'd been in danger of randomly falling for anyone if the conditions had been right.

"You make me feel like an idiot."

"I'm not trying to, I swear. It's just that you seem to have put a whole lot of energy into this thing and why? It's not like you and Haylee dated, or that she chose Dean over you. If you'd had a relationship, I could see not being over it. But you didn't. This is random, literally like getting hit by lightning."

As if to illustrate a point, the sky chose that moment to flash with far off light.

"People do get hit by lightning."

"I know, but you have like a one in fifteen-thousand chance in a lifetime. It's not all that common. That's what I'm saying."

"Wow. Not only are you in charge of my physical therapy sessions, you're giving me a little tough love therapy about my love life. Maybe I should have taken the pill," he joked.

"I told you so."

He stretched out and put his leg on the coffee table, trying to get some relief from the pain. The muscles were tight, the bones aching deep inside. He could feel the heat in his leg where the aching made everything unhappy and hot.

Scarlett moved until she was closer. "I can massage it for you if you think it'll help."

His entire body went taut at the idea. But he nodded. "Worth a try."

Her small hands touched his skin, and he had to swallow. "It's inflamed," she said softly. "What have you been doing?"

"I don't know. Walking up and down the stairs. Trying to strengthen these damned muscles. Doesn't seem to matter, still hurts like a bitch and nothing gets better."

"It will, Mal. Patience," she said, fingers digging in gently but firmly. "So tight. I think we need to ice it for the swelling."

"I've got a couple of cold packs in the freezer."

"Okay. Let me try to loosen these knots a bit first, then I'll get one."

He stared at the top of her head, at the way her

hair shone in the dim light, and he itched to touch it. To distract himself, no doubt. "It's going to storm," he said as the sky flashed again. This time the rumble of thunder wasn't far behind.

"I know."

"Just wanted to mention it in case you wanted to be back in your bed before it starts."

Bed. Just saying the word made a shiver roll down his spine. What the fuck was that about?

"I'll stay as long as you need me. You woke me up, so I'm up. When I'm ready to crash, I'll sleep on your couch if I have to."

"I have an extra bed. You don't have to sleep on the couch."

"Okie doke." She kept digging into his muscles, firm and soft, easing the tension. The bone-deep ache didn't abate, but at least his muscles weren't knotted with unrelenting pain anymore. They still hurt, but it wasn't a stabbing pain.

Scarlett ran her hands up his thigh, toward his groin, and his breath halted in his chest. He found himself wishing she'd keep going, but of course she ran her hands in the other direction again. His dick didn't get the message though. It throbbed to life despite his best attempts to keep it from doing so.

Thank heavens the light was dim. He only hoped Scarlett didn't notice the growing bulge in his athletic shorts as she worked her way up and down his thigh. He thought maybe her movements slowed at one point, but he wasn't sure. She wasn't looking at him, and he wasn't sure if it was deliberate or not.

The tension was thick between them, though maybe it was all in his mind. He was beginning to think it was, that he was losing his grip on reality, when she looked up and their gazes locked. Her eyes were wide, her chest rising and falling a little faster than he expected. Her fingers stilled as her tongue darted over her lips. Mal's dick strained against the confines of his shorts.

"I'd better, uh, get that ice pack."

Chapter Fourteen

SCARLETT SCRAMBLED TO HER FEET AND HURRIED INTO the kitchen. What was the matter with her? She'd been massaging Mal's leg when the sensuality of touching his skin got through the professional veneer she tried to maintain and set up a humming in her belly.

Since that moment, all she could think was how firm his body was, how sexy. And what a waste it was that he thought he was in love with someone he'd never even kissed before. How the hell did his mind get so twisted around that he let himself believe he loved a woman he'd never shared a single intimate moment with?

She understood that people fell in love for all kinds of reasons, and there were always unreciprocated feelings happening in this world, but how did you love someone you'd never spent significant time with, whether it was real time or time spent talking and texting each other about anything and everything?

He'd never had that relationship with Haylee. Everything he felt was based off one lightning bolt in one moment. It made her want to shake him.

Though maybe she was the one who was wrong. Maybe it happened exactly like that and she'd just never met the right person. Maybe Mal'd had the terrible misfortune to meet the person who did that for him when she belonged to someone else.

God, what a sucky situation.

"Stop thinking about it," she grumbled under her breath as she pulled the freezer open. She found the ice pack, grabbed a towel from a drawer, and wrapped the pack in it. Then she got herself a beer. Because, why not? Before she returned to the sitting room, she rubbed the cold bottle over her forehead, her chest, and slipped it between her breasts.

It gave her the shot of reality she needed. She had no business getting worked up over Mal, no matter how handsome he was. No matter how kind and safe. He wasn't free to be hers, and she wasn't looking anyway.

When she walked into the room, he was still sitting with his leg propped up, looking out the window at the lightning. Her heart did a little flip thing in her chest that she didn't appreciate. But he was gorgeous and she couldn't help it. Despite his injury, every line of him was hard and beautiful. He hadn't gone to flab in the past few weeks. Knowing him the way she did now, she knew he wouldn't allow it.

"Got your ice," she said cheerily.

"Thanks."

"Why don't you move to the couch and stretch your leg on the cushions? I'll take the chair."

She waited for him to move, then bent to put the ice on his leg. Her hair slipped over her shoulder, dangling on his skin. He gathered it up gently and held it. "Tickles," he said.

"Sorry. Now you know why I wear a ponytail at work."

He twisted her hair around his hand. "It's soft."

That heated feeling was starting to return to her body with a vengeance. She finished getting the ice in place, then straightened. Mal let go of her hair and she retreated to the chair, grabbing the beer she'd set down and taking a swallow.

"Changed your mind about that drink, huh?"

"Yep. I'm not at work, it's the middle of the night, and nobody's going to tell on me."

He grinned and lifted his own bottle. "Not me, that's for sure."

She reached over to clink bottles with him, then sat back to prop a foot on the coffee table. It was nearly two in the morning and she wasn't all that tired. The dozing she'd done on her couch had filled the need, apparently. She'd pay for it tomorrow, or today really, but at least it was Saturday.

"Thanks for the massage," he said. "I think it helped."

"Ice will help, too. And not overtaxing your leg. That will help most of all."

"I'm trying, Scar. It's hard. I want to be back at work. I hate being idle. I need to get cleared to return."

"I thought you were supposed to return to a desk job for a while."

He nodded. "I am. Next week if the doc signs off on it Monday morning. But I really want to return to the field."

Scarlett ran the rim of the bottle beneath her lip, enjoying the bite of cold on her skin. She didn't understand why anyone would want to return to a job where they could get shot again, but that's why she wasn't a candidate for the military. To each his own.

Except she really didn't want Mal to take another bullet. She thought of what Haylee had said. "Did you really save Dean's life that day?"

He was quiet for a moment. "I like to think so." He didn't elaborate and she didn't push. If he wanted to talk about it, he would.

The wind whipped up outside, blowing the branches of a hydrangea bush against the glass. "You've figured out my darkest secret," he said. "And I still don't know anything about you."

Scarlett nibbled the inside of her lip. "You know things about me. You know about my parents, my job, and the fact I love to thrift."

He snorted. "Because that really equates to the fact I'm an asshole who fell for my buddy's girl."

"You aren't an asshole. At least not about that. If you were actively trying to undermine their relationship, yes, asshole territory. But you aren't. As far as I can tell, if Haylee left Dean tomorrow and knocked on your door, you'd turn her away because you are definitely a *bros before hoes* kind of dude when it comes to your teammates."

Now he was laughing. She was glad of it because he had enough going on with the pain and trauma of his injury tonight to spend any extra time wallowing in guilt.

"You're funny, Scar. I really like you. And I just want you to know if that motherfucker who put the fear in your eyes ever shows up here looking for you, I'll make sure he doesn't come back again."

She didn't know whether to shiver at the leashed violence in his voice, or to feel grateful for it. She chose grateful since it was merely a hypothetical at the moment.

"Thanks, Mal. I like you too."

"Good to know." He was silent for a moment. "It's funny, but you're right. No matter how many times I've dreamed about her coming to me, I'd turn her away if it happened. So long as Wolf loves her, she's off limits."

"Sometimes we want what we can't have—and when we can have it, we no longer want it. People are perverse that way."

"You think I want her because I can't have her?"

"I don't know. Do you?"

"If I knew the answer, would I be asking you if that's what you thought?"

Scarlett sighed. "When I was twelve, this boy a grade ahead of me—a very cool, very handsome boy —sat beside me on the school bus. He held my hand for all of five minutes. I spent the next year thinking I was in love with him, writing his name inside all my notebooks, contriving to run into him at school, desiring him. He never spoke to me, and he never sat next to me again. He certainly never held my hand. If anything, I wanted him more. Until my dad moved us away and I had to get over it, which took probably another year of pining and being certain he was my soulmate."

"I'm not twelve, Scarlett."

"I know that. But not being able to have something makes us want it more sometimes. If that boy— his name was Mark—if he'd held my hand again, talked to me, sat with me, I'd have probably been convinced I was in love then too. But it would have burned out faster. If I'd gotten what I wanted, I'd have discovered much sooner that it wasn't the right thing for me."

"You think? Maybe you're right. Still, it doesn't go away quickly, does it?"

"Nope. But the important part, the part you need to think about, is that it *does* go away. Might go easier if you didn't see her all that often."

"Hard to do since the team is close."

"Yeah, guess so." She finished the beer and set the bottle on the table. Her belly was pleasantly warm, her limbs languid. It made her mouth loose, but she didn't much care. "You're a beautiful, sexy man, Mal. You should be banging babes and breaking hearts from one continent to another. The world is too big to narrow yourself to one sweet but utterly undeserving woman."

———

MAL WAS a little stunned at the words coming from her mouth. He was also a little turned on by them. He tried to focus on the important part, which was the part about Haylee. But he kept thinking of the part about him. The part where she said he was beautiful and sexy.

"What do you mean undeserving?" he asked, swinging his mind back to the topic at hand.

"Undeserving of *you*, Mal. She's got Dean. She doesn't get you too."

"She doesn't want me."

Scarlett crossed one leg over the other where it rested on the coffee table. She had long legs. Slender legs. She was wearing a pair of shorts and a T-shirt, nothing exciting, but the more he watched those legs, the more he thought about how they'd wrap around his hips and hold him tight while he thrust into her body.

"No, she doesn't want you. She doesn't even know you exist that way. So why waste your time pining? It's just like Mark Whatshisname when I was a kid. He had no idea I was sick over him, that I dreamed of him and of our life together. He went about his business without a second thought. Hell, he probably held my hand on a dare. A dare! It was everything to me and nothing to him. Waste of time," she finished with a mutter.

He wanted to laugh. And protest. She was really taking the wind out of his sails, making him feel kinda dumb in the process. "Are you comparing me to a pre-teen girl?"

Scarlett flailed her hands. "Well, yeah, I guess so. It's just a waste, that's all. You *can* get over these things. I mean sure, I was a kid, but the situation was darn near the same. A boy I had a lightning bolt for wasn't interested in me and never gave me a second thought. I spent two years wallowing in it until one day it was over and he wasn't important anymore. Somehow, you have to make her not important anymore."

A wicked thought flared in his brain. "Maybe a lot of hot, dirty sex would do the trick."

"Maybe so. You need to get out there and get back on the pony, so to speak."

"Or I could find a friend with benefits. A little mutual back scratching to satisfy an itch."

He saw her squirm. Hope burned bright.

"Are you suggesting that you and I…?" Her voice

trailed off in a whisper. Then she laughed. "Of course you aren't. I'm not your type."

His skin was on fire. His dick was waking up again. "Why would you say that?"

"I'm tall and skinny, not packed with curves. That *is* your type, right?"

Hell, was it? He didn't even know anymore. "My type is female, Scarlett."

She huffed. "*That's* flattering. I can be your type if I'm willing to fuck you into forgetting your crush? Or just fuck you whenever you want *her*—but can't have her—so any wet pussy will do? No thank you."

Oh shit. "That's not what I said, Scar."

She popped her arms over her chest. "It is what you said. You need a lot of hot, dirty sex to get over a crush and any willing female will do—"

"You weren't upset at me until you tried to tell me what my type was and I countered your assumption."

She glared at him. "That is not what happened."

"It is what happened. Jesus, we aren't dating or fucking and yet we're arguing like a married couple. What the hell is that about?"

She kept glaring—and then she laughed. Not just any laugh, but a belly laugh that had her doubling over and snorting. It wasn't feminine or cute. But it damned sure was funny. He tried not to, but then he was laughing too. Laughing until tears leaked from his eyes and the throbbing in his leg didn't bother him nearly as much because, shit, she was just so damned adorable—and really good for his state of mind.

"I don't know what it's about," she finally got out between giggles, "but it's funny."

"Are you drunk?" he asked after a couple more minutes of laughter—his and hers.

"No! It was one beer. I'm not that much of a lightweight."

"But you feel it."

"I'd be lying if I said I didn't."

"Thought so."

"Don't be smug or I won't massage your leg the next time."

"I'm not being smug, baby. Swear."

"Did you just call me *baby?*"

"Slip of the tongue," he said, enjoying himself just a little too much. "Want to get us another couple of beers?"

She seemed to consider it. Then she hopped up and grabbed his bottle. "Don't get any ideas," she called out as she walked into the kitchen.

She returned with two cold bottles, handing him one before flopping onto the chair. "Drinking makes me sleepy, not horny, so if you were thinking another beer would make me more agreeable to your suggestion, not happening. Just so you know."

He reached over to clink bottles with her. "Duly noted."

"Time and distance does the trick, Mal. Not sex."

He lifted the bottle to his lips. "Beg to differ, Scar. Sex cures a lot of ills."

"Or makes them worse."

"You're full of sunshine, aren't you?"

She grinned at him. "It's my job to keep it real."

Rain spattered the roof for a few seconds before the sky opened up and the deluge poured. It was a satisfying sound. Soothing.

Just like being with Scarlett.

Chapter Fifteen

Scarlett drifted awake slowly. She was warm but cramped, yet she didn't want to open her eyes. Sleep felt too good, and she had such a feeling of safety and contentment at the moment. If she got out of bed, it would change. The world, and all her problems, would come crashing down on her once more.

She sighed and snuggled into her pillow. A moment later, she realized her pillow was harder than usual—and it was breathing.

Her eyes popped open as panic filled her brain. He was wearing a shirt, thank heavens. If he wasn't naked, then they hadn't….

She lifted her gaze to his face. Mal's eyes were closed. His features were relaxed in slumber. Somehow, it made him even more handsome than he was when fully awake and teasing her over something. Pain wasn't etched on his face at the moment, and she was glad for that.

But she also needed to move. His arm was draped over her, his hand resting on her hip. He was on his back and she was snuggled into him like a second skin. How the hell had that happened?

It took her a moment to remember. They'd drank another beer, which meant three total for her, and she'd definitely been feeling it. The sky had still been pouring and there'd been no way she'd have made it up the stairs to her apartment. Mal had mentioned the guest room, and she'd intended to go there. Instead, when he'd said he was staying on the couch because he wasn't tired yet, she'd sat down next to him. She didn't know what she'd intended, but she'd apparently fallen asleep because here she was, plastered up against him.

Carefully, she eased herself downward, intending to slip from beneath his arm and escape as quietly as possible. But his grip on her tightened and his eyes opened. Scarlett held her breath, not knowing what to say. Should she apologize for falling asleep on him and forcing him to shift them onto the couch for comfort? Should she say nothing? Pretend like she didn't know what had happened?

Mal smiled at her, and her heart flipped. "Morning, Scar. Sleep okay?"

"I, uh, think so. You?"

"I slept cuddled up to you, so yeah, I slept fine."

"I'm sorry," Scarlett blurted. "I didn't mean to fall asleep on you."

His hand hadn't moved from her hip. He splayed

his fingers, not touching her inappropriately, but still sending bolts of lightning through her body. Scarlett bit her lip to stop a moan from escaping.

"I liked it," he said. "It's been a long time—no, that's wrong. I don't think I've ever slept with a woman without having sex with her first."

She remembered last night and his teasing suggestion they start a friends with benefits arrangement. She'd pretended to be offended, but in truth she'd been excited. Too excited.

"I guess there's a first time for everything."

"Apparently so. Hey, you hungry?"

Scarlett's head was reeling. Not only with a slight headache from the beer but also with the whiplash from Mal shifting gears on her so quickly. Yet his hand was still on her hip, still sending those spirals of need echoing through her system.

"Um, yeah, I am."

"I've got eggs and sausage and toast. Or we could go somewhere for pancakes."

"I think I need a shower and some Tylenol before I eat anything." And a few minutes to get her head on straight. As enjoyable and confusing as lying there with Mal was, her problems hadn't gone away overnight. She still had to worry about Josh finding her. Had meeting that guy last night made the possibility stronger? Or was it simply a coincidence?

"You can use my shower. I've got Tylenol in the medicine cabinet."

"I need clean clothes, Mal. But thank you."

His hand eased off her hip. The only thing holding her in place now was her own reluctance to move. Which meant she needed to get up immediately. She stood and straightened her clothes. Mal sat up, his body looking hard and perfect in the morning light. Except for his leg, which was scarred and swollen compared to the other smooth thigh. She'd seen his injuries many times in the course of working with him, but something about them this morning tore at her heart in a way it hadn't before.

"It's fine," he said softly. "Doesn't ache this morning."

"Good. That's good." *You're babbling, Scarlett.*

"The massage helped. Thanks."

"You're welcome. But try not to overtax it today, okay? And take a pain pill if it starts to hurt."

"Yes, ma'am."

Scarlett rolled her eyes at him. "Right. You're going to do what I say without complaint now when you wouldn't do it before? Not sure I buy it, Mal."

"Promise, Scar. You were right yesterday. Today, I'll take it easy and follow instructions. But I have a request."

"What's that?"

"That when you go take your shower and get dressed, you don't skip out on breakfast with me. Don't make an excuse not to come back."

A pinprick of guilt stabbed her. She would have done exactly that simply because she needed to process everything about last night. Like how she'd ended up sleeping next to him and, worse, enjoying it. Not to mention the whole friends with benefits discussion.

"I won't."

"Promise? Because if I scramble eggs and fry sausage for two people, and you don't help me eat it, I'm going to have to work out extra hard to get rid of it. Then my leg will hurt again."

Scarlett smacked him lightly on the arm. "You jerk. Guilt tripping me is not cool. Fine, I'll be back. Give me twenty minutes or so."

"I'll start the timer."

———

MAL WASN'T sure if she'd come back, no matter what she'd said, but when he saw her emerge from her apartment and walk down the stairs, he hoped she was coming his way instead of heading for her car. He was standing at the kitchen sink, washing up the dishes he'd left yesterday, and thinking about how nice it had felt to sleep next to a woman.

Next to Scarlett.

She'd gotten adorably tipsy last night, and though he'd ached with a different kind of pain when she'd sat down beside him and put her head against his shoulder, the last thing in the world he would ever do was abuse her trust. He'd sat there while she mumbled that he was a nice guy, and sexy too, and how much she wanted to do the friends with benefits thing but she was scared, and he didn't do anything inappropriate. She'd fallen asleep and he'd taken them both down to the couch since he knew he wasn't going to be able to carry her to the guest room.

It'd been torture at first, but eventually he'd fallen asleep. And then he'd wakened with a soft, female body beside him, his hand on her hip, her blue eyes wide on his, and he'd wanted nothing more than to strip her naked and explore every inch. It'd taken a supreme act of will to force his dick to stop throbbing. The last thing he'd wanted was a raging woody for her to see.

There was a soft tap at the door. "Come in," he said, and she walked into the kitchen, smelling like vanilla and roses. Her hair was wound up in a messy bun on her head, and she wore a pair of cut off jean shorts with sandals and a tank top. Her limbs were long and slender and he imagined them wrapped around him while he fucked her. It was enough to start the throbbing in his dick again. "Want to dry for me?" he asked.

"Sure." She grabbed a dish towel and started drying the dishes, stacking them neatly on the counter.

"Just need to get these out of the way so I can make a new mess."

Scarlett laughed. "I'll clean up while you cook so there won't be a mess. How's that?"

"Sounds good to me."

She stood beside him, taking dishes to dry. He

loved the way she smelled. There was more than vanilla and roses. There was sunshine, too. Scarlett was a puzzle to him. Someone with darkness in her past, someone who carried a lot of fear, and also someone who made the sun shine with her presence. He felt happier when she was around. Maybe it was because they'd forged this friendship, or maybe it was the fact she knew his darkest secret and didn't judge him for it.

No, she'd basically called him a teenage girl over the whole thing, which had both shocked him and made him think. What if she was right? What if it was merely a matter of time and distance?

"That storm blew right through last night," she said. "You wouldn't even know it'd happened this morning other than a few branches on the ground."

He looked out the window. The sun shone and the trees and bushes danced in a soft breeze. There were a few branches on the ground, like she said, but considering how violent the storm had seemed last night, it was remarkably calm now. As if it'd never happened.

Yet he felt that storm in his soul this morning. He felt it in the way his feelings swirled inside him, and in the way he wanted to sweep Scarlett up and kiss her senseless. Not the best plan, though, so he kept those impulses at bay and weathered the storm's battering ram deep inside.

"That's how it goes sometimes."

"I like the afternoon thunderstorms in Maryland.

I like the thunder and the way they roll over quickly, giving you that relief from the heat for a while."

"Until the sun comes out again and the humidity stews you in your clothes."

"That's true. I didn't expect it to be so humid here, not compared to Florida, but it really is."

"All that water surrounding us. The Chesapeake Bay, the Potomac and Patuxent." He finished the last dish and handed it to her. "You ready for breakfast?"

"Starved."

He broke the eggs into a bowl and turned on the flame. "What are your plans for the day, Scar?"

She shrugged. "I've pretty much put everything away in the apartment, but I still need to hang those pictures. And I thought I'd hit up another couple of thrift shops, see what else I could find. What about you?"

He put sausage in the pan to cook and beat the eggs with a fork. "I was thinking about going fishing, maybe fire up the grill later."

"Where do you go fishing?"

"There's a pond on the neighbor's property, right through the woods behind us, and he lets me use it. I don't keep anything, but I enjoy the peace of casting a lure and reeling it in. Coffee?"

"Yes, please. I can get it." She went to pour coffee into a mug and then rummaged in the fridge for cream. He was glad to see her do that instead of asking for permission. Meant she was comfortable. "Do you need a refill?"

He glanced at his cup. "Sure. Just black for me."

She filled his cup and set it beside him, then leaned against the counter to sip her own. She held the cup with two hands as she brought it to her lips. He didn't know why he noticed that, but he did. He was noticing a lot about Scarlett lately.

"Thanks for, um, being nice about me falling asleep on you."

"Why wouldn't I be nice? You were tired."

Her cheeks looked a little red. "Yes, but I'm pretty sure I said some things I wish I hadn't."

"You mean like telling me I'm sexy? I rather enjoyed that."

"Oh good grief," she muttered. "I knew I shouldn't have had that third beer."

He slipped sausage onto a plate, popped bread into the toaster, and started on the eggs while Scarlett washed up the bowl and fork he'd used. "You were having fun. Nothing wrong with that."

"I know I told you the beer wasn't going to make me change my mind about sex, but honestly it wouldn't have taken much persuasion once I started the third one. So thanks for not taking advantage of that."

"Trust me, Scar, if we ever get naked together, I want you sober. I want you to know exactly what you're doing, and I want you to know it's me you're doing it with."

She shot him a look. "*If* it happens, and I'm not saying it will, I'd want the same from you."

"I promise you, if you ever let me strip you out of those cute little shorts, I'm gonna be present for it. In fact, I'm not drinking another drop of alcohol in your presence just in case."

She snickered. "You're a goof."

"But you like goofs."

Her eyes sparkled. "I honestly do."

"I have an idea," he said.

One eyebrow lifted. "What's that?"

"How about I help you hang those pictures after breakfast and then you go fishing with me?" He didn't know why he wanted to hang out with her, but he did. The thought of spending the day alone wasn't appealing. It carved out a hollow spot in his belly and he didn't like it. Ordinarily he'd call one of his teammates, or Shade from the HOT SEAL Team, and make a plan to hang out. But those ideas weren't as appealing as spending time with Scarlett.

"I have a better idea."

"Impossible," he teased.

She laughed. "Come thrifting with me, and then we'll go fishing. The pictures can wait."

He made a face just to keep her laughing. "I dunno, Scar. Shopping?"

"Come on. It'll be fun. Not to be critical or anything, but you could use a few more homey touches around here. You might find some stuff if you hang out with me."

"You mean you don't like the blanket I hung over

the window in the living room? I'll have you know that's the ultimate in thrifting."

"It's a good effort, but I bet we could do better. Maybe find some matching sheets or curtains for all the windows, not just one. Does the sun come in that particular one every evening?"

"How did you guess?"

She snorted. "No reason."

He finished the eggs and put them on plates while Scarlett buttered the toast. Then they carried everything to the built-in breakfast nook and sat down to eat.

"Okay," he said, forking up some eggs. "I'll go shopping with you. But don't get carried away trying to help me decorate. A couch, television, and remote are all a man needs in a room."

"You do you, buddy," she said, taking a bite of her sausage. "Mmm, delicious."

He loved the way she made that sound in her throat. He wondered if she'd make it with a different kind of sausage in her mouth. *Bad, Mal. So bad.*

Maybe so, but he really wanted to find out.

Chapter Sixteen

SCARLETT CAST A LINE INTO THE WATER AND FELT strangely content. The events of last night—that guy in Buddy's insisting he knew her—had receded to a low-level hum in her brain instead of the full-frontal panic she'd been dealing with in the immediate aftermath. Logic and reason had had time to work and she no longer felt as if Josh was going to show up to terrorize her any minute.

She wasn't the same person. She didn't have the same color hair, or the same name, and she'd left no trail to her door. She'd untagged herself in Justine's photo, and she'd sent a text asking her friend to remove the picture. Justine had complied, with an apology for uploading it in the first place, so now it was gone. There was no way for Josh to track her down. A single picture, tagged to someone he didn't even know, wasn't going to do it.

A few feet away, Mal stood on the bank, throwing

his own line into the water and slowly reeling it back in. He stood with his injured leg cocked, taking the weight off it, but he stubbornly wouldn't fish from a chair. They'd brought chairs, and sandwiches and drinks, but so far they hadn't utilized them.

Scarlett watched Mal fish. The movements of his wrists and hands as he cast out and reeled in, the play of muscle beneath his skin, the concentration on his handsome face as he studied the water. He wore a baseball cap and white T-shirt with athletic shorts and hiking boots. On any other guy, it might look ridiculous. On him, it looked strangely appealing.

Like so appealing there was a constant thrum in her belly, a tendril of attraction that wanted to flare into a bright flame if she'd let it. It didn't help that she'd been spending so much time with him lately. Part of her thought she should say no to his invitations to eat breakfast together, or go shopping—though that had been her invitation—or fishing. But another part was having *fun*.

And enjoying the company of someone who didn't pressure her in any way. It was easy with Mal—except for this niggling attraction that simmered inside. She supposed she shouldn't be too surprised she could feel this way. She'd thought that Josh had broken her, but really it was him who was broken. He'd dampened her spirit, but he hadn't ruined it. She felt it unfurling again, like a flower bud cautiously peeling back its layers.

She reminded herself that caution was not only

good, but necessary. Mal wasn't emotionally available. Despite their conversation about Haylee and his crush, he wasn't going to instantly get over it just because Scarlett told him he needed to take a different approach. They'd said a lot of things last night, and he'd put forth the idea of friends with benefits after beer got involved, but that didn't mean today was magically different. He was still a man with feelings for someone else.

So why was she here again? She reeled her line in and cast out once more, watching the lure sink into the water with a satisfying plop. She hadn't been fishing since she was a teenager and her dad took her out. Not that she'd really wanted to go, she recalled, but looking back, she was glad she had. Fishing together was one of the few memories she had of her dad where he hadn't been stressed out about surviving and providing for her. She'd loved her dad, and resented him too, but as an adult she understood the pressures he'd been under.

"Nice cast," Mal said.

"Thanks. You get any bites?"

"No. You?"

"Not yet."

"Patience, Scar. This is a good pond, I promise."

"I trust you."

Saying those words made her feel warm inside. It wasn't only that she trusted him about the pond, it was that she trusted him in general. And that was a big thing for her after Josh. Still, she told herself she'd only known him a little over a month now. She'd only known Josh for about two weeks before they'd started dating, but he'd begun showing his paranoid side fairly quickly. Not that she'd recognized it at first. She'd been flattered by his protectiveness when in reality that protectiveness was a form of control. Mal's protectiveness was different. It took her feelings into account.

A few seconds later, a fish hit her line and she instantly set the hook, remembering how to do it by muscle memory rather than conscious knowledge. "Got one," she called.

Mal pulled his line and headed her way. The fish might be tiny, but it fought hard enough to make her think she had a whopper on the other end of the line.

"Whoa, nice bass," Mal said as the fish jumped out of the water.

Scarlett twisted the other way, still reeling, recognizing the fish's maneuver as a way to shake the lure. But it didn't happen and she finished pulling it in. Mal reached down to grasp the fish by the lip and lift it out of the water. He removed the hook and held the fish up.

"Damn, girl. He's a good five-pounder."

Scarlett beamed. "He's pretty, isn't he?"

"Here, hold him and I'll get your picture."

Her stomach fell. "No, that's okay. I don't need a picture."

Mal was still smiling, oblivious to the turmoil inside her. "You sure? Don't want proof for when you brag about him and somebody says you're exaggerating?"

"No, I'm good." She dragged her phone from her back pocket. "I'll get a picture of you with him instead."

He shrugged. "Hardly seems fair, but okay."

She snapped the pic, then took the fish when Mal handed him over. It was definitely heavy. After admiring the fish for a few more seconds, she knelt and set it back in the water, moving it from side to side for a second before letting go. With a flash of its tail, the fish was gone and Scarlett straightened again.

"Good job, Scar. I admit when you said you'd been fishing before, I didn't think that meant you knew how to cast a lure or set a hook."

"My dad loved to fish. I went along reluctantly a lot of times, but I paid attention when he taught me what to do."

"He gave good lessons."

She felt a lump form in her throat. "He did."

"You ready for a sandwich?"

"Yep."

They sat in the chairs and Mal opened the insulated bag he'd brought. He handed her a scented antibacterial wipe to clean off her hands while he did the same. When she was done with that, he gave her a bottle of water and a sandwich, then got his own. Scarlett stretched her legs out and opened the baggie. The sky was blue, with billowy white clouds. There were some darker gray clouds too, but they were distant. Probably raining over the Chesapeake, she decided.

She took a bite of the sandwich, surprise filling her at the taste. Peanut butter and jelly. No wonder he'd asked her if she had any allergies. When she glanced over at him, he was watching her.

"Good?"

"Yes. I haven't had peanut butter and jelly in years. Makes me think of my childhood."

"Really? I love PBJ. Eat it all the time. Why haven't you had any for years?"

Scarlett shrugged. "I don't know. Just haven't."

Which didn't make a lot of sense since she couldn't cook, but she always opted for lunchmeat and cheese instead. Maybe she needed to get back to the basics.

"Man, you have missed out."

She laughed. "Apparently so."

"You're an adult, Scar. You can eat Captain Crunch for dinner if you want. Chocolate cake for lunch. The world is your oyster."

"Funny enough, I'm not a fan of oysters. Please don't ever make me an oyster sandwich."

"There go my dinner plans. I was thinking oysters on the half shell with tabasco and crackers."

Scarlett stuck out her tongue. "Bleh."

"No sense of adventure," Mal admonished. But there was a twinkle in his eye that told her he was teasing.

Warmth flowed through her. She was enjoying this

day. So much. The fear she'd felt last night when that man thought he'd recognized her was fading in the bright light of day. Josh wasn't lurking around a corner, waiting to attack. He wasn't coming for her. There was no way he could.

She leaned back in her chair and continued to eat the sandwich, watching the clouds drift overhead. It was hot, but not too hot in the shade. She'd worn her tank top and cut-off shorts, but she'd put on hiking boots because she was no dummy and snakes were always a possibility around water.

The longer she sat, the sleepier she felt. Mal didn't say anything else for several minutes. She closed her eyes, thinking to catch a quick cat nap. When she opened them again, she was startled that it was no longer bright out. A gray cloud loomed, blotting out the sun and blue sky.

Mal stood nearby, packing up his chair and the fishing gear. Scarlett got up to help. "That happened fast," she said.

He looked up, arching a brow. "You think?"

"Well, yeah. It was sunny just a minute ago."

"You've been napping for forty-five minutes, Scar."

"What? No way! That chair isn't comfortable enough."

"Nevertheless, it happened."

"And you let me sleep while the sky got dark?"

"You needed it. Besides, I wasn't done fishing."

Scarlett snatched up her chair and folded it before stuffing it into the bag. "We could get wet, Mal."

"So?"

She slung the chair over her shoulder and grabbed the insulated bag that had contained their picnic. Mal had his chair along with the rods and tackle box. They'd walked to his neighbor's pond, despite her misgivings over his leg, but he'd insisted it wasn't far and he needed the exercise. And it hadn't been far, but when the sky was threatening to open up any minute, it might as well be a mile.

"We should have driven," she grumbled as they started trudging toward his house.

"Are you afraid you'll melt?"

A raindrop splatted on her shoulder. "No, I'm afraid of being struck by lightning."

"It's not that kind of storm. Have you heard any thunder?"

She thought about it. "I was napping. How do I know?"

"It's rain, Scar. Nothing more."

As if in contradiction the wind picked up, swirling through the treetops almost violently. But there was no thunder, he was right about that much. Still, the rain dumped down all at once with surprising intensity as the wind whipped around them.

"Shit," Mal said. "It's a squall." He grabbed her hand and hauled her toward the trees, moving faster than she would have thought he could at this stage of his recovery. But Mal was nothing if not determined.

She would have protested going into the trees, but she knew as well as he did that it was either shelter against a thick trunk or stand in the field unprotected as the wind buffeted them.

Unfortunately, as they were hurrying for shelter, Scarlett tripped on a root and sprawled onto the now soaked ground before Mal could save her. He was there, though, pulling her up with strong arms and tugging her deeper into the trees. When he came to a clearing, there was a small building perched on a rise. She wondered that she hadn't seen it on their way through before. He led her over and tugged open the door. She followed him into what seemed to be a tiny cabin. He put the rods and tackle box down, then took the chair from her shoulder and leaned both of them against the wall. She set the insulated bag down beside the chairs.

"What is this?" she asked, turning around in the space. It was clean, though plain, with a twin-sized mattress and an iron headboard, a table by the window, and a door that led to a tiny bathroom. She could tell because she could see a toilet.

"It was supposed to be a She-Shed, or so the woman who sold the house to me said. She was a writer of some kind, and she had to get away from her family to work."

"What do you plan to do with it?"

He wiped rain from his face and shrugged. "No idea. I've left it alone since moving in. The bed and table were here already."

An empty potato chip bag and a soda can lay on the floor beside the bed. He picked the can up and crumpled it, frowning. "Neighbor kids must be using this as a hideout. I probably should put a lock on the door."

"Do you really care?"

He shrugged. "So long as they clean up their mess and don't break anything? Not really."

"I didn't think so." She started to pick up the bottom of her T-shirt and wipe her face but Mal stopped her. "You don't want to do that. Your shirt's muddy."

She looked down at the unfortunate fabric. "Only on the front. Unless you've got a towel around here, I don't think I have a choice."

"Let me look." He went into the small bathroom and came out again with a ragged old towel that looked like it had seen better days.

"I don't know about this," she said as he handed it to her. "At least I know my shirt went through the wash this century."

He shrugged. "It's not muddy."

She sniffed the towel. It was musty so she dropped it and pulled up her shirt instead. "I'll use the inside," she told him as she wiped it across her face. Belatedly, it occurred to her that she was flashing Mal since she had to pull her shirt so high to get to the clean part. She hurriedly finished and dropped it so she was covered again. When she looked up, Mal was watching her, his brows drawn together as if he was thinking hard about something.

"Sorry," she said. "Didn't mean to flash you."

She had a bra on, but it was thin, white cotton lace and she hated to think that the rain had made it see-through. She wasn't going to check though. *Just brazen it out.*

"I didn't mind. You can do it again if you want to."

The air in the small room seemed to grow thicker. Her nipples chose that moment to tighten. Any second and they'd be poking through the wet fabric of her shirt. She crossed her arms self-consciously. "If the sight of my bare abdomen and plain bra is all that thrilling, maybe you need to get out more," she joked.

He took a step toward her. He loomed in the space, his body big and solid. But he didn't frighten her. No, the feeling zipping through her was some-thing much more pleasant than fear.

"I'm afraid I saw more than your bra, Scar. It's a little see through at the moment." His voice was husky, and she swallowed at the heat contained in it.

"Oh."

He put a finger under her chin and tipped her face up so she had to look at him. "I liked what I saw. I'd like to see more."

"Mal," she whispered, doubt and desire mingling into one big confusing ball in her stomach. She swal-lowed again. "I don't think it's a good idea."

"Okay," he said. "Maybe you're right. But I'm still

thinking about it, and I'm thinking about kissing you again. Does that bother you?"

She knew if she said yes that he'd drop his hand and take a step back. Mal wouldn't press her. He wouldn't use his strength against her. For that alone, she adored him.

"No," she said softly. "It doesn't bother me."

He stepped closer, until he loomed large. She was no match for his strength, but she had something more. She had a voice, and Mal had integrity. All she had to do was speak. Tell him to back up, stop touching her.

But she didn't. She gazed up at him, into a face that made her heart skip beats. She wasn't consciously aware of moving, but she lifted her hand and spread it over his jaw. His skin was warm and wet where rain dripped from his hair onto his cheeks. She traced a thumb over his lips, telling herself to stop but unable to do so.

His mouth was firm, his lips full and soft. She traced back and forth, back and forth. His eyes gleamed hot. Outside, the wind howled against the cabin, the walls creaking and cracking as they withstood the pressure.

"Hell of a storm," she said, her throat tight. Her nipples ached. Her pussy too. It'd been a long time since she'd desired a man. Towards the end, she'd given in to Josh because it was easier, but she hadn't enjoyed it. Not for a long time.

To feel herself wanting now was miraculous.

He took her other hand in his. A current of surprise rocked her but she didn't pull away as he dragged her hand up to his chest and pressed it there. For a moment she'd thought he'd been planning to put it on his crotch, but of course she'd been wrong. Instead, she could feel the strong, rapid beat beneath her palm.

"We're friends, Scarlett. I don't want to do anything to endanger that. But holy shit, babe, you're making my heart thunder like I'm running for my life. I fucking want you. So damned much. Maybe it *is* a bad idea, and maybe it'll cost me your friendship if I act on it, but I have to let you know. I want to do things to you. Hot, dirty things. I want to taste you and touch you and lose myself inside you. There. I said it."

He closed his eyes and tilted his head back, his nostrils flaring as he breathed deeply and slowly. Maintaining control? Regaining it? She didn't know which, but it was sexy as hell. And all for her. He wasn't emotionally available, she knew that, but this heat and desire wasn't for Haylee. It was for *her.* Scarlett Reed—Erin Rose. Shy little Erin who'd never had a boyfriend until she'd graduated high school and went to college. Erin, who'd lost her virginity to a computer nerd who'd never called her again. She'd grown a bit since then, matured and stopped being so shy. She'd had boyfriends in the years since, none serious until Josh had tried to take over her life.

Mal wasn't trying to take over her life. She

dropped her gaze over his torso, over the shirt clinging to him like a second skin, and down to the dark athletic shorts he wore. She drew a sharp breath. He was hard, his dick bulging against his shorts. For her.

Suddenly, she wanted nothing more in this life than to experience everything Mal had promised her.

Was it a bad idea? Probably.

Was that going to stop her? Doubtfully.

"Mal."

His eyes opened, his gaze dropping to hers. She closed the remaining distance between them, pressing her body against his, smoothing her palms over his chest as she held his gaze. Between them, his dick strained. His Adam's apple slid slowly down his throat and back up.

"Are you sure?" he asked.

Sweet Mal. Sexy, handsome, desirable Mal. Tortured Mal.

"Yes," she whispered. "Now kiss me."

Chapter Seventeen

MAL DIDN'T KNOW WHAT WAS HAPPENING TO HIM, BUT this need lashing into him was all-encompassing. He'd been having fun with Scarlett—shopping, fishing, cooking breakfast.

Sleeping on the couch.

Fun.

It was supposed to be nothing but some harmless fun, yet here he was, aching like he hadn't had a sexual release in years when in fact he'd jerked off in the shower that morning just to relieve some of the tension that had been coiling tight in his belly and balls.

He wasn't supposed to want Scarlett. Scar. His sweet, funny friend. His sassy, smart-mouthed physical therapist.

He wasn't supposed to want her, but he was harder than stone and she was plastered against him, their bodies wet from the sudden storm. The heat coming off her was incredible, or maybe that was him.

With a groan, he dropped his mouth to hers, lips and tongues meeting in a sensual clash that threatened to suck him under. He'd been staring at her ass in those short little shorts all afternoon. Studying the way her T-shirt clung to her breasts, wondering what was under there.

He'd gotten a peek when she'd wiped her face with her shirt. Her bra was white, lacy, and simple. She didn't have big tits, but what she had intrigued him. Surprisingly dark nipples, bigger than he'd expected, poking through the thin cotton. He'd wanted to suck one through the fabric and listen to her beg. He hadn't, of course. That was going too far.

Until now.

Now he had her permission. Her participation.

He intended to rock her world. Scarlett deserved to feel good, and he was just the man to make sure she did. His leg ached, but it wasn't as bad as it would have been two weeks ago. He *was* getting stronger. Besides, he wasn't going to let a little pain stop him from the pleasure that waited for him inside Scarlett's lithe body.

She wrapped her arms around his neck, arching her slender form against him, and he flexed his hips, grinding his cock into her. She tasted like peanut butter and that gorgeous sunshine he associated her with. Her lips were soft beneath his, her tongue wet and hot. She kissed with an enthusiasm that caused his pulse to ratchet higher.

Mal spread a hand over her back, slid it down her body until he could grasp one hip and pull her tighter to him. She lifted a leg and wrapped it carefully around his good one. He groaned at what that did to the pressure against his cock.

"If I'd known kissing you would be this good, I'd have tried a lot sooner," he said against the skin of her neck as he licked and sucked his way from one side to the other.

He put his hands beneath her T-shirt and dragged it over her head, pausing for a second to gaze at her. Her blue eyes were a little wary, as if she expected him not to like what he saw.

"Fucking beautiful," he said, palming a breast before scraping his thumb over the nipple. So damned perfect.

He'd meant to suck her through the fabric, but that would no longer do. Instead, he dragged a cup down and licked the rosy tip like it was the best damned ice cream cone he'd ever had.

Scarlett clutched his shoulders and made a sound in her throat that would have undone a lesser man. It made him want to make her do it again, so he sucked her nipple into his mouth and tugged rhythmically.

"Mal," she gasped, her fingers curling into his skin. "Oh my god…"

"So gorgeous, Scar." He blew on her nipple then

dragged the other cup down and sucked that one until she moaned.

"I don't have a condom," she blurted as he reached for the button of her shorts.

"I do," he said, grateful as hell he'd put a fresh one in his wallet recently. Not that he'd expected to use it anytime soon, but he liked being ready. Just in case a hot, sweet, sexy woman he'd been lusting after said yes when he least expected it. Like now.

She tugged his shirt up and he finished the task by jerking it over his head and dropping it.

"How do you happen to have a condom?"

He unbuttoned her shorts and pushed them downward. "Do you really want to talk about this right now?"

She licked his nipple and he sucked in a breath. "I don't know. Maybe. Did you think you were getting into my panties today?"

He let out a strangled laugh as she swirled her tongue around his other nipple. "No, I didn't. But I like to be prepared."

"For random rainstorms and weakened willpower?"

He couldn't help but laugh again. "Scar, you're killing me. I'm so fucking horny I could blow at any second and you want to talk about why I have a condom."

"Why do you think I'm talking about it? I'm horny too—and just as likely to blow."

Everything inside him went tight. "Then we need to make sure we do that together."

She stepped back and shimmied out of her shorts. Her panties were white cotton, modest, but somehow the sexiest thing he'd ever seen. She hooked her thumbs into the waistband, then hesitated. "I know I'm going to regret this when it's over. Not because I don't want to do it," she said. "But because it's going to change things between us."

His dick throbbed. His pulse pounded. He stared at her, his throat tight and utterly dry. "We won't let it," he practically croaked. "We're friends. First and foremost."

"Friends with benefits." She ran her thumbs around the waistband, teasing him. "I know you aren't going to get emotionally involved with me since you're in love with *her*, but just so you know, I'm not going to get emotionally involved with you either. I've had enough of men trying to control me through emotion, so don't worry I'm going to fall in love with you or anything. Not happening."

Mal wasn't quite sure why her words disappointed him. They shouldn't. He should be fucking thrilled, but somehow he wasn't. "Don't make it seem so mercenary, Scar. There'll be emotion involved with us because we like each other. I care about you even if I don't love you. I think you care about me, too. That's a lot more than a hookup between strangers."

She wriggled her hips and pushed her panties

down just until the top of her pubic hair was revealed. His jaw went slack.

"I want to see stars, Mal. I want it to feel so good I can't help but be loud. Embarrassingly loud. I want to forget my own damn name while I see those stars. If you aren't prepared to make that happen, then maybe we don't need to do this."

How the hell did she make him want to laugh and groan all at once?

"Drop the panties, Scar," he growled. "I'm about to show you constellations."

———

IT MIGHT BE A BAD IDEA, but Scarlett was too far gone to turn back now. Besides, even if she'd had a sliver of doubt, the look on Mal's face when she dropped her panties would have erased it. He was definitely present and thinking of her rather than someone else. The flare of his nostrils, the flexing of his jaw, the hot spark in his eyes—it was all for her.

"Red," he said almost wonderingly, his gaze centered entirely on her pussy.

Shit. She'd been so engrossed she'd forgotten. "Now you know," she told him flippantly, her heart pounding in contrast to her tone. "I decided I wanted to be blond for a while."

He moved her until the backs of her knees hit the mattress, then skimmed his hands down her body, his touch reverent. "You're a gorgeous blonde, babe, but I think you'd be a gorgeous redhead too."

She should say something to him about calling her babe, but the words wouldn't come. She liked it, even if she knew she shouldn't let him do it.

"You have too many clothes on, Mal."

"I do, don't I?" He grinned as he shucked off the hiking boots and shorts. His underwear made her drool. Black boxer briefs hugged his thighs, and his dick was a long ridge angling up and to the left. She wanted to see so she reached for the waistband and dragged it down.

"Whoa," she said as he sprang free. "Now that's impressive, Malcolm McCoy."

She wrapped her hand around him and he groaned. "God, Scar, you're not like anyone else."

"Not like anyone else is good," she said before dropping to the mattress and taking him in her mouth.

His breath hissed in. "Babe, this isn't the plan—"

She swirled her tongue around the head of his cock and whatever he was saying died in his throat. She hadn't meant to take control, but she'd been overcome with the need to taste him. She closed her eyes as she licked the length of him and then sucked him into her mouth again.

"I want to let you finish, God knows I do, but I need to be in you when I come, baby."

Mal pushed her back and knelt in front of her, spreading her legs wide with his broad shoulders. She wanted to ask him about his leg, but she knew better than that. He was to the point in his therapy where he had to bend it and put weight on it. Still, she noticed he'd pushed it out to the side where he could keep it straighter while he put most of his weight on his good leg.

"That's not getting inside me," she said as his intent became clear. She didn't want him in that position for too long, no matter how good it would feel for her.

He grinned. "No, but it'll make you see stars."

"Not fair, Mal. You wouldn't let me finish you, but you plan to lick me?"

"Can you or can you not come multiple times without a break in between?"

A small shiver rolled through her. "Pretty sure I can."

He arched a brow. "Pretty sure? What kind of men have you let in your bed, Scarlett?"

"The wrong ones, apparently," she grumbled. Her body was on fire, she needed his touch, and yet something about bantering with him was also necessary. It's who they were together, she realized.

"Oh, honey. I'm about to fix that for you."

She put a hand on his head and tugged him toward her pussy. "Then stop talking and start doing."

He spread her apart with a thumb and finger, then gently traced around her clit without touching it. She was going to die.

"You're so wet for me, babe."

Scarlett lay back on the mattress and closed her eyes, not sure she could watch without expiring of pleasure. "You forgot my name, didn't you?" she gasped as he touched the tip of his tongue to her clit.

"Shut up, Scarlett. Just feel."

He licked her slowly at first, then faster, sucking and nipping at all the right moments. Scarlett arched her back, pressing her hips into his face as the pressure began to build inside her. One moment she was climbing toward the peak and the next she'd dropped off the cliff. Her orgasm hit with blinding speed, stealing her breath and curling her toes.

Mal held her in place and kept licking until she pushed hard against his shoulders, forcing him to stop. He looked smug as their eyes met. "Did you see any stars?"

She was still shuddering from the force of her climax. "I believe I did."

He rose with that smug look still on his face and reached for his shorts. He fished his wallet from the pocket and took out a condom. Watching him rip it open and roll it onto his cock was one of the sexiest things she thought she'd ever seen.

"You still good for this?" he asked as she turned and scooted up on the bed so he could join her.

"Oh yeah. Definitely."

Outside, the wind didn't howl quite so much and the cabin didn't creak. But the bed did when he put his good knee on it and positioned himself over her. "You want to be on top?"

She loved that he asked. "Do you want me to? Would it be more comfortable?"

He snorted. "Scar, this isn't any more strenuous on me than those damned squats you've been making me do at rehab."

"No, I know. Just checking. Remember that conversation about not pushing it too hard."

"I'm not."

She grinned. "Okay then. You can be on top. I want you to do all the work."

He snorted. "Does this count as one of my workouts then?"

"If you do it right it does."

He slipped an arm beneath her hips and tugged her into place beneath him. Then he let his gaze drop down her body. She felt more than a little self-conscious beneath his perusal, but his dick stayed hard and that was what counted.

"I hope you know that one time won't be enough. There's a lot I didn't get to do to you yet."

She gripped his arms, heavy with muscle, and ran her hands up them and then down across his chest before tracing the lines of his abs—such tight, perfect abs. "We'll see, Mal. I can't promise anything beyond this moment."

She reached down to cup his balls and he hissed in a breath. "Dammit, Scar."

He took her hands in both of his and pushed them above her head. His body was heavy on hers, but he managed to shift his weight in such a way that he didn't crush her. She felt a tiny flare of panic, but she pushed it down again. This was Mal, and Mal wouldn't hurt her.

Scarlett wrapped her legs around his hips as he began to push inside her. "Oh my god," she groaned.

"Am I hurting you?"

"No. I just..." She swallowed. "I like it. The pressure. You're big—a-and it feels *so* good. Like all I have to do is wiggle my hips a little bit and I'll come again."

"That's the idea, baby." He slid deeper inside until she was so full of him she thought she'd explode. "I need to move, Scar. Hard if that's okay. And if it's not, I'll take it easier. But damn I want to make you scream my name a few times before we're done."

"It's okay, Mal. I trust you. Please, please make me come again."

He nipped her collarbone, then sucked her nipple before letting it pop out of his mouth and grinning. "You're gonna come, Scar. A lot."

Chapter Eighteen

MAL WAS BONELESS. SPENT. HE WAS STILL DEEP INSIDE Scarlett, his cock twitching with the aftermath of his release. He'd rolled to the side and taken her with him. Because he was still so damned hard, he hadn't slipped out of her body when he'd moved. She moaned and then licked his nipple, her hair a beautiful mess that hid her face from view. He pushed it back, needing to see her. If she was licking him, then she probably wasn't hurt or devastated, but damn, he'd kind of lost control there for a few moments.

He'd driven her against the headboard so hard she'd gripped the iron and pushed back against him, keeping them anchored in the middle. The bed had squeaked like it was about to fly apart, but all he'd cared about was making Scarlett come.

And she had. Spectacularly. She'd let go of the headboard with one hand and dragged his mouth to hers before she'd stiffened beneath him, her back and hips arching upward even as he kept driving into her. Sinking into her wet little pussy again and again, all thoughts of the world outside these walls disintegrating. All he'd known in those moments was the desire to be the best damned lover she'd ever had.

She'd shook and moaned and, yeah, she'd gotten loud. He liked that. A lot. Maybe that was why, when his own orgasm hit, he saw those stars she'd been talking about. Lots of fucking stars.

"You okay?" he asked, his breathing a little more ragged than he'd like. Damn his inability to run and keep up his fitness right now.

"Mmm," she said, eyes still closed as she lay against his chest.

"You don't appear to be hurt," he continued, "So I'll take that as a yes."

She skimmed her palm over his abs. "Not hurt. Drained."

He closed his eyes, contentment stealing over him for the moment. "Me too."

"I don't think I can move, Mal."

"Nope, me neither. Let's stay here until the storm blows through."

"I think it already did."

He listened. The rain wasn't pounding the roof anymore and the wind didn't whistle. "Then let's stay until we can both walk again."

Scarlett lifted her head, looking instantly concerned. "Is it your leg? Does it hurt? Want me to massage it?"

He pushed her hair behind her ear. "I meant that I'm worn out from servicing you, Scar. Not that my leg hurts."

She frowned and then swatted him, but it was playful. "Servicing me? What are you, a mechanic? A waiter?"

"More like a stallion servicing a fine little filly," he drawled in his best Texas accent.

Scarlett rolled her eyes. But then she laughed, and he found himself laughing with her. "You're a mess, Mal. But I like you."

"I like you too, Scar. I really like being inside you. Tasting you." He skimmed his fingers over her pussy, down into the wet seam and over her clit. She gasped. "I can't believe you're a redhead. I really want to see that."

Her lashes dropped over her eyes. "You're seeing it, aren't you? Red pubic hair."

"I mean on your head."

"I'm not done being blond."

She sounded tense. He wasn't quite sure why. "When you're done then. Is that where you got your name?"

"Yes." She rolled away from him and sat up, and he felt oddly bereft when they were no longer joined. "Maybe we should get back home while it's not raining much anymore."

He gripped her by the shoulders and pulled her down, curving his body around hers. "I'm sorry, Scar."

She was stiff at first, but he could feel it when the tension drained out of her. She was more pliable in his arms.

"For what?"

"Asking questions you don't want to answer."

She sighed. "It's complicated."

Everything with Scarlett was complicated in one way or another. Eventually. "Then you can tell me when you're ready."

"And if I never am?"

His belly twisted at the thought. Why did he care? He didn't know, but dammit, friends were supposed to share things with each other. "Then I guess I have to accept that."

His phone buzzed from his shorts on the floor. He'd forgotten the outside world until then and he wasn't ready to let it back in just yet.

"You going to get that?"

"Nope."

"What if it's important?"

"I doubt it is. I'm not active right now, so I'm not going on a mission."

"You have parents. A sister."

He sighed. "Fine," he said, reaching onto the floor and dragging his shorts up until he could fish the phone from a pocket. The name on the screen said Sky Kelley. Definitely not a call Mal could take right now. He pressed the button to send it to voicemail and then kissed Scarlett's bare shoulder. "It's one of my teammates. I'll call him later."

And pray that Hacker had found some information Mal could use to protect Scarlett from her worst fears.

———

SCARLETT HAD THOUGHT she'd want to escape as soon as she could after giving in to her stupid hormones, but it turned out what she wanted worse than escape was more Mal. When the storm had passed over, they made their way back to his house. He'd given her his T-shirt because hers was so dirty, and she'd spent the trip staring at the muscles rippling in his bare back as he led the way. By the time they reached his house, all she needed was a little encouragement to send her inside with him instead of going up the stairs to her place.

That encouragement came in the way of a kiss and a request to shower with him. How could she say no?

They'd shed their wet clothes and stepped beneath the spray, mouths already joined and hands exploring sensitive skin. By the time they'd ended up in his bed, she'd already come three times. Another three times there and she'd been unwilling to move even though she'd told herself she definitely needed to say goodbye and go back to her place.

Instead, she'd fallen asleep. It wasn't dark when she woke, but the room was in shadow which told her it was getting late in the day. Mal lay beside her, sheet thrown off and leg cocked, eyes closed. She lifted on an elbow to study him in the dim light.

He was so damned beautiful. Even his scarred thigh couldn't detract from his perfection in her eyes. She studied his leg, wanting to touch it but not daring because it might wake him. He'd gotten that injury from trying to protect Dean Garner. Because he hadn't wanted Haylee to lose the man she loved even though it might benefit him if Dean were out of the way.

She thought of Josh. If he'd been the one in this love triangle, he definitely wouldn't have tried to save his rival. In fact, he'd have probably tried to eliminate him. Scarlett shivered at the thought. For the longest time she hadn't wanted to admit that Josh was capable of such a diabolical thing, but she knew he was. After her brakes had failed on a rain-slicked night and her car dove into the lake, she could no longer kid herself.

All she'd tried to do was move on. She'd finally found her courage and told him it wasn't working and she needed her space. He'd seemed to accept that, but of course he hadn't really. That was when the harassment began, though it'd been so subtle she hadn't realized what was happening at first. She'd thought she was crazy when things in her apartment weren't where she'd left them, but it'd been Josh using the key he'd stolen to get in while she was at work. He'd been watching her, recording her, and enjoying himself as he played with her mind.

She drew in a breath and blinked away tears. It'd

been months of hell. She'd thought her trust was irreparably broken, but here she was in bed with a man. Not just any man, but a military man. A big, lethal special operator just like Josh.

Not like Josh.

Mal was nothing like Josh. He was honorable. Trustworthy. He wouldn't lie to her or manipulate her. He wouldn't gaslight her.

He shifted, his eyes opening. When they met hers, her heart flipped in her chest.

"Hey," he said.

"Hey yourself."

He reached up to pull her down for a kiss. "How're you feeling, Scar?"

She loved his tenderness. His thoughtfulness. Josh had pretended to be thoughtful, but they were always grand gestures. Sending a huge bouquet of flowers to her work. Ordering a takeout feast to be delivered to her place and then showing up with wine and flowers so they could have dinner after she got off work. Nice things. Expensive things. But not from the heart. Never that.

His gifts were meant to impress, and he'd wanted praise for them. Lots of praise. It'd taken her a long time to realize he needed that praise like a junkie needed a drug.

"A little sore," she said truthfully. "I need to build up to Olympic-level sex instead of trying to do everything all at once."

He grinned. "Not quite everything, babe. I can still think of a few things we didn't do."

She patted his shoulder. "Not right now, Mal. I need parts of me to recover first."

He cupped her breast and thumbed her nipple. Of course it responded to him. "Does this mean you're thinking about doing it again?"

She couldn't think with the electricity sparking through her body at every scrape of his thumb over her flesh. "Maybe so. Be a shame to lie in my own bed with a vibrator when I could have you take care of business for me."

His hand stilled, his eyes going a little wide for a second. "You have a vibrator?"

"Show me a single girl who doesn't."

He rolled her beneath him in a quick move that made her squeak. "I'd kind of like to watch you use it. But then again, I'd hate to watch you come when I wasn't the one who'd made you do it."

She ran her palms up his sides, loving the feel of him. "Then you use it to make me come. Though I gotta say, I prefer your cock to my vibrator."

He flexed his hips against her. "Speaking of cock, he's growing interested."

Scarlett laughed. "You're kidding. How is this even possible?"

"I'm a man in my prime, babe. And I've got a helluva lot of pent-up energy from being sidelined from my job."

"Mmm, lucky me. But aren't you hungry? I'm starved. Peanut butter was a long time ago."

"I can think of something I want to eat," he said, waggling his eyebrows.

Her insides liquified. "Death by sex. That's your plan, isn't it?" she teased.

"Nah," he told her. "Come up here and put your pussy in my face. You can suck me while I eat you. We'll give the old girl a break from all that pounding."

Scarlett snort-laughed. "God you're silly."

"I like it when you laugh," he said, grinning down at her. "I like it even better when you yell my name while you come."

Hot embarrassment heated her cheeks. She hadn't meant to be so vocal, but he'd made it impossible not to be. "I don't usually, um…"

He cocked an eyebrow. "Really? Damn, that makes me even happier I could make that happen. Now come up here and let me do it again."

———

MAL WATCHED Scarlett walk across the backyard to the garage. He was torn between wanting her to turn around or keep going. He wanted her back so he could go to sleep tonight with her beside him. He also wanted her in her own place for a while so he could process everything that had happened today—and so he could call Hacker and find out what his teammate might have learned.

After they'd sixty-nined their way to nirvana, they'd gotten dressed—her in one of his t-shirts and only her panties, which had made it hard for him to focus—and headed to the kitchen so he could fix dinner. He'd opted for fried potatoes and oven-baked chicken with green beans and biscuits. It was one of his mother's signature meals, and he'd learned it well. Scarlett had washed dishes as he worked. She'd also asked questions about what he was doing, and she'd watched with wide-eyed amazement as he'd made biscuits from scratch.

He hadn't made biscuits from scratch in a long time since it was so damned easy to buy frozen ones and pop them on a baking sheet, but he'd wanted to impress her. He still didn't know why.

After they'd eaten and talked some more, she'd said she needed to get home. He'd wanted her to stay, but he'd stopped himself from asking. Which was how he found himself standing at the back door watching her climb the stairs to her apartment and wondering when he was going to get into her panties again.

Because he definitely wanted to. Making Scarlett come was one of the most fun things he'd done in a long time.

When she closed the door behind her—without turning around to see if he was looking, he noted—he sighed and went to retrieve his phone from the counter. He hit the call button without listening to the message. Hacker answered on the third ring.

"Hey, man. What's up?"

186

"Sorry I missed your call. Scarlett was with me and I couldn't answer."

Hacker made a noise. "That was six hours ago. Did you listen to my message?"

"No. I called as soon as I could."

"Wait, you mean she's been with you all this time?"

Mal could hear the curiosity in Hack's voice. "We went fishing."

"Okay. Wouldn't be my choice if I were you, but whatever."

"Scarlett and I are just friends."

"Okie doke. Whatever you say. Probably a good thing anyway."

A prickle of dread danced across the back of his neck. "Why do you say that?"

Hacker sighed. "There is no Scarlett Reed, Mal. She doesn't exist before three months ago when she took the job at Riverstone."

Mal's stomach twisted. A hard knot formed there, sitting like a lead weight. "She couldn't get a job doing what she does without a background check. Her credentials had to be vetted. You don't just walk into Riverstone and get hired without proving who you are."

"I know that, but she's managed it. Either she found someone to fake it all, or else someone at the hospital knows who Scarlett really is. Probably Dr. Puckett, because it'd have to go through her since she's in charge."

Mal agreed with that. If the rumors were true, nothing got by Stacy Puckett. The woman was formidable.

"I've checked in Florida and she doesn't exist there," Hacker continued. "It would help if we knew which hospital she came from. Then we could check out women who'd left in that timeframe. In the meantime, I'm trying to check for restraining orders against military men, but there are more of those than you'd expect. It'll take time to look at them all, assuming she filed one in the first place."

Mal was reeling. Not because Scarlett had lied, but because she had help lying. Which meant that whatever had happened in her past was serious enough she'd needed a new identity. But he also felt betrayed in a way because she knew his deepest, most shameful secret and he didn't know hers. He'd thought she'd been opening up to him, but she hadn't been. Not really.

He'd just spent the afternoon buried inside her body and he didn't know who she was.

And how's that any different from a one-night stand? You don't know those women either.

True, but he didn't usually care about them. He did care about Scarlett. They were supposed to be *friends*. "I'll see what I can find out, but whatever hospital she came from, she worked with patients from Eglin."

"There are a few options. Bliss is still checking

things out on her end. She might find something I can't. I'll let you know."

"Thanks, Hack. I appreciate it."

"We're family, Mal. You know that. I'll do anything I can for you. We all will."

They finished the call and Mal walked to the back door to look up at the apartment. It was starting to get dark now, and there was a light on inside. He wanted to go up there so badly, wanted to demand answers and hold her close—but he wouldn't.

Not yet. He needed time to think first. Time to get over the anger simmering low, or at least wall it off from the rational side of his brain. It was going to take patience to get the truth from Scarlett.

He wasn't sure he had a lot of that left right now.

Chapter Nineteen

"WHAT HAVE YOU GOTTEN YOURSELF INTO," SCARLETT muttered to herself as she moved around the apartment, tidying things that were already tidy and putting away the stuff she'd bought earlier. She'd never gotten around to hanging pictures. Maybe she'd do that now.

Except all she could think about were the past few hours in Mal's arms. In his bed, with his body driving into hers, his mouth fused to hers, and the world seeming to stand still for all that time. She'd had fun. More than fun.

She was both the most relaxed and the most jumpy she'd been in months. Relaxed—because how couldn't she be?—and jumpy for all the usual reasons. She wanted to go knock on his door and spend the rest of the weekend wrapped up in him.

But she couldn't. When she'd said it was time for

her to get back home, he hadn't stopped her. He hadn't said, "Scar, stay with me. I need you."

No, he hadn't said anything other than goodnight. Tears pricked her eyes and she swallowed them angrily. She was *not* getting emotional over that man. She'd lapsed, but damn it had been fun. If he asked again, she might just say yes. Or maybe she'd find her strength and she wouldn't.

Because she liked him more than she should. He fixed dinner for her, shopped with her, made her come until she was boneless, but that didn't mean she needed to let herself get goofy. For him, it was a friends with benefits arrangement. His feelings for Haylee hadn't changed. She thought he could, and maybe would, get over that, but it wasn't going to happen overnight. Not that it mattered to her. She wasn't looking for a relationship anyway.

Not after the last time.

Once she finished cleaning, she got her computer out and sat down on the couch to find a movie. She resisted the urge to pick up her phone and text Mal, ask him if he'd like to watch with her, but it wasn't easy. What was it about him that made her want to spend time with him? Yeah, he was sexy and he definitely knew how to use what he had—that tongue, dear heaven—but it wasn't just that.

She felt safe when he was near. She liked not being alone, and she liked the way he made her laugh. The world didn't seem quite as lonely then. For a girl who had no one left in her life, the allure of being with someone like Mal was almost too much.

"Stop it, Scarlett," she said to no one. "Find a movie and settle down."

Her phone dinged, making her jump with the sudden noise. She picked it up, her silly heart hoping it was Mal.

It was not.

Unknown Sender: *I'll see you soon.*

Scarlett's stomach squeezed hard as she whipped around to look at the windows. There was no one there. It was still light enough to see into the trees, and there was no one staring back at her. God, she needed curtains. She'd picked up some patterned sheets at the thrift shop today, fully intending to use them as curtains, but of course she hadn't had a chance to do it yet.

Scarlett stared at the message again, but nothing else happened. There was no new message, no call. Just a random text from an unknown number. She dragged in a breath. It didn't mean anything. Not really.

She told herself all the reasons why she didn't need to freak out. People called the wrong number sometimes. It happened. They texted the wrong number too. Which clearly this person had realized since there was no follow up to the first text.

Still, it rattled her to get such a random text. *I'll see you soon.*

Such an innocent combination of words, but it

made the well of panic she carried deep inside bubble toward the surface. Someone could have been reminding a friend about a date in the calendar, for heaven's sake. Besides, how would Josh get this number?

She'd been rattled since the man at Buddy's said she looked familiar, but really, she had to *be logical* about this. She'd treated a lot of patients during her time in Florida, and he could have been one of them. The chances he knew Josh, and then called and told Josh he'd seen someone who resembled her specifically, and then Josh somehow magically got her phone number and texted her, were rather astronomical. Especially since that had only happened *last night.*

Scarlett shook her head and set her phone down. *Be reasonable.*

She took a deep breath and continued to scroll for a movie to watch. When her phone dinged again, she was ready for it this time. But it was Mal, and her insides melted just a little at the sight of his name. Maybe it was relief, or maybe it was something more. She hoped not.

Mal: *It's Saturday night. You sure you want to sit up there all alone and watch something on your computer like a sad girl who can't get a date?*

Scarlett laughed. How did he manage to chase the shadows away with his nonsense? She typed back, *I'm not sad. I like watching movies.*

Mal: *Yeah, but alone? I've got a big tv down here. Come watch with me. I'll even let you pick.*

Scarlett: *Even if it's a chick flick?*

Mal: *Even then.*

Scarlett: *You have an ulterior motive.*

Mal: *Never! What makes you say such a thing, Scar? Just bc I'm sitting here with a box of condoms on the table beside me doesn't mean a damned thing. I swear.*

Scarlett wasn't surprised at the little flare of desire deep inside. It was like her libido had been hibernating all winter and was now wide awake. *I thought we discussed the fact the beaver needs a break.*

Mal: *<laughing so hard I'm crying emoji> And I thought I demonstrated there are plenty of other things I can do to make the beaver happy. So do you want to join me or not?*

Scarlett stared at the screen. She shouldn't do this. She really shouldn't. Getting involved with Mal was a bad plan. But she was lonely, and he made her laugh.

She closed her laptop and typed back, *Be right there.*

———

MAL BLINKED AWAKE right after dawn. Beside him, Scarlett snored softly. She was lying on her belly, her head buried beneath a silky wave of blond hair, her form blessedly naked as he let his gaze wander from the curve of her ass to the side mound of the breast he could see.

He thought about skimming kisses up her spine and waking her with a stiff cock poking between her legs, but she was sleeping soundly and he figured she needed it. He hadn't had much of a plan when he'd invited her over to watch television with him, but what he had involved sex and conversation and more sex.

So far, the plan had skewed to sex. The conversation had been lacking in information about anything she'd done before moving to Maryland, unfortunately. But today was a new day.

Mal got out of bed and crept to the bathroom, his injured leg stiff and aching. He didn't want to take a pain pill yet, so he took Tylenol instead. He stared at himself in the mirror while he brushed his teeth. Everybody said his leg would get better, but what if it didn't ever get better than this? What the hell would he do with himself if he couldn't go on missions anymore? What would his life be without HOT?

Not that they'd kick him out if he didn't recover. Mendez and Ghost would give him a desk job and that would be the end of it. He'd be able to finish his military career and retire in twenty if he wanted, or he could leave the service when his time was up instead of re-upping.

And do what?

He spit out the toothpaste and rinsed. That's what he didn't know. Who was he without HOT? What was he without them?

"Hey," a gravelly voice said, and he turned to see Scarlett with her mussed up hair and sweet smile.

"Hey. I thought you were sleeping."

"Oh, I'm going back to bed. Gotta pee. But you looked serious. Everything okay?"

"It's fine, Scar."

She frowned. "Is it your leg? Does it hurt?"

How the hell did she always know? Then again it was her job to know.

"It's stiff. I took Tylenol."

She nodded. "That'll help. Don't get too upset, Mal. You're only a few weeks out from surgery. And you're doing amazing, so don't worry that things aren't where they used to be yet. It'll get there. Sooner than you think, probably."

Frustration hammered him, but it wasn't her fault so he didn't snap at her. "Everybody says that. It doesn't feel that way, though."

She patted his shoulder. "I know. Trust me."

The words twisted in his gut. Trust? He wanted to ask her what she knew about trust, but he knew that wouldn't get him anywhere. If he pushed, she'd never tell him anything. And she'd go back to her place and never let him inside her sweet body again.

"I'm going to make coffee," he said. "If you don't fall asleep again, join me on the back porch. It's cool and there'll be wildlife in the yard."

"Mmm," she said, waiting for him to clear out so she could use the bathroom. "Maybe. Pretty tired though. You wore me out."

He dipped to put a kiss on her forehead. "I like wearing you out."

"I like it too," she said as she closed the door on him.

Mal went downstairs and put on the coffee, then he opened the back door and stepped onto the screened in porch. This was one of the things he loved most about this property. The view encompassed the garage and apartment where Scarlett lived, when she wasn't in his bed, and a long stretch of grass with small trees and bushes planted by the previous owners. Behind that were the woods separating him from the neighboring property where the pond was. The former She-Shed was in those woods. He thought of discovering the delights of Scarlett's body there yesterday and knew he was going to clean the place up and make it into the kind of space he could take her for a romantic retreat without televisions or internet connections.

Mal blinked. Romantic retreat? What the hell?

He shook his head. He was officially losing it. Romantic retreats were not something you did with a booty call. Scarlett was his booty call. He was hers. No romance necessary.

When the coffee was done, Mal poured a cup and went to sit on the porch. He opened email on his phone and discovered another from Hacker.

Still looking for more information, but Bliss found an abstract of a police report about a woman whose BMW went into a lake nearly four months ago. She thought her ex-boyfriend had tampered with her brakes. Bliss is working on getting names, etc. It might be nothing, but it's worth a look. No new HOT recruits lately, so whoever that guy was Friday night, he's not HOT.

Mal sighed. There were a lot of Special Ops assignments in the DC area, so the guy could be assigned to any of them. Too bad Scarlett hadn't gotten a name from him, but she'd been too rattled by the fact he thought he knew her. Mal thought of Scarlett lying naked in his bed, her red pubic hair so fiery compared to the blond of her head. If she'd been a redhead in Florida, which no doubt she was, it might have been enough to confuse the guy when he'd spotted her at Buddy's.

Mal typed a quick reply and sent it, then settled in to watch the birds picking worms from his yard. A couple of deer grazed on the edge of the property. He loved seeing that. There was a time when he'd hunted deer, but these days he didn't have the desire. He'd rather watch them and let others do the hunting.

After he finished his coffee, Mal went into the dining room—where he had no dining table but had instead put some weights and a treadmill—and did his workout. He moved slowly through the exercises, especially the ones involving his legs, telling himself that he was getting stronger every day. His leg didn't ache too much right now because the Tylenol had kicked in, but it would later. It ached a lot in the evenings after using it for hours, but it was still strong enough to carry him through the day. He no longer needed a cane, and even though Scarlett might yell at him for it, he didn't take pain pills if he could help it. He didn't want to be addicted to them.

Tomorrow, he was returning to work—or so he hoped. A desk job at HOT, if the doctor cleared him in the morning at his appointment, but his real goal was to get back into the field as soon as possible. The quicker he got his strength back, the quicker it would happen.

He finished the workout, wiping sweat from his face, and looked up to find Scarlett standing in the door, leaning against the jamb, a cup of coffee in her hand.

"Morning," he said, his gaze roaming her face as if he could see the truth there. He'd gotten distracted last night, but he wasn't going to let it happen today.

"Morning," she said. "You're working hard at that."

He dropped the towel around his shoulders and shrugged. "I have incentive."

"Your job, I suppose."

"Yes. I need to be with my team again."

"You will be, Mal. Just give it a little time."

He went over and dropped a kiss on her forehead before stealing her coffee cup and taking a sip. "You're speaking from experience, right?"

"Yes," she said as he handed the cup back. "I've worked with plenty of vets and active duty."

"What hospital did you work at?" he asked. "I don't think you ever said before."

"No, I didn't. Does it matter?"

He thought of Hacker's words. *There is no Scarlett Reed.* "Maybe it does."

She looked instantly wary. "Why should it? Do you think I'm lying?"

He studied her. "About your experience? No."

Her entire body had gone rigid. "What do you think I'm lying about then?"

He picked up a lock of her blond hair and twirled it gently around his finger. "I don't know, Scar. Maybe you aren't lying so much as not telling the truth. I thought you trusted me."

She pulled from his grasp and headed for the kitchen. "You know what," she said, setting the cup down. "I think I'm just going to go home and shower there. Thanks for the sex."

Frustration pounded through his brain. He wanted to reach for her, spin her around, press his mouth to hers and stop her in her tracks. But that wouldn't get them anywhere except naked again. And how the hell was he going to help her if she wouldn't open up to him? Not to mention he was seriously pissed that she wouldn't tell him the truth after everything they'd shared. After she'd exposed all his secrets and made him examine them under a microscope.

"You're welcome, Scar," he drawled. "Always happy to be your fuck buddy since it doesn't look like we're actually friends at all."

She spun. "Is that what you think?"

He stepped into her space, glaring down at her flashing eyes and dark scowl. "Friends share their secrets, honey. They don't hide them and lie about them, especially when it's obvious they aren't telling the truth."

"How dare you," she growled.

"Give it up, Scarlett. Or is that even your name?"

She looked like he'd slapped her. "Why do you say that?"

"Because I asked my friends to help protect you after that guy scared you the other night. And guess what Hacker told me? There is no Scarlett Reed. She doesn't exist."

Her expression collapsed. "You went behind my back. Oh my god."

"If you'd tell me what was wrong, I wouldn't have to," he growled back at her.

She searched his face for a long moment, not speaking. And then she spun and ran from the kitchen, out onto the porch, and across the yard. Mal closed his eyes and swore.

Way to go, genius.

Chapter Twenty

Scarlett told herself she was acting like an idiot, but the knowledge that Mal had gone behind her back—Mal, who she'd believed was different—was like a blow to the belly. She couldn't breathe. Damn him for spying on her. She ran up the steps to her apartment and yanked her key from her pocket.

But when she went to insert it in the lock, the door creaked open instead. Scarlett's heart stopped beating. She knew better than to go inside. Instead, she backed away, fear clawing up her insides as she stumbled onto the steps and ran down them again. Had she pulled the door all the way shut last night? Was it her fault?

She bounded onto Mal's porch, the screen door banging behind her, and pounded on his back door. He yanked it open immediately, his brows drawn low. One look at her face and he dragged her inside, shoving her behind him as he locked the door and peered out. When he didn't see anything, he turned to her.

Scarlett hugged herself tight. What the actual fuck was she doing? He would think she was crazy.

He put his hands on her shoulders and squeezed lightly. She was happy that he wasn't thinking about their fight in that moment. He was more concerned about her.

"What's wrong, Scarlett?"

"M-my d-door. It was open."

He frowned. "The apartment door was open?"

She nodded.

"And you remember locking it last night?"

"I always lock the door, Mal. It's something I do since… Since my ex. I never leave my door unlocked. I m-mean maybe I didn't pull it tight enough and it opened during the night. It could happen. But I know I locked it."

Mal was still sweaty from his workout, but he reached into a drawer and pulled out a gun. "You stay here and I'll go check it out."

Fear sliced into her. "No, don't go. Please."

"It's fine, honey. You'll be okay and it won't take me long. Lock the door behind me and watch me from the window."

How could she tell him it wasn't herself she was worried about? Not while she was here in his house. It was the idea of him going up there, and Josh waiting for him. Not that she knew Josh was there, but what if he was? He was capable of *anything*.

A tear spilled down her cheek. "Mal, please."

He reached into the drawer and handed her a gun in a holster. "Do you know how to use a weapon?"

"My d-dad taught me."

"Then you know what to do if anyone but me comes through the door."

She nodded.

"I'll be back in a few minutes."

"Okay," she whispered.

Mal disappeared outside and she locked the door behind him, watching from the window as he ascended the stairs and flattened his body along the side of the building before kicking the door open and entering with weapon drawn. Her heart hammered in her chest as she pleaded with God to let it be nothing. Let Mal come back safe. Don't let Josh be there.

Within moments Mal exited the apartment, shutting the door firmly behind him and descending the stairs at an even pace. He didn't hobble or limp, and she was happy to see that for him. She twisted the lock on the back door and he came inside, shutting it behind him and twisting it again.

"There's no one inside. Your computer is still there, and your purse too. I think maybe the lock didn't catch all the way and the door blew open during the night when it rained again."

She put a hand to her heart and concentrated on slowing the speed of it. Of course it would be something simple like that. She felt so stupid. "Thank you."

He took the gun from her and went to put both of

them away. Then he came back and pulled out a chair at the kitchen table. "Sit, Scarlett."

She sat. He sat in the chair nearest hers. "Do you want to tell me what you're scared of or do you want to continue to pretend like it's nothing?"

Scarlett dropped her forehead into her hands and studied the table surface. If she told him everything, she'd have someone who knew. Someone who could maybe keep an eye on Josh from afar with his contacts. She squeezed her eyes shut, her pulse racing as sweat beaded on her skin. But maybe it was the right thing to do. Yes, she was pissed at Mal for digging into her life, but since he'd seen her reaction to the man at Buddy's, could she blame him for asking his friends to get involved?

She sat up and leaned back in the chair, fixing him with as steady a gaze as she could manage. He watched her with placid green eyes, and she gradually felt her heart rate slowing.

"My dad's nickname for me was Scarlett. Because of my hair. My mom was a redhead too, but my dad had dark hair. He called me Scarlett from the time I was a little girl. He was the only one who did, though. When I needed to disappear, I thought it would be easier to use a name I was used to. Could I have another cup of coffee?"

Mal got up to get it silently, returning with two mugs and the pot. He fetched cream from the fridge, pouring some into her cup until her heart ached because he knew exactly how much to use. Scarlett picked up the mug with both hands.

"My name is Erin Rose. Rose is my last name, not a middle name, which is another reason Dad called me Scarlett. He got a kick out of it. My middle name is Colleen. My mom's grandparents came from Ireland." She let out a laugh that shook with sadness. "She always loved everything Irish. Reed is her maiden name, from her dad's side obviously. Her mother was an O'Toole."

She felt like she was babbling, but Mal merely listened. He never tried to hurry her along or ask questions. She knew he wanted her to get it all out, and that he would ask questions eventually, but she appreciated that he let her tell it in her own way.

"I worked at the The Orthopedic Center. It's a sports med facility in Fort Walton Beach. That's where I met Josh. Joshua Wright. He's a technical sergeant in the Air Force, and he was stationed at the Special Operations unit on Eglin. I don't know what he did, but he claimed to be an operator. Like a green beret or a Navy SEAL, he said. He had laparoscopic surgery to repair a torn labrum, and I met him when he came to his rehab appointments. He seemed like a normal guy, really, and he flirted with me from the beginning. I didn't agree to go out with him the first time he asked, but he was persistent."

She took a shaky sip of coffee. *Damn it.*

"He seemed normal at first. Attentive. A real gentleman. I fell for it all. The grand gestures, the overly concerned act, everything. And then, when we'd been going out for a month, he hit me. I was stunned, but of course he apologized and swore up and down it wouldn't happen again." Scarlett gripped the mug tight, hating Josh. Hating herself. "But of course it did."

"Scarlett," Mal said, his voice sounding more ragged than she expected.

She reached for his hand on the table and he wrapped hers up, squeezing it comfortingly. "I wasn't battered in the sense he beat the hell out of me and I had to go to the hospital. His abuse was much more insidious. A lot of it was mental. He tore me down, Mal. Told me I was nothing. And because I didn't have anyone—no parents, no real close friends—I believed him. He said my coworkers were jealous, or plotting to have me fired. All kinds of bullshit I shouldn't have believed, but I did. And when I finally got smart, when Dr. Saunders—she's the doctor I worked for—when she took me aside and talked to me about her concerns over Josh and how he treated me, well, I tried to break it off."

"But it didn't work."

She shook her head. "No, not really. He'd already worked so hard to separate me from everyone. He manipulated me in every way." She gritted her teeth, anger surging at the memories. "And when I told him I didn't want to see him anymore, he started doing other things. He used the key to my apartment that he'd stolen, and he regularly entered when I wasn't home. He moved things around, stole things, then denied it was him. He was always so careful. If I called the police, they found nothing and thought I was making it all up. I stopped calling them."

"Did you speak to his commanding officer?"

She shook her head. "I tried calling once. I left a message with his secretary about what was going on, but he never called back. I didn't expect him to since Josh and I weren't married. I know the military is very particular about things like that. I wasn't Josh's dependent, so therefore I wasn't worth the commander's time. I didn't try again."

"Did Josh tamper with your brakes?"

Scarlett felt the icy grip of fear wrap around her heart. "How did you find that out?"

"Hacker found something about a woman whose car went into a lake."

Scarlett thought of those moments when she'd lost control. When the rain beneath her tires had turned into a slick sheet that carried her off the road and into the lake. If she hadn't seen a video about how to break her window in an emergency, she'd have never gotten out alive. But she had, and she'd even managed to drag her purse with her. A passerby had stopped and called 911, staying with her until they arrived.

"There was no proof it was him. My brake line had a hole in it, but it was small and the fluid apparently leaked out over days. They barely found it when they examined the car after it was pulled from the lake. But I knew." She sucked in a breath. "I told Dr.

Saunders. She was the only one I could trust. She called Dr. Puckett and helped me get the job up here."

"Puckett knows who you really are."

"Yes. She's been helping me get things switched over to Scarlett Reed. You'd be surprised how easy it is to use a new name when you have help with paperwork."

Mal reached out and took one of her hands gently into his. "I know this is hard for you, Scar, but you didn't have to hide it from me."

"It's hard to trust anyone, Mal. Even a guy as great as you. I thought Josh was great at one time too."

He stared at their joined hands, frowning. "I get that. I'm not insulted by it because you'd be dumb to pretend like it wasn't possible that I'd turn into a dick given time. But I won't, Scar. It's not who I am."

She sighed and set the cup down. Then she leaned forward to cup his cheek. His skin was warm, and her body reacted to that simple touch. "A man who throws himself in front of a bullet to save his friend, especially when that friend has something he wants, isn't capable of being anything but honorable and decent. Believe me, I know that. But dragging you—dragging anyone—into the insanity of what my life has turned into after Josh wasn't something I intended to do. I just want to forget it happened."

"But that's the trouble, Scarlett. You haven't

forgotten. You aren't forgetting. You're terrified he's looking for you. Terrified he'll find you."

She trembled inside. "I am. I don't know what he's capable of, but from the moment I went into that lake, I knew it wasn't good. I'm afraid if he finds me, he'll kill me," she finished on a hoarse whisper.

Mal dragged her onto his lap and held her. She didn't try to stop him. She *wanted* him to hold her. He made her feel safe, even if she knew she really wasn't. He couldn't be there every minute of every day. That was the problem in the end. No one could be there all the time, and Josh was patient. If he found her, he'd wait for the best moment to make his move. He'd bide his time, and he'd have a plan.

"Not happening, Scar," Mal said fiercely. "You've got me now. And when you've got me, you've got a whole team of people just like me. We're the best at what we do, honey. We'll find him, and we'll put the fear of God in him. I swear it."

Scarlett lay her head against his shoulder and closed her eyes. She wanted to believe it could be that easy. But she didn't. "I got a text last night. From an unknown sender. It said *I'll see you soon*."

His arms tightened around her. "You think it's him?"

"I don't see how it could be. I have a new phone, new number. It has to be a wrong number, and yet for a minute I was terrified."

"Give me the number and I'll see what I can find

out. It's probably nothing, like you said. But you'll feel better once you know."

She would feel better. But only until the next text came, or until she encountered the next unlocked door.

Chapter Twenty-One

MAL'S PLACE WAS HOPPING THAT AFTERNOON. IT WAS Sunday, which meant everyone had to work tomorrow, but it didn't matter. He'd called his team and they'd arrived. They'd brought their ladies—the ones who had ladies—and they'd brought food. It was an emergency meeting of Strike Team Two. The business wasn't HOT business, but it was important business nonetheless.

Brooke, Haylee, and Eva had taken Scarlett beneath their wings in the kitchen, and Bliss was hanging out in the backyard with the guys since she was one of the team. Wolf was flipping burgers on the grill, and they were all talking about Scarlett's problem. Saint and Muffin had gone through Scarlett's apartment again, looking for anything Mal might have missed in his quick pass through. They were detailing what they'd found to the gathering.

"Someone could have popped the lock," Saint

said. "It's not definite, but there are scratch marks on the jamb that look recent. You been doing work up there, Mal?"

Mal shook his head. "Nope. I put new locks in before Scarlett moved in, but I haven't had a reason to touch them since. The door sticks sometimes when it's been raining. It's wood and it swells. You have to shove it hard to open or close when that happens. The whole building is old."

Saint frowned. "Yeah, could be what's happened."

"There are footprints at the bottom of the stairs," Muffin said. "But I can't distinguish between them. Scarlett's been up and down those stairs. You have too. If there are others, then the prints are mixed in with both of yours."

Mal shoved a hand through his hair. The door swelling made more sense than someone breaking in, and yet Scarlett had been so terrified. She'd relaxed as the day wore on, but he could tell she was still on edge.

"I've got the cameras," Noah "Easy" Cross said. "I'll put them up where they aren't likely to be noticed and train them on the house and garage. Can't hurt."

"Thanks, Easy. I appreciate it," Mal said.

Hacker had a laptop open on a nearby table. "And here he is. Joshua Calvin Wright. He's thirty-two, a technical sergeant in the Air Force, and he's definitely assigned to the unit on Eglin. But he's not an operator, or at least not these days. He's a desk jockey." Hacker glanced at Mal and grimaced.

"Sorry, Mal. I know you aren't going to be on a desk forever."

Mal ignored the prickle of unease that flared to life inside. "Nope, I know it too. This week it's a desk. A month from now, who knows?"

Wolf reached over and clapped him on the back. "You'll be out there with us again soon. You're too damned ornery not to be."

Easy snorted. "Tell me about it. When I joined the team, he told me I had to memorize everyone's coffee preferences and serve you every morning before training."

"And that's one reason why we call you Easy," Mal laughed. "It was too easy to convince you it was a tradition for the new recruits."

"Never again," Easy said with a grin.

"Man, you did such a great job," Harley said. "I miss having someone bring me coffee every morning."

Easy rolled his eyes. "What, Eva won't do it for you?"

"Hell no. I take Eva her tea every morning before I leave for work."

"Awwww," the guys said in unison.

Harley wasn't rattled at all. "Go ahead and make fun. You'll see. When you find the woman you love more than life, you'll find out just how far you'll go."

"Damn straight," Wolf said.

"Sky?" Bliss prodded with a laugh.

He glanced up from his computer, looking slightly confused at the interruption. "Huh?"

They all laughed. Bliss went over and put her arms around his neck and kissed him on the cheek. "Nothing, babe. You find anything else?"

"Haven't unlocked that police report yet, but I don't guess we need to since Scarlett's confirmed it was her in the car."

She'd told them a few more things too, like the fact she'd tried to get a restraining order but there'd been no evidence of prior assaults or threats. Therefore, the restraining order had been denied. No matter how scared she'd been, how convinced she'd been that Josh was entering her apartment and spying on her, there'd been no hard evidence. She'd said it all with her eyes downcast, as if she'd expected they wouldn't believe her either, but Mal had pulled her into his arms in front of everyone and hugged her. She'd asked him once before how he knew she wasn't the crazy one. He'd told her he knew because she was asking him.

It made him angry for her that no one had believed her before now. That she'd doubted herself and her sanity because of it.

No one had believed her, except Dr. Jessica Saunders. Thank God the doctor had or Scarlett wouldn't have escaped. And who knows what Wright might have done to her then?

"Any idea where Wright is at the moment?" Mal asked.

"Not yet," Hacker said. "He's still stationed at Eglin so far as I can see. But I'm digging."

"I am too," Bliss said, though she was holding a phone and not a computer. "I've got a couple of calls out. Waiting on information."

"I found the phone number you gave me," Hacker said. "It's a burner."

"Fuck." He didn't want to have to tell Scarlett that. Burners weren't in themselves ominous. Hell, his grandmother used a burner, otherwise known as a prepaid cell phone, because she didn't want or need a monthly plan. Lots of people did. But Scarlett would have felt a lot better if Mal could have said the number belonged to Jane Doe from Baltimore who'd probably been texting a friend.

"Are those things about done?" Muffin asked, nodding at the grill. "I'm starved."

"Yeah, yeah, don't get your shorts in a wad," Wolf said.

The back door opened and the ladies came outside carrying all the fixings for burgers as well as the casseroles they'd brought. Mal met Scarlett's eyes. She smiled, and he knew she was okay for the moment. He let his gaze slip to Haylee. She was wearing a pink sundress with sandals, her naturally curly hair hanging loose down her back, and she looked like an angel. But looking at her didn't hurt the way it usually did.

Interesting.

She caught his gaze once she'd set down the plates and came over to loop her arm through his. It was a casually friendly gesture, like always, but his heart

didn't ache for once. "I like Scarlett," she said softly.
"She's smart and kind."

"She is," Mal said, looking at Scarlett as she
helped Brooke and Eva shift the dishes on the outdoor
table. Mal didn't have a picnic table, but it didn't
matter. Saint had brought a big plastic table with legs
that unfolded, Wolf had brought another, and
everyone brought an extra chair or two. It was a team
effort, but a far pleasanter one than they usually
encountered when they worked together.

"Pretty too," Haylee added.

"Very," Mal said, and meant it.

Haylee looked up at him, one beautiful dark
eyebrow arched. "I'm glad you noticed."

"Why wouldn't I?"

Haylee shrugged. "No reason. Now please don't
do something dumb."

Mal wanted to sputter. "What makes you think I'd
do that?"

Haylee laughed. "You're male. It's encoded in
your DNA."

Wolf turned and caught her eye and Mal felt her
slipping away from him. And that was okay. She gave
his arm a squeeze and went to stand at her fiancé's
side. Wolf put an arm around her and kissed her
quick before turning back to the burgers. "Can you
get me a platter, babe?" he asked her.

"Yep. One platter coming up."

Once the burgers were on the table, people started
fixing plates. Hacker closed his computer and joined

Bliss, who handed him a plate with a bun on it. Mal picked up a plate, grabbed a bun, and let his gaze stray to Scarlett, who stood off to one side with Muffin. She was laughing at something Muffin said, which made Mal's gut clench suddenly because what if his teammate decided he wanted to ask her out? Then what?

Scarlett was Mal's friend with bennies, not a romantic connection, so he couldn't say no if someone else wanted to date her. Or could he?

The acid boiling inside told him he damned well wanted to. And who said he couldn't anyway? He was a grown ass man. He could do what he wanted.

And what he wanted was Scarlett. He finished filling the plate with a little bit of everything, and then went over to where Muffin was leaning in to say something to her.

"Hey, Scar, I brought you some food," Mal said.

She looked up, smiling at him. Warmth spread through his body.

"How sweet. Thanks, Mal."

"I put a bit of everything on the plate. Just in case."

She took it from him as Muffin caught Mal's eye. Mal knew he was communicating clearly when Muffin excused himself and went to grab his own food. Scarlett nodded toward Mal's empty hands. "Shouldn't you get some for yourself?"

"Yep. They won't eat it all, though. Did I get it right with the burger?" He'd gotten all the things he liked, which was pretty much everything. Plus mayo and mustard. No ketchup.

"Perfect," she said with a smile. "How did you guess?"

He shrugged. "Lucky, I suppose. It's also the way I like it."

She shoved her fork into the mac and cheese, sighing as she tasted it. "Everything is good. I like your friends."

"They like you, too."

Scarlett seemed to frown a little. "I feel like I over-reacted about the door. They're here because I panicked."

He decided not to tell her about the phone number until later. There was no sense giving her something to worry about when she was finally relaxing again.

"You didn't overreact. Besides, I'm glad you told me everything, and I'm not sure you would have if you hadn't been scared."

She dropped her chin. "No, probably not. I'm used to taking care of myself."

He tweaked her nose affectionately. "You're used to going it alone. You don't have to do that anymore. We're here for you."

Her smile wavered a fraction, and he knew it was emotion making it happen. "Thank you. But I really hope I never need their help."

Mal gave her a look. "It's about more than Josh,

babe. *We're here for you* means more than protecting you from a dangerous situation."

She looked as if she might tear up, so he gave her a little bump on the arm with his fist and grinned to keep things light. Inside, his heart was throbbing, but outside he pretended to be cool. "Gotta get some food before I starve," he said. Then he leaned in and whispered in her ear. "Gotta keep my strength up so I can service you some more."

Scarlett giggled and leaned into him, bumping her shoulder to his bicep. "You're a goofball."

"But you like goofballs."

"I really do," she said.

"Does that mean I'm forgiven?"

After a moment, she nodded. "Yes."

"Excellent. I'm looking forward to the makeup sex," he said where only she could hear. Her cheeks reddened and he laughed. "Stop blushing or they'll know you've been doing me."

"Mal!"

She was still blushing, and he wanted to kiss her in front of everyone. Claim her. That was a new feeling. He didn't do it, though.

"Keep it up and all I'll do to you is wrap my hands around your neck later," she added. "Then I'll squeeze."

"I got something you can squeeze. But it's not my neck." He waggled his eyebrows at her and headed for the food, laughing the whole way.

————

SCARLETT HADN'T THOUGHT she could be comfortable with so many people she didn't know well, but it turned out she could. Mal's teammates, and their girlfriends-slash-fiancées, were easy to be around. They accepted her as if she were one of their own. She knew she wasn't, and she tried to keep reminding herself of that when they laughed and joked about things she wasn't a part of, but someone always let her in on the joke. It wasn't always Mal, either. Sometimes it was one of the ladies, and sometimes it was one of the big, buff military men who ought to make her cringe but somehow didn't.

They sat around the tables eating burgers, mac and cheese, deviled eggs, potato salad, and a couple different vegetable dishes, drinking beer or wine or water, and laughing like the best of friends until it got dark and the party moved inside.

Scarlett didn't stay by Mal's side the whole time, but she often found her gaze straying to him when they were apart. She'd seen him talking to Haylee much earlier, but that was the only time she'd seen them together. Scarlett hadn't expected the pang of jealousy she'd felt at the sight of Haylee's arm looped through his, but it'd reared its head and sank its claws into her as she'd watched them out of the corner of her eye.

And then Haylee walked away, and though Mal watched her for a few moments, he didn't seem to linger in his study of her. Instead, his gaze sought Scarlett's. She'd felt relief, and that troubled her.

Why did she care if Mal watched Haylee or not? Yes, she wanted him to get over his feelings because it was healthier for him, but that shouldn't make her want him to look at her instead.

But she did. She wanted it badly, and when he did look at her, their eyes locked and she couldn't help but smile. He always smiled back. It was like sharing a secret with someone—which she supposed they did since they were having sex and his team didn't know it.

Or at least she thought they didn't know it, though Haylee had asked a couple of pointed questions after Mal had looked in their direction earlier. Not to mention how red Scarlett had gotten when Mal was teasing her. Who knew how many of them had noticed it?

"So," Haylee had said. "How's it going living so close to Mal?"

"Fine," Scarlett had replied. "He's quiet."

"I heard you two went fishing yesterday. How'd that go?"

"About how you'd expect. We caught some fish, let them go, and that was that."

She left out the storm, and the little shed in the woods. What an experience that had been. Just remembering made her body start to tingle.

"Mmm. Mal's a handsome guy, don't you think?"

If Scarlett had thought Haylee was at all interested in Mal, she'd have been depressed. As it was, she knew the other woman was head over heels for Dean Garner. The questions were an attempt at matchmaking or Scarlett was the queen of England.

"He's not bad," Scarlett had said, more to mess with Haylee than anything.

Before Haylee could grill her some more, Brooke carried over a tray of her homemade cupcakes. Scarlett had used the opportunity to escape. By the time the evening wore down and everyone got in their cars, Scarlett was yawning and trying to hide it behind her hand. She and Mal stood outside, watching the last car pull out of the driveway. Once the headlights were facing the opposite direction, Mal put an arm around her and pulled her to his side.

"You doing okay?"

"I'm fine. Been a long day."

"It has." He turned her and held her by the shoulders. "I want you to stay with me, Scar. I think you'll be more comfortable in my house. And if you don't want to sleep in the same bed, I'll live. Somehow."

She laughed. "Will you?"

"Yes, though I'll lie in my bed and stroke myself while I think about you."

"Oooh, kinky."

Mal snorted. "Honey, if you think that's kinky, you've got some things to learn."

"Maybe I do." She sighed. "I really like my apartment, and the things I've bought to decorate it with—

but I *would* feel better staying with you tonight. Maybe for a couple of nights."

She knew that his team had put up cameras, but she still didn't want to be alone. A camera wouldn't save her if Josh was out there waiting.

Mal looped an arm around her. "It's okay. I get it."

"They didn't find any evidence of tampering, I know that, but that's how it was before, too." Which was why she was grateful they'd believed her enough to put up the cameras.

"Hacker found the phone number," Mal said. "It's a prepaid cell phone, which means nothing other than I can't give you a name and tell you for certain it was an accident. Lots of people have prepaid cell phones. My grandmother does, and she'd be very likely to text someone she didn't mean to text."

Scarlett's belly clenched. "Okay. It's not what I wanted to hear, but I know it doesn't mean anything."

"It doesn't. Though it's also how someone like me would make contact if I didn't want a person to know it was me."

"I know that too," she said softly.

"Do you think he's tracked you to Maryland?"

Scarlett thought about it. The only person who knew where she'd gone was Dr. Saunders, and she wasn't going to share it with Josh. If he'd been trying to find out the information, Jessica would have texted to let Scarlett know. "Logically, no. But my animal brain keeps wanting me to run."

"I know, honey. But don't run. Stay with me."

She loved the way he said those words. For a moment she could pretend he was asking her to stay with him for always. But he wasn't, nor did she want him to.

Liar.

"Let's get inside. We both have to go to work in the morning," Mal said.

He was very likely going to a desk after he saw the doctor, which she knew he didn't like, but at least he'd get to return to work. It was a start. "I have to go upstairs and get my clothes, Mal."

He looked at her blankly. Then he grinned as it dawned on him. "Oh, you mean for tomorrow. Sure, let's go up and get your things. But you won't need any clothes tonight—not if you're sleeping in my bed."

"We'll see," she said, turning and heading for the stairs. "Maybe I'll try out that guest bed after all."

She would do no such thing, but it didn't hurt to keep him guessing.

"That's fine," he said. Grumbled really. Her heart filled with emotion over how easily he agreed. She was teasing him, but he'd said it was okay if she wanted to be alone and he meant it.

Scarlett turned after she'd climbed a couple of steps. Mal was below her and their eyes were on a level. She wrapped her arms around his neck and kissed him. His hands splayed over her back, one sliding down to cup her ass. She shuddered plea-surably.

"On second thought, I think I'll spend the night with you."

"Good choice," he said on a growl. "Now let's get your stuff so I can strip you naked and make you come."

Chapter Twenty-Two

EVERYTHING SEEMED BETTER IN THE LIGHT OF A NEW day. Scarlett, her body still languid from the night before, hit the shower after Mal and got ready for work. He'd wanted her to join him, but she'd pointed out they might both be late if she did. He'd laughed and said she was right. Then he'd gone downstairs to make coffee.

When Scarlett walked into the kitchen, two things hit her at once. First, he was wearing a uniform. Army camouflage, with his name tape on one side, U.S. Army on the other, and his rank on his sleeves. There was a unit patch on one pocket, and an American flag on one arm. She hadn't seen him in uniform before, and the sight did things to her pulse. Good things, not bad.

Second, he'd made more than coffee. He'd fixed her a bagel sandwich and wrapped wax paper around half of it so she could hold it easily. There was egg, cheese, and mayo, and she bit into it with relish while trying to cover her awe at the sight of him in uniform.

"Good?" he asked with a laugh.

"Very. It's nice to have something besides cereal or toast for breakfast."

"You know they make frozen breakfast sandwiches, right? Pop them in the microwave and you've got a warm meal."

"I tried that once. I think I did something wrong because it was chewy on the outside and frozen in the center. No thanks."

Mal laughed. "I really need to teach you how to cook, don't I?"

His words made happiness blossom inside her. She imagined being with him long enough for cooking lessons. But there was a cloud to her joy. A cloud she was determined not to think about this morning. No Josh. And no Haylee.

"You can try," she said, taking another bite of her sandwich.

He leaned over and kissed her. Then he handed her a go-cup of coffee. "We could ride together," he said. "I'll take you to work and pick you up after."

She was tempted. "No, I need my car." If she needed to pick up something on her lunch break, or stay late because she ended up taking on extra patients, then she had to be flexible.

"Okay. Just thought I'd offer."

"I'm fine, Mal. Really. I had a minor meltdown

yesterday, but you and the others made me feel better. Thanks again for calling them."

"Anytime, Scar. We're your posse now."

She smiled. "I like that idea."

Mal grabbed his keys and his own cup. "You ready to get in the car and start the trek?"

"Yep. I'll finish the sandwich on the way."

"I thought you might say that so I wrapped it in wax paper."

She loved how thoughtful he was. It was the little things. Even though he didn't love her—wouldn't love her—he cared more than Josh ever had. That she believed.

They went outside, Mal locked the door, and then he walked her to her car though it was right beside his. "Have a good day," he said before kissing her soundly.

"You too, Mal. Don't overdo it."

"Promise I'll be good," he said, crossing his heart like they were kids swearing to keep a secret.

Scarlett climbed into her car and started it up, happiness a bright bubble inside her. Maybe her life really was getting better. She had a good job doing what she loved, a group of new friends, and a man who made her feel incredible and cared for.

It was about time something started going right for her. But how long would it last?

———

IT WAS odd being back at work and not hitting the training hard. His appointment this morning had gone well and the doctor had cleared him to return. But Mal was relegated to a desk for the time being, though he was allowed to hit the range for stationary shooting. He couldn't do the training course outside, and he wasn't allowed to do any of the shooting exercises that involved moving across terrain.

He participated as much as possible, though. He kept up with the equipment, the timers, the targets. Whatever was needed. He could walk around the building without a cane, but his leg started to ache when he stayed on his feet too long. He remembered Scarlett's command not to overdo it and tempered his expectations. He wouldn't take a pain pill at work, but he popped Tylenol when necessary.

"Good to have you back," Mendez said as he stopped by Mal's desk. "You listening to your physical therapist's instructions?"

"Yes, sir," Mal replied. He pictured Scarlett, arms crossed and looking smug when he told her later that it was the first thing his commander had asked him. She'd get a kick out of it for sure.

"I know it's hard, but they know what they're talking about. I need you back to full strength as quickly as possible, and that only happens when you do what you're told. Try to rush it and you'll make things worse."

"Yes, sir. I've been told that, sir."

Repeatedly, in fact. Mendez nodded and

continued on his way. Ghost—the HOT deputy commander—stopped by an hour later and said much the same thing. Mal nodded and replied that he was being careful, doing everything he was supposed to do, and looking forward to a full recovery. When Ghost left, Mal shook his head. It was almost like Scarlett had called them both and told them what to say. He knew she hadn't, but it was amusing to think so.

He picked up his phone and sent her a text. He hadn't seen her in a little over four hours now so he could legit get away with a message without seeming like he was hovering. He sent something sure to raise an eyebrow and then waited eagerly for her reply. *What are you wearing?*

Her reply was swift. *The same thing I was wearing when you said goodbye to me this morning.*

Sweet, sassy Scarlett. He knew her name was Erin now, but he could only think of her as Scarlett. When he'd asked her what she preferred to be called when they were alone, she'd said Scarlett. He was glad because it seemed right to call her that.

And what will you be wearing when I get home tonight? he typed back.

Scarlett: *Whatever I want.*

Mal laughed. The woman did not miss a beat. *And then you'll be wearing me.*

Scarlett: *Maybe. First you have to feed me.*

Mal had a vision of feeding a naked Scarlett as if she were a goddess and he were her servant. He didn't mind the idea at all. He pictured her pink lips nibbling grapes from his hand and felt a flame kindle inside. A flame he quashed before it turned into something embarrassing.

Mal: *I can do that. How's steak on the grill?*

Scarlett: *Mmm, steak. Sounds delicious. How's work going? You behaving?*

Mal: *Yes. I'm not taxing my leg, so don't worry. Work is fine. They won't let me overdo it even if I wanted to.*

Scarlett: *Good. Hey, gotta go. Patient arriving.*

See you tonight. Mal sent the message, then pulled up the spreadsheet he'd been working on. An hour later he went to lunch with his teammates, then they were back at work for the rest of the afternoon. Mal didn't consciously watch the clock, but as the day wore on, anticipation began to build. Soon he'd be on his way home, and then he'd spend the evening with Scarlett. It was a new feeling to anticipate going home with such pleasure, but he liked it.

At around four-thirty, Hacker's phone rang and he picked it up with a happy, "Hey, Baby." A few seconds later, he swore. When he hung up, he was on his feet. Everyone else shot up from their seats as well, Mal included. It was ingrained in him, even if he felt a twinge in his leg muscles from the strain of the day.

"What's up, Hack?" Saint asked as they converged on the big table where they could spread out maps or other documents as required. Not everything was digital. It was still incredibly important that the teams work in analog as well. You couldn't count on electronics to the exclusion of everything else, so they continued to train as if their devices would fail.

Hacker was frowning. "It's about Scarlett's problem," he said, and Mal's gut twisted. "Joshua Wright took leave two weeks ago and hasn't been seen since."

"Shit," Mal said. Had Wright somehow managed to track Scarlett in spite of all her precautions?

"There's more. Bliss finally found Dr. Saunders. She was in a car accident three weeks ago. Her car ran off the road in a heavily wooded area and hit a tree. She was intoxicated when it happened."

"That's similar to what happened to Scarlett, only it was a lake and she wasn't drinking," Mal said as ice formed in his veins. "How is the doctor now?"

Hacker shook his head. "I'm sorry, Mal. She was declared brain dead and taken off life-support a little over a week ago. She had alcohol and anti-depressants in her system, but it appears to be the blunt-force trauma of hitting the tree that led to her death. She wasn't wearing a seat belt."

Mal was still only a second, then he rushed back to his desk and grabbed his phone, dialing Scarlett. He didn't know where Wright was or if he'd found Scarlett's whereabouts, but Mal's gut told him something wasn't right. The guys watched helplessly as the longest few seconds of his life ticked by.

A computer-generated voice answered, reciting the number he'd reached and telling him to leave a message. Mal ended the call and typed a text. If Scarlett was with a patient, she wouldn't check her phone.

He knew from his own experience with her. It could be that simple. Probably was that simple.

Scar, call me. It's important. Don't go anywhere until you do.

"I need to get over to the hospital and tell her what's happened. Then I need to set up a perimeter at the house in case he tries to come for her there."

Saint nodded. "We'll take care of the perimeter. You go get your girl, Mal. Let me know when you've got her."

Mal grabbed his keys and took off, the words *get your girl* echoing in his head as he pushed his leg to the breaking point. Pain didn't matter. Progress didn't matter.

Scarlett mattered.

———

SCARLETT WAS TIRED. It'd been a long day working with patients, and she was ready to head for home. And Mal. Her heart filled as she thought of Mal waiting for her, steaks sizzling on the grill. It was nice to have someone to go home to, even if it was only temporary. It was nearly five, and it would take her an hour in traffic to get there. She didn't enjoy that part of living in the country, but everything else was pretty splendid.

Scarlett cleaned up the area where she worked with patients, then grabbed her purse and walked into the hallway. At the other end of the corridor a man stood in shadow, facing her. Her heart skipped a quick beat until she scolded herself. Not every shadowy man was dangerous. He was a patient, or he was meeting someone. Scarlett reached into her purse for her phone. When she couldn't find it, she took her purse off her shoulder and dug through the contents. She had to look away from the man to do it, and when she looked up again he was gone.

Naturally.

Her phone wasn't in her purse. Scarlett frowned. And then it hit her that she'd been in a meeting with the physical therapist before her last patient. She'd had her phone with her, and she'd probably set it down. She remembered looking at the clock on Scott's wall and jumping up to head back for her next appointment. She must have forgotten the phone then. Scarlett turned and traipsed toward his office with a sigh. All she wanted was to be on her way, but it was always something when you were in a hurry.

When she reached Scott's door, she knocked. There was no reply so she tried again, louder. Then she twisted the knob. The door was locked.

"Damn it," she muttered, remembering. Scott had already left for the day. It was Monday and that was his day to get his daughter from school. She could try to find the custodian and get him to unlock the room, or she could just live without her phone until tomorrow.

In the end, she decided to go home. It was one day, and she wasn't wed to her phone like a lot of people were. If she didn't have it to scroll the news, so what? She still had her computer. She'd tell Mal when she got home. He'd probably insist on bringing her to work tomorrow, but that was okay. She'd get by without her car for a day.

Scarlett badged out and made her way toward the parking garage. It was still light out so she wasn't nervous about walking through the garage alone. And she wasn't alone because there were other people heading to their cars as well. She reached her car, gave it a quick walk around out of habit—nothing out of place, no new scrapes or broken glass anywhere— and got inside.

The car started easily and she backed out of her space, heading toward the exit. She turned on the radio, tuned into the news, and eased into traffic. In an hour, she'd be standing at Mal's side, leaning into him for comfort and smelling steak on the grill. She told herself not to get too used to the idea of Mal being her rock, but for now she could indulge the desire. He would be there, waiting, and he wanted her. She'd figure out the rest later.

Scarlett let her mind wander as she drove, thinking about Mal, about everything that'd happened this weekend, about how life could change so dramatically in an instant. One minute they'd been friends, and the next they'd been soaking wet in a little shed, ripping off clothes and having wild sex like they'd been starved for the contact. She hadn't meant to say yes, but then she had and nothing had been the same since. She craved him, craved his touch, and it worried her what that meant in the end.

He was in love with someone else, after all. Had been for months, so it wasn't going away easily. Though he hadn't spent a lot of time staring at Haylee yesterday. Not that she'd watched him for every moment, but whenever she'd looked at him, he'd been looking at her. It'd made her feel good inside.

Maybe that's all this was. Feeling good for as long as it lasted. She would have to be happy with that.

After forty minutes in traffic, Scarlett turned onto a quieter country road. There were fewer cars out here, and already she felt her spirit start to soar at the sight of green fields and trees. She liked the country, no doubt about it. Suburbia was too confining, even if more convenient. But being in the country, she felt freer. Her dad had moved them a lot, but the places she'd been happiest had been in the country where she could explore and play without worrying about trying to fit into a new neighborhood hierarchy. Her most miserable childhood memories had been in suburbs when she was the new kid in town.

She glanced into the rearview. Behind her, another vehicle followed at a distance. Someone else heading home after a long day too. Sometimes when she made the turn, there were no other cars on this road. Sometimes there were. Maybe it was Mal, though she couldn't tell if it was his truck yet since he was still too far back.

Her favorite part of the drive was coming up. For about a mile, on both sides of the road, the trees closed in and formed a thick, tunnel-like canopy. It was beautiful, especially when the sun shone down and dappled the road at midday. At this time of day, it wouldn't be as bright because the sun was sinking in the sky, but it was still beautiful. There was a creek with a bridge about halfway through the tree tunnel. She sometimes wished she could stop and look at the creek, but there was literally nowhere to do so. A ditch ran along both sides of the road, and it wasn't possible to pull off the road at any point.

As she drove into the tunnel, she switched on her headlights. She'd noticed that unless there were head-lights, it was sometimes difficult to see another car when you'd gone from the bright light before the tunnel to the dim light inside.

Scarlett glanced into the rearview, surprised at how close the car behind her had gotten. It wasn't Mal's truck. She slowed, intending to let the driver pass since he seemed in a sudden rush. The car sped up, then whipped into the left lane at the last second.

"Idiot," Scarlett muttered as the driver started to pass. But then the car cut suddenly toward her again. Scarlett squeaked as she slammed on the brakes and tried to avoid a collision. It was too late, though. The car's bumper slammed into the rear quarter-panel of her Kia, sending her off the roadway and toward the ditch.

Scarlett came to a stop with the hood of her car

facing downward, her breath scissoring in and out of her lungs. She was alive. She didn't think she was hurt, though her airbag had deployed and slammed into her chest. Her heart was in her mouth and adrenaline pumped through her system with the speed of a rocket. Nothing felt broken or bleeding, though she expected there would be bruises.

Her door ripped open and she turned, expecting to see anyone but the person who stood there looking at her with a smug expression.

"I told you I'd see you soon."

Chapter Twenty-Three

SCARLETT STILL WASN'T ANSWERING HER PHONE. MAL swore as he dropped his cell into the cup holder and pressed his foot to the gas. Traffic at this time of day was hell. Nothing for it, but he didn't like the ball of nerves settling in his belly. Knotting tight. Insisting something was wrong.

He pulled into the hospital parking garage, found the first available slot, and hurried inside, heading for the rehab wing. It was after five but there were still people around. He went to the desk where he usually checked in for his appointments. The receptionist looked up.

"Hey, Mal."

"Hey, Darcy. Is Scarlett still around?"

"I think she left about fifteen minutes ago or so. You just missed her."

Shit. So why wasn't she answering her phone?

"Was she with anyone?"

Darcy frowned. "I don't think so. I didn't see her leave the building, but she said goodnight as she walked by the desk."

"She wasn't upset or anything?"

"Didn't sound like it. Is everything okay?"

He forced a smile and nodded. "Yeah, everything's fine. I thought we were meeting here after work. Must have gotten my wires crossed."

"Sorry."

"No problem. It's not your fault I'm an idiot."

She laughed. "You are not an idiot. But stuff happens, right?"

"Yep, stuff happens. See you later, Darcy."

"Bye."

Mal stopped by Scarlett's treatment room and peered in. Everything looked normal, so he hurried for the door as fast as his legs could take him. His leg was cramping, but he ignored it. Until he found Scarlett, he didn't care if it hurt. He got inside his truck, took a pass through the garage to look for her car—not there—then headed out again. As soon as he was clear of the garage, he called Hacker.

"Did you find her?" Hacker asked.

"No. She's already gone. But she's still not answering her phone. Do you think you could triangulate its position for me?"

Maybe she'd turned it off to save battery. He didn't know all her habits, and anything was possible. It would explain why she wasn't answering.

"Yeah, sure. Give me a little time and I'll find out where the last known location was."

"Thanks."

"Saint, Wolf, Muffin, and Easy are headed for your place. I'm waiting on Bliss but I'll be there too."

"Appreciate it, man."

They ended the call and Mal sped toward home. The knot in his belly hadn't eased a bit, though he told himself the fact she wasn't answering her phone didn't mean she'd been kidnapped. Batteries died. Shit happened. But when he found her again, after he kissed the hell out of her, he was planning to lecture her to always have backup chargers and never to turn her phone off without first telling him she had to do so for some reason.

He pictured Scarlett when he delivered that news. She was going to sass him over it, but he wasn't relenting. They were friends, and you had to let your friends know when you were going to be out of touch. It was the right thing to do, otherwise you made people worry.

Mal's phone rang a few minutes later. "Her phone's still at the hospital," Hacker said without preliminary.

Mal swore. "Her car's not there, though." He had to decide, quickly, whether to turn around and head for the hospital or whether to keep heading for home.

"She must have left her phone by mistake."

It had to be the case. If Scarlett was still in the hospital, where was her car? Besides, if she had her phone with her, she'd answer her calls now that she was finished with patients for the day. She would have called him back. She wouldn't ignore the voice message he'd finally left or his numerous texts. It wasn't like her, just like he'd known deep inside that turning her phone off wasn't like her either.

"I don't like it, especially now that we know Wright isn't at work. I don't suppose you've found any credit card transactions to pinpoint him yet?"

"No. He's an operator, Mal. Even if he's a benched one, he's had the training. He won't use a card if he's on the move. His last charge was for gas two and a half weeks ago."

That's what Mal was afraid of. He clenched the wheel in frustration as traffic slowed to a crawl. If Scarlett had told him the truth sooner, he'd have figured out where Wright was before now. He understood why she hadn't, but it didn't make keeping her safe any easier.

"We need to find him, Hack."

"I know that, buddy. Bliss and I are working on it. We'll stop by the hospital on our way to your place, make sure Scarlett isn't there after all."

"The receptionist said she'd left."

"Maybe so, but until you actually catch up with her, you're going to wonder. It won't take us long. I'll find the exact location of the phone and we'll solve that detail, okay?"

A small current of relief washed over him, but it didn't last. He wasn't going to feel better until he saw

Scarlett's face again. Until he heard her say something sassy to him.

"Thank you," he replied, his throat tight.

The call ended and traffic started moving again. Mal pressed the gas and prayed the uneasiness in his gut was nothing more than the result of not being able to talk to Scarlett. She could have forgotten her phone. She could have started her drive, realized she'd left it, and kept on driving because going back for it would take too much time.

It *could* have happened that way. But he wasn't sure it had.

———

SCARLETT TREMBLED with fear but she was determined not to show it. Not to let all those months of confusion and abuse petrify her into inaction. She had to stay alert, had to make a move if she got a chance.

But what chance would she get? When she'd looked up to see Josh standing over her, the emotions flooding her had threatened to overwhelm her system. There'd been fear, of course. Anger. Disbelief. How could he be here? How could he have found her? Ambushed her so suddenly?

He'd dragged her from the Kia and forced her into the sedan he was driving. Then he'd zip-tied her wrists together before slamming the door and getting into the driver's seat. Now they were barreling down the road in the direction she'd been traveling. She had no idea where he was taking her.

"Josh," she said. Pleaded.

"You thought you could leave me, Erin. Thought you could disappear without a trace. You thought it was over between us," he said, ignoring her. "But it's not over until *I* say it's over."

Scarlett tried to make herself small. She didn't know what good it would do, but she had a deep desire to fold in on herself. Tears hovered beneath the surface. Her throat was tight with fear. He wasn't angry because she'd tried to leave him. He was angry because he didn't like to lose. This was a game to him. A sick, twisted game to prove he was the smarter of them. The better. It had always been about control with him. About being the best.

"Where are we going?"

He shot her a glare. "Too late to worry about that, Erin." His nostrils flared. "You thought you could fuck that guy and I wouldn't know it? Been fucking him like a bitch in heat all weekend. Jesus, I thought you were better than that. Turns out you're nothing but a whore."

Her belly turned inside out. He'd been watching her. Of course he had. He'd been there, somewhere, and he'd known. Nausea rolled through her.

"You broke into my apartment. You left the door open to scare me when I went back."

Just like before. To make her doubt herself when others examined the scene and told her it wasn't a break-in. Not that the guys had said it wasn't, but they'd said there was no evidence it had been. She should have known. She should have gotten the hell out when she'd had the chance.

Except Josh had already been watching her when that guy had recognized her in Buddy's on Friday. He'd already been there, waiting. It'd been too late and she hadn't even known it.

"Yet here you are. Too stupid to figure it out."

"How long have you been here?" she asked. "How long have you been watching me?"

Had he been watching when she'd gone for drinks with Justine, Neil, and Ricky? That had been almost two weeks ago.

His nostrils flared. "Long enough."

What did that even mean? He wouldn't tell her, though. She knew that much. "Did you key my car door?"

He snorted. "Please. I could think of better things than scratching your shitty Kia."

Despair pounded in her temples. "Let me go, Josh. This doesn't have to get out of control. Just let me go and get on with your life."

His expression was cold. Superior. "Get on with my life? I did everything for you. I treated you like a fucking queen and you lied about me to everyone. Tried to get me in trouble with my command. Then you ran away when nobody believed you. I was planning to take care of you for the rest of your life, but you had to go and listen to that bitch Jessica Saunders. She poisoned your mind."

Scarlett's stomach was a cold pit of despair. There was nothing she could say, no amount of reason he would listen to. No matter what, Josh believed his own press. He believed the lies he spun out, and he believed she was the person who'd cold-heartedly betrayed him. Everything he'd done was justified in his mind. Everything he planned to do. He was the injured party. The wronged party. He rewrote history, and he made everyone believe it was the truth.

She didn't know what he was planning, but whatever it was, he'd get away with it. He always did. He wasn't here without a well-thought-out plan. He wasn't impulsive. He was diabolical.

And she was going to suffer.

A tear slipped down her cheek. Before long another fell, and then another. She couldn't stop them. Couldn't stop the sobs that took over and shook her body.

Josh had found her. He'd tracked her down, stalked her like prey, and now he'd trapped her. Whatever he did next, it wasn't going to be good. She wasn't going to escape this time.

———

MAL WAS NEARLY home when he came to a traffic jam in the tree tunnel. Maybe not a jam, precisely, but three cars were stopped, hugging the side of the road as closely as they could while still blocking the lane he was traveling in. Instead of going around, something made him stop and climb out of his truck to see what the problem was. A blue Kia Sportage lay almost on its side, the hood pointing downward into the ditch. His heart stopped as a sharp pain sliced his chest.

Two men stood by the road while a third clambered around the Kia. "Nobody here," the guy said. "They must have gotten out and walked down the road for help. Found a work badge." He held up a lanyard with a badge dangling from it. Mal didn't need to see the picture to know.

"That's my girlfriend's," Mal said, his voice feeling very far away.

"Seriously, buddy?" one of the guys standing nearby said.

"Yeah, seriously." His insides were ice. "Her name's Scarlett and she works at Riverstone Hospital."

The guy looked at the laminated plastic. "Yep. Scarlett Reed." He came up the side of the ditch and thrust the badge at Mal. "She's not in the car, so she must be fine. Probably flagged down help, or she's walking."

Mal hurried back to the truck and jumped inside, dialing Saint as he shot down the road toward home. Saint picked up on the second ring. "You find her? She's not at your place yet."

"No. Her car ran off the road in the tree tunnel. She's not there."

"Shit," Saint swore.

"He's here," Mal said with deadly certainty. "He's got her. We have to find where the sonofabitch would go."

He didn't know how Joshua Wright had managed it, but he had. Mal had no doubt.

"Copy that. Get here as soon as you can. We'll figure out our next move. We'll find her, Mal."

"I hope so."

Mal threw his phone down and shoved the gas pedal hard. He was doing eighty when he approached the turn to his house. He slammed the breaks and whipped into the drive, bumping along the dirt and gravel until he skidded to a halt in front of the house. A cloud of dust swallowed him up as he opened the door.

The guys were standing on his porch, waiting. They could have picked the lock to get inside, but courtesy made them wait. Mal hurried up the steps and shoved his key in the lock. The team spilled inside behind him, fanning into the kitchen to set up an ops center on the old table that'd come with the house.

Hacker wasn't there yet, but Easy opened his laptop and logged in. Hacker was the best there was, but Easy wasn't far behind. He wasn't called Easy just because he'd been gullible about the coffee. Most things came easily to him—computer programs, solutions to problems, new skills, women.

"What have you got?" Saint asked.

Easy was scanning the monitor. He slapped a

hand on the table. "Yes! Someone triggered the camera at two this afternoon."

Mal swallowed the hard knot in his throat. "You didn't get a notice about that when it happened?"

"We were at work, Mal," Saint said gently. "You know Easy didn't have access."

"Sorry, man," Easy said. "It's not HOT equipment. The range isn't as good as what we have there, plus we were inside the SCIF at that time."

Mal closed his eyes and grounded himself. They couldn't take cell phones or laptops into the secret parts of HOT HQ. It wasn't Easy's fault. "I know. I'm just worried."

Wolf looped an arm around Mal's shoulders and squeezed. "We'll find her. Whatcha got, Easy?"

They all gathered so they could see the screen. A white Chevy Malibu pulled into the driveway. Mal squinted at it. "Can you grab the plate off that shot?"

Easy's fingers were already flying across the keyboard. "On it."

A man got out and looked around. He was wearing jeans and a dark T-shirt. He had dark hair and he stood for a second before walking up the stairs to Scarlett's place. Mal watched as he shoved a pick into the lock and opened the door. A few minutes later, he was walking out again. He had a bag with a strap slung over his shoulder.

"We need to see what he took," Saint said. "Muffin?"

"On it." The big man slipped outside while they kept watching.

Wright slung the bag into his car, then stared at Mal's place. He swaggered over to the door and tried the lock. Then he picked it as well.

"Shit," Mal swore. "He could have placed a listening device." Red-hot anger swelled in Mal's chest. "I'm going to find you, you son of a bitch," he growled.

Wolf grabbed a scanner from Easy's bag. "I'll do a sweep. If he bugged you, we'll know."

Wright wasn't carrying anything, but a bug was small enough to fit in a pocket. Some cameras were too, but Wolf would sweep for that as well. Muffin walked through the back door. "Her computer is gone. It's hard to tell if he took any clothes. Everything else appears to be where it belongs."

"Wolf's sweeping for bugs. Wright entered Mal's house," Saint said.

Mal stalked into the living room, needing something to do while his teammates scanned the footage. He stopped and turned, looking at the room for anything out of place. There were fresh scuff marks on the coffee table, like someone had propped up his boots and dug the heels in. It took Mal a minute to notice the edge of a piece of paper sticking out from under the cushions of his couch. He reached down and fished it out carefully.

It was a sheet of white paper, probably from the legal pad he kept on his desk upstairs. He unfolded it as fury battered his insides. The son of a bitch had broken into his house. Strolled around like he owned the place. And left a note where Mal would eventually find it.

You lose, asshole.

Mal ground his teeth together, then continued through the house, looking for more messages. In his room, Wolf was staring at the bed. The sheets were pulled back, and there was a yellow arcing stain all over the bedding. Wolf turned.

"Uh, I think he pissed on your bed."

Mal had been angry in his life, but he wasn't sure he'd ever been this angry. It wasn't the piss. It wasn't the defilement of his things.

It was Scarlett. The threat to her safety. The defilement of her, when she was one of the sweetest people Mal had ever known. Why hadn't he told her that? He'd focused so hard on the friends with benefits angle that he'd missed there was more to it than that. She *was* his friend, goddammit, but she was also one of his best friends. He couldn't fail her. If he did, he'd lose her forever. He couldn't bear that.

"Sick fuck," Mal growled.

Wolf just shook his head slowly. "Definitely. I haven't found a bug yet. Almost done."

Mal held up the note so Wolf could see. Wolf swore. He looked like Mal felt. Coldly furious.

"He plans to kill her," Mal said. "But first he plans to torture her."

"You can't be certain of that," Wolf began.

"I can," Mal snapped back. "He's already tried once before. He won't fail this time."

"Then get back downstairs and help with the planning," Wolf said. "I'll finish the sweep."

Mal couldn't move. He could only stare at the sheets, the callous way Joshua Wright had ruined the bed. It was a message aimed straight at Mal's heart.

Wolf strode over and put a finger in Mal's face. The corners of his mouth were white. "We aren't letting this happen, Mal. It's not what we do. Go. I'll take care of this."

Mal lifted his gaze to his friend's. He nodded once and left the room. He wouldn't enter it again until they found Scarlett and brought her home.

Chapter Twenty-Four

JOSH DROVE UP TO A RATTY MOTEL THAT SAT BY THE highway in a small Maryland town. Scarlett didn't think they'd gone more than twenty miles beyond Mal's place, but she wasn't sure since she hadn't been out this way before. And when you were terrified for your life, every moment felt like an eternity.

Josh didn't bother to stop at the front office. He drove around the side of the building and straight up to a parking spot in front of a door. The motel was old, one story, the kind of place where some people lived full time and where it was almost certain there were drugs and prostitution going on.

A disheveled looking man sprawled in a lawn chair by another door, a dirty tank top covering his chest, greasy hair flopping across his eyes, and a cigarette hanging from his mouth. He held a beer bottle in two fingers. It dangled along the side of his lawn chair. He watched with slitted eyes as Josh climbed from the car and went over to stick a key in the door. Josh unlocked the door and returned to the passenger side of the car.

He opened her door and bent down to look her in the eyes. "You make a fuss at all and you won't like what happens. Nobody here is going to help you, so don't try it. You'll just piss me off more."

Scarlett bit her trembling lip. Her eyes were puffy from where she'd been crying, and her nose was blocked. She could barely breathe, let alone scream.

But she wanted to. God how she wanted to.

Josh flicked open a knife and she flinched. But all he did was cut the zip ties from her wrists. She rubbed the ugly red indentations, trying to get the circulation back before he did something else to her.

"You hear me, Erin?"

"Yes," she forced out, her voice little more than a whisper.

He straightened and tugged her to her feet. He held her arm casually, but she knew he could tighten his grip at any second. Make her feel pain.

The man sitting next door watched them, tipping his chin slightly when Josh nodded to him. Scarlett tried to tell him with her eyes that she wasn't here willingly. Tried to send fear across the space separating them in the brief moment she could make eye contact. The man lifted his beer and sipped, then looked away and sucked on his cigarette again.

Message not received. Scarlett's shoulders slumped as Josh pushed her into the room and shut the door behind them. The room was dingy, the walls stained with water spots and the furniture worn. There was a green carpet, so old that it had been worn flat, and the air smelled stale and musty. The bed was covered in threadbare white bedding, and Josh pushed her toward it. When she resisted, he shoved her hard and she sprawled across the bed, her hair in her mouth and eyes. She pushed it out of the way and scrambled up against the headboard, her heart hammering.

"Please don't," she said as he reached for her. "Please."

She couldn't bear having him touch her now. Couldn't bear it if he tried to strip her naked and have his way with her. Not after Mal.

Josh looked at her with contempt. "If you think I'm sticking my dick in you after what you've been doing, you'd be wrong."

He grabbed her arms and bound them with a set of stainless steel cuffs he'd dragged from his pocket, then he shoved her against the headboard so hard she bounced.

"Fucking bitch," he said.

Scarlett's breath was ragged as she tried to get control of her emotions. *What would Mal do?* He'd be cool and calm. He'd ask questions. Look for weaknesses. Most of all, he'd be strong and stoic. She knew that because of how he handled his injuries. And how he handled his forbidden feelings for a friend's fiancée.

"What are you going to do, Josh?"

He walked away from her and flopped into a chair, legs outstretched. He pulled a knife from his belt and flicked it open. Then he closed it. Opened it again. *Flick, flick, flick.*

Scarlett swallowed. He was trying to intimidate her. He might use the knife on her, but not yet. He wanted her to feel the fear first. He'd spent months making her fear before.

"I'm going to make you regret what you did to me," he finally said.

"I didn't do anything to you. You're the one who did things to me. You broke into my apartment, and you tampered with my car."

He huffed a soft breath. "So delusional, Erin. I'm not a mechanic. I wouldn't begin to know how to start a slow leak in your brake line. I definitely wouldn't know how to time it so you lost your brakes during a rainstorm and skidded into a lake. That'd be pretty extraordinary, wouldn't it?"

He was smug. Superior. He always had been. How had she missed the signs in the beginning? Always bragging about his job, about his abilities. Trying to impress her. He had impressed her, unfortunately. She knew better now.

"I think the timing was lucky, yes. But you definitely did it."

"Nobody else thinks so, do they?" He flicked the knife again. "With the exception of your favorite doctor friend. She was very reluctant to tell me where you'd gone. But she did in the end."

A chill spread through Scarlett's body. "What did you do?"

His face was a cold mask. "I didn't do anything, Erin. I merely suggested she tell me where to find you."

Scarlett's chest tightened. Dr. Saunders would have texted her. Warned her. Something was definitely wrong if she hadn't. "Where is she?"

Josh shrugged. "Not sure. They had to use the jaws of life to cut her out of her car, though. I heard about it on the news."

Anger and despair flooded Scarlett, followed by a blinding numbness. Jessica Saunders had been a friend when she desperately needed one. The one person who'd seen through Josh's bullshit and did what she could to help Scarlett escape. And now she was hurt, possibly dead, and it was all Scarlett's fault for dragging her into this mess. For being unable to extract herself from a bad situation without intervention. For being weak.

No.

She heard Mal's voice in her head, telling her it wasn't her fault. That we didn't get through life alone and we needed a posse sometimes.

"We're your posse. We'll be there for you."

He'd told her that, but how was he going to find her now? How were any of the guys going to help her? She didn't have her phone, didn't know where she was, and she was cuffed in a locked room with a psychopath.

Josh reached down and slipped a laptop from the bag he'd brought inside. It took her a second to realize it was hers. He flipped it open and grinned evilly at her. "Password?"

She thought about denying him, but he'd only hurt her if she did. He'd already been pissed that she'd left her phone at work. He'd upended her purse when she'd told him she had done so, then threw it into the back seat of his car. She didn't know why he cared, but he had for some reason. There was nothing vital on her laptop anyway. She didn't have credit cards or online banking anymore. She gave him the password and he logged on.

"What are you doing?" she asked as he studied her computer. She couldn't see the screen.

"Just reading your messages. You and Mal. He has no idea what a bitch you are, does he?"

She didn't answer that. Her heart thumped as it sunk in that he was reading her messages. Reading. Her. Texts.

Of course.

He'd wanted to see her phone so he could see the texts. But she had iMessage on the computer, which meant all the messages were there when the computer connected to Wi-Fi because Mal had an iPhone too.

Maybe she could get to the computer and text Mal if Josh left her alone for any length of time. She didn't need her phone to do it. For the first time since Josh had grabbed her, she felt a tiny tendril of hope.

Josh lifted his phone and took a picture of her. She squinted when the light flashed in her eyes.

"Think I'll send him a photo. Do you think he'll care? Or is he just drinking the milk for free?"

About a minute later, she heard the whoosh of the message from her computer. He'd transferred the photo to her computer instead of using his phone. He wasn't stupid, and her hope died on the vine. Josh wasn't going to let her near the laptop. Worse, if he was sending Mal a photo of her, then he intended to involve Mal somehow. She didn't know how, but Josh was going to make everything look like her fault.

"Why are you doing this? I'm the one you're angry with. Don't get him into this. He doesn't deserve it."

"Oh, so now you care about some poor guy's reputation and career?" He sat back in the chair, glaring at her. "Why would *I* be angry? Because you lied? Because you tried to ruin *my* career with those lies?" He shook his head. "I'm not angry, Erin. I'm furious." His face twisted. "Did you know I got benched? Pulled from active rotation and put on a desk while I had to go to psych evals. Evals I passed, by the way. Because I'm a lot smarter than you gave me credit for. Than anyone gave me credit for."

His nostrils flared as he sucked in a deep breath. The hatred on his face as he lunged at her made her gasp. He grabbed her shoulders and shook her hard enough to rattle her teeth. "I'm not letting some skinny, whoring little bitch ruin everything I've achieved. No fucking way. You're going to pay for everything you've done, Erin. You and Mal both."

"He's got nothing to do with it," she said, her voice shaking. "Why would you make him pay for something I did?"

Not that she'd done anything wrong but she couldn't let him hurt Mal. Why? Mal had been nothing but good to her. He was her friend. Her lover.

The man she was falling in love with. Her heart ached at the revelation. *Poor, stupid Scarlett…*

Josh straightened and tugged his T-shirt. As if he'd pulled on a mask, he appeared coolly controlled again. "It's nothing personal. I just need someone to take the blame for your death." His smile was pure evil. "Wrong place, wrong time, I'm afraid."

He flicked open the knife and shot her another malevolent grin. "Time to start paying up, bitch."

———

HACKER AND BLISS had just arrived. Bliss handed Scarlett's phone to Mal. "It was inside a locked office. Sky broke in to retrieve it."

"The phone was inside the PT's office," Hacker said. "Not hers. Maybe she thought it was in her purse when she left work."

Of all the times to lose your phone. Mal shoved a hand through his hair and stared at Scarlett's phone in his hand. But would it have made a difference if she'd had it? Wright would have taken it from her when he ran her off the road. None of them had any doubt that's what had happened. Muffin and Wolf had gone to inspect the scene and returned with the news that Scarlett had been forced off the road by a white vehicle. They knew that because of the paint embedded in the side of her Kia.

Hacker was busy setting up on the table with Easy, who was searching for information about the Chevy Malibu that Joshua Wright had been driving. It wasn't a rental, and it wasn't Wright's personal vehicle. He usually drove a black Toyota Forerunner. The plates on the Malibu didn't belong to the Malibu. Not that any of them were surprised. Wright had changed the plates. It was something an operator would do when trying to avoid detection, so it was no surprise he had. It was possible he'd changed the plates again since this afternoon—and possible he'd changed cars too. But, for now, they were going to look for a Chevy Malibu. It was all they had to go on.

Saint had a map spread out at one end of the table. He traced a line with his finger. "This is the main route south. We don't know that he's taking her to Florida, but it's possible he wants to return there. If you were abducting someone, what would you do?" he asked the room at large.

"There are a lot of old motels along that route," Muffin said. "It's a scenic alternative to the Beltway and I-75 south. If I were trying to avoid pursuit, I'd pick the rattiest shitholes I could find instead of places along the highway."

"Yep, me too," Easy said. "I'd probably change cars—or plates anyway—at those places too. Middle of the night when people are asleep."

"The interstate would be faster, and you might get more anonymity with the amount of traffic at the hotels you find along the way," Hacker said. "You'd have a bigger pool to choose from when it came to switching plates or stealing a new ride."

"You'd take the risk of more cops patrolling though," Wolf replied. "I'd take the back route, and I'd probably stay put for a couple of days first. Just to throw off the scent and make my pursuers look further afield."

Mal didn't say anything at first. All the options were viable, and each one had its benefits. Finally, gripping Scarlett's phone, he spoke. "What if your plan wasn't to abduct, but to dispose? But first you intended to make your victim suffer, either physically or through fear."

Bliss bit her lip and looked away. The guys wore varying expressions of fury and concentration.

"I'd find an abandoned house or I'd rent a room at one of the shitty motels," Bliss said, surprising them all. "I mean seriously shitty, like the kind of place where people cook meth and dwell in despair. I wouldn't call too much attention to myself by flashing money around, but I'd slip cigarettes or alcohol to the residents for information or just to get them to keep their mouths shut. I'd keep my prisoner there, and I wouldn't feed her—or not much anyway. And I'd torment her with bits and pieces of her life that she'd never see again. I'd also threaten to hurt people she cared about if she tried to scream for help. I'd break her down bit by bit, physically and mentally, until the fight was completely gone."

Bliss blinked and stopped speaking, dropping her gaze to the floor. "Jesus, honey," Hacker said, dragging her into his arms.

Mal didn't know if she'd been reciting something that had happened in her past, or something she knew had happened to someone else, but he was aware Bliss had come from a criminal family that dealt meth and other drugs in the hills of Tennessee. She'd likely seen some shit in her life before she'd escaped.

"I think she's right," Mal croaked out, his voice as hollow as he felt inside. "Wright doesn't intend to let Scarlett live. He tried to hurt her before, he very likely caused the accident that killed Jessica Saunders, and he's traveled a long way to find Scarlett. He's been stalking her for days, and doing it so quietly that she was the only one who felt like something was wrong. He wanted to scare her, and he succeeded." Mal squeezed her phone in his hand. "And I fucking missed the signs."

"We all did," Saint said. "Don't beat yourself up. Muffin and I went through her place, and we didn't find any concrete evidence that anyone had been there. It's a failure on all our parts."

Bliss started to type on her phone. "I've got a contact in the state troopers' office. I'll get a list of all the shitty motels from here to the 301 bridge, and I'll ask if his people can be on the lookout for a white Malibu with this plate number, though I'll tell him it's possible the plate will have changed by now."

She walked from the room, her fingers still flying. A moment later, she was talking to someone.

Hacker looked after her for a second, then turned his attention to his laptop. "Some of those places have security cameras these days. I'll see if I can hack into any of them when she gets me that list. I'll start with the closest and move outward. Easy, can you start at the bridge and move backward?"

"Copy that."

Mal's heart thumped a beat. They were trying. His team wouldn't give up, no matter what.

"I'm going to call Brooke," Saint said. "Maybe she and Haylee can pick up some pizzas since you live in the middle of nowhere. We can work on this until we have to be back at the base tomorrow morning."

Mal didn't know what to say. His throat was tight and a sick feeling sat like a weight in his gut. He nodded his thanks. An hour later, Brooke and Haylee arrived with the pizzas. Haylee came over and gave Mal a hug—after she kissed Wolf, of course.

She was soft and smelled good, but he didn't ache when she touched him. Didn't feel that gut-deep despair and longing he usually felt. She squeezed his hand. "I'm so sorry, Mal."

He looked at where their hands joined—and felt

nothing except warmth and comfort. The longing wasn't there. He squeezed back. "Thanks, Haylee."

"I know you guys will find her. It's what you do. Scarlett is strong and determined. She'll make it out of this alive."

He squeezed her hand again, softly. "I know."

He didn't know, but he couldn't say that. Couldn't voice the fear he felt. If he lost Scarlett, then what? She was important to him. He'd sort out why later.

His phone dinged in his pocket. He let go of Haylee's hand and fished it out. The usual people who texted him were in the same room. It could be his sister or his mother, though. His dad never texted.

But it wasn't any of them. It was Scarlett. How the hell?

He swore when he realized there was a picture attached. Everyone looked at him.

"What is it?" Wolf asked, coming to Haylee's side.

Mal turned the phone around so they could all see the photo. The atmosphere in the room was suddenly charged as they stared helplessly. Scarlett was still dressed in her scrubs, and her eyes were red and puffy. She'd been crying. She was scared. He hated that for her. He'd promised her she'd be safe, but she wasn't. And it was his fault.

Mal had a strong desire to murder Joshua Wright if he ever caught him. Murder him and burn the body.

"He's using iMessage on her computer," Hacker

said excitedly. "Is there anything else in that photo we can use as a clue?"

"Just Scarlett," Mal said, anger still swirling hot inside. Wright had been careful not to allow any background to show. Nothing but Scarlett's face and shoulders.

"Can you trace where they are, Hack?" Saint asked.

"Not through iMessage. The encryption is end-to-end." He looked thoughtful. "Do you happen to know the passcode for her phone, Mal?"

"I might. I saw her key it in, but I wasn't paying much attention at the time." They'd been in bed and he'd still been thinking about the sounds she'd made as he'd sucked her clit only minutes before. Soft, mewling sounds that grew deeper and hungrier as he drove her toward orgasm.

He wanted to do that again. More than that, he needed Scarlett safe and well so he could wrap her in his arms and hold her close.

"Can you try to open it? If I can get inside, I can see if she's got *Find my iPhone* turned on. If we're lucky, it's on and all her devices are registering locations."

"And if I mess it up?"

"You'll get locked out, but you get six attempts before it locks up for a minute. The time increases incrementally with each failed attempt. You get a lot of them, but it'd be better if you could get inside sooner."

Mal nodded. He pictured Scarlett keying in the numbers and repeated what he saw. The phone didn't open. He frowned and concentrated, trying again to see her tapping the screen. She'd done it fast, but if he thought about it, he could slow it down and piece it together. He knew he could.

Mal pressed the numbers more slowly, picturing Scarlett's thumb moving across the phone. He hadn't asked her why she didn't have the facial recognition turned on, but he was glad she didn't. He'd have never seen her entering the code otherwise.

He pressed the last number, holding his breath— and the phone opened up. Mal breathed out as he handed it to Hacker, blood thudding in his temples.

"Good job." Hacker scrolled through the phone, tapping the screen as he went. "Holy shit, it's turned on. Now we gotta hope all her devices are connected."

"Can you see the laptop yet?"

"Just a sec…" Hacker frowned at the screen. A second later he grinned. "There it is. Smart girl, Scarlett." He went back to his own computer and sat to type in the address. The guys converged, waiting. Hacker's eyes gleamed with excitement. "It's a motel about twenty-three miles from here. The George Washington Inn."

He spun the laptop and showed them the buildings on Google Earth. There was a main office in front near the highway entrance, and two wings that formed a V behind it. A pool sat empty in the center of the V, weeds growing out of the cracked concrete.

"The laptop is somewhere in this wing," he said, pointing to the right side. "I'll have to pinpoint it when we get there, but this is within about twenty feet or so of the true location."

Muffin whooped. "Damn, man, let's go get her!"

"Roger that," Saint said. "We'll plan the op on the way. Check your weapons and let's bug out."

For the first time since this nightmare began, Mal started to hope. But they weren't in the clear yet. So many things could go wrong before they got to Scarlett. They had to reach her before Wright broke her. Because there was no doubt in Mal's mind that's what he intended to do.

Break her spirit, and then break her body.

Chapter Twenty-Five

SCARLETT HAD STOPPED PAYING ATTENTION TO THE blood trickling down her skin and dripping onto the dingy white coverlet. She'd had to stop, or she would go crazy. Josh had gagged her, then he'd run a chain through the handcuffs, wrenching her arms above her body and binding them to a hook in the ceiling. It amazed her, in an abstract way, that there'd even been a hook. In a motel? A cheap motel?

But it occurred to her that he'd put the hook there himself. He'd been in town for days, planning everything down to the smallest detail. The hook was over the bed so that she dangled on top of it, her knees touching but not able to sink into the mattress and take some of the weight off her arms.

Josh had turned on the television, a fucking Jerry Springer marathon on some stupid channel somewhere, and cranked the volume. The dysfunctional lives of America's underclass played out again and again on the screen while Josh used the histrionics to cover any screaming she might do.

Like when he'd made the first cut. He'd sliced her scrubs from her body, ripping them open and throwing them onto the floor. Then he'd carved his first mark into her belly. She couldn't see what he did, but she'd felt the sting of pain and the hot trickle of her own blood as it dripped down her body.

"An M," he'd said, studying his work. "We'll do the A next, of course. And an L. We want the police to know who did this to you, don't we? What a sick fucker he is, am I right?"

Scarlett had been sobbing by then, begging him through the gag to stop. The pain wasn't unbearable at that point, but the idea he was carving words into her body had terrified her. She hadn't thought of scars or anything like that. She'd been thinking of how long it would go on. How many words he intended to carve. Flaying her with a thousand tiny cuts.

Now, Josh was sitting back and studying her body. He hadn't folded the knife up, which meant he wasn't done yet. She hadn't realized it at first, but it was a different knife than the one he'd originally flicked at her. This one had come from the bag where he'd carried her laptop instead of from his belt. He was also wearing latex gloves. When he'd snapped them on, before he'd cut her clothes off, adrenaline had surged through her body, making her shake uncontrollably. Josh had only laughed.

Her voice wouldn't work anymore because she'd screamed into the gag until she was hoarse. She tried to speak around the gag now, while he was still, but the words were unintelligible.

"Looking great, Erin. Really. I put his name there where the police can see it, but everything else is just a design. Stars. Moons. But I've saved the best. Not sure if it's last or not, but you're making a pretty big mess now so maybe it will be." He stood, knife in hand. "We're going to put a nice big flag on your back—and then I'm going to call your loverboy and arrange to meet. Not here, of course. But I'll bring him here, don't worry. You can say your goodbyes before your tragic murder-suicide."

Scarlett's throat was closing up again as tears welled. She hated crying because it made her sinuses swell, and it was hard to breathe. The gag made it worse. She didn't know what Josh's plan was for killing her, but it was entirely possible she'd suffocate before he got that far.

He stepped around behind her and she cried out, shaking so hard the blood trickled faster down her skin. "Going to have to get rid of this," Josh said.

Her bra pulled tight and then fell loose on her breasts as he cut the strap. It wasn't going to come off because she couldn't lower her arms, but that didn't matter because she felt as naked as if it were gone. Somehow that made her feel more vulnerable, which was crazy considering she was hanging from the ceiling in only a bra and panties while a psychopath carved things into her skin.

Her arms burned, her shoulder sockets were numb, and pain filled her every conscious thought. Scarlett tried to picture Mal, tried to believe he was coming for her, but she didn't know how he would find her. He'd texted back because she'd heard the ping of her computer, but Josh hadn't replied to him. Or maybe someone from work had texted her. Justine maybe.

It didn't matter. Nothing mattered anymore. Josh traced a finger along her back, and Scarlett twisted, crying out in pain as she tried to get away. She didn't know why she reacted so viscerally to the touch of his skin against hers, but in her mind his finger was a blowtorch etching yet more of his evil onto her body.

"Such smooth skin, Erin. Unmarked by any violence. People like me are scarred because we fight to protect ungrateful bitches like you who go about their lives while we risk ours. You have no idea what it's like to sacrifice yourself for your country. None at all. You go about your selfish, self-absorbed life—and when you decide I'm not good enough for you, you tell my commander that I'm harassing you. You tell the police that I'm the one at fault because you drove into a lake. You try to get restraining orders against me, but I've done nothing to you. And all the while, I carry the scars of battle on my body. I drag my sacrifices around like a ball and chain while you run away, unconcerned about the trouble you've caused for me."

Scarlett dangled above the mattress, her body twitching, her arms on fire, tears leaking from her eyes, and wanted to die. Then and there. Just die. It wasn't what Mal would do if he were the one hanging from the ceiling, being tortured. He would fight, like he'd fought to protect Dean Garner and keep him safe for Haylee. Mal wouldn't give up.

But she wasn't Mal. She was weak, and she was tired, and she wanted it to be over. She wanted to close her eyes and make it all go away.

"I think we'll make this one a little deeper," Josh said, his evil voice so close that his breath tickled her ear. "You need to really feel it this time."

The point of the knife slipped into her skin, down between layers of tissue and muscle, and Scarlett screamed hoarsely, her voice weak and useless. Nausea rose into her stomach, her throat. Her vision grew black at the edges. Darkness swallowed light.

And then, mercifully, she was gone.

———

MAL and his team rocketed down the highway, heading for the George Washington Inn. They'd piled into two vehicles, and they were on speaker the entire time as they made plans for how to infiltrate the motel and rescue Scarlett.

Mal had Scarlett's phone, the sound turned off, and he kept checking it for the last known location of her computer like Hacker had told him to do.

The MacBook hadn't moved, but Mal wasn't entirely sure that Wright hadn't shut it off and changed locations.

He prayed that wasn't the case, and he kept the team informed every five minutes where the laptop was. It was dusk by the time they reached the motel. The office loomed in front of them as they turned off the highway. There was a plate glass window with a neon sign that said *Vacancy*. A balding man sat behind a desk inside, laughing at something playing on a television that hung on the wall.

On either side of the office, there was a covered drive that led to the two wings behind. They drove beneath the roof and emerged into an area with a courtyard and the fenced off pool. A couple of doors were open, and people sat outside in lawn chairs, smoking and drinking while kids ran up and down the sidewalk.

"Second to last room on the right side. That's where the signal is," Hacker said. "It's as close as I can get, but the rooms are small and it could be any of the three rooms sitting beside each other. I need to get closer and use the infrared camera."

This wasn't a sanctioned operation, but Hacker was the kind of guy who had his own very interesting equipment. Not that he wouldn't have gone back to HOT HQ and retrieved something else if they'd needed it.

The two vehicles moved slowly across the parking lot. People looked at them with interest, but nobody got up or went back inside. "There's the Malibu," Easy said. "In front of Room 1302."

"That's where the signal's coming from."

They kept driving past the room, then parked around the side of the building. Hacker stepped from the vehicle. Mal held his breath while his teammate walked around the back of the wing. There were windows on that side, but they were small and set up high. Presumably bathroom windows. A few minutes later, Hacker was back.

"I've got two heat signatures in that room. One has its arms lifted over its head like it's hanging from the ceiling, but its not moving. The other one is across the room. I think it's safe to assume the signature with the arms in the air is not Wright."

"Agreed," Saint said.

"We've got to get in there," Mal said on a growl. "She's not moving."

"We aren't dealing with your average criminal here," Wolf said coolly. "He's had spec ops training. He could kill her before we get to her if we aren't careful."

Mal's phone buzzed. He scanned the text quickly. "He wants to me to meet him at Carl's Diner in an hour." Mal swore. "I'm not waiting an hour for him to leave that room."

"Agreed," Saint said. "We've got to get her out of there now."

"Too bad we don't have any flash bangs," Muffin muttered.

"We need to breach," Mal said. "While he's separated from her. Take him out."

"It's a risk," Wolf said. "But I agree. We don't know what kind of shape she's in, and every second counts."

"Keep texting him," Saint said. "We know he won't be near her or have a weapon in his hand if he's answering texts on her laptop."

Mal wanted to be the one to enter the room and save Scarlett. Every masculine instinct he had beat hard within him that he needed to rescue her. But logically Saint was right. Distract the asshole and let his team enter. It was the only chance Scarlett was going to get.

"I'm going in," Mal said. "But I'll keep texting him until we do."

"Fine."

Because Saint knew there was no arguing the point. They all did. His team wanted him back as much as he wanted to be back. At least on this rescue mission.

They exited the vehicles and moved toward the door. A man walked out of the room beside 1302, then stopped short when he saw them. He seemed undecided for a moment, but then he turned and went back inside, slamming the door behind him.

Hacker was looking at the heat signatures on his camera. They watched him, waiting for his signal. Wolf and Easy took up position in front of the door. They'd be the ones to kick it in. Muffin took the window. His job was to make sure Wright didn't exit out of it.

When Hacker gave the go-ahead, Wolf and Easy kicked the door in. Mal was right behind them as they entered. Wright launched himself from his chair, throwing Scarlett's computer at them and grabbing for a weapon lying on the table. Wolf rushed toward Wright, tackling him before he could secure the weapon in his hand. Wright crashed into the wall as a knife clattered to the floor. Wolf spun Wright around, shoving his face into the sheetrock. He dragged out a pair of steel-lined zip ties to secure Wright's arms behind his back.

"I'll fucking kill you," Wright yelled.

"Yeah, yeah," Wolf answered. "Not if I fucking kill you first, douchebag."

Mal swore as he scrambled onto the bed and grabbed Scarlett's limp body. He needed to take the weight off her arms, and he needed to free her. She didn't stir, and panic rose in his throat. He felt for her pulse, his heart throbbing in his chest, anger flaring hot. If he had a free hand right now, he'd draw his weapon and put a bullet between Joshua Wright's eyes. Wolf knew it too because he swept Wright's legs out from under him and slammed him onto the floor, making the man a less handy target for the moment.

"She's alive," Mal said. "Help me get her down."

"Jesus," Saint said as he got his first real good look at Scarlett after securing the room.

Mal could only swallow helplessly. The bed was a

bloody mess, and so was Scarlett. Her body was covered in bright red marks all over her arms and torso. Blood oozed from dozens of cuts. Mal tried to process how someone could do something like this to his sassy, sweet friend, but it was impossible. Wolf moved to put his body between Mal and Wright's. His eyes locked with Mal's. They were hard and sympathetic, but also determined. He wouldn't let Mal kill Wright no matter how much Mal wanted to shoot the fucker and watch his head explode.

"Good god," Muffin said from the door.

Easy was there suddenly with a key he'd taken off Wright while he lay on the floor. He unlocked the cuffs and Scarlett's arms dropped as she sagged into Mal's embrace. She moaned but didn't open her eyes. Mal held her close, anger and fear and something else swirling hot inside him.

"I've got you, baby. I've got you. You're safe now."

"We need to get her to the hospital," Saint said. "And I need to call Ghost."

Mal cradled Scarlett against him as he gingerly moved from the bed and stood. He knew why they had to call Ghost. They weren't involving the police in this one if they could help it. But if they did involve the cops, then let Ghost liaise with the civilian authorities to make sure Wright was charged with the most severe crime he could be charged with.

Mal stopped for a second before he walked out the door. Wright stared up at him angrily.

"You didn't get to her in time, asshole," Wright

spat. "Erin will bear scars for the rest of her life, and she won't ever get over me. She'll always remember."

Mal resisted the urge to kick Wright in the face, but only barely. "*Scarlett* is stronger than you think. She'll get over what you did in time because she's better than you are. Better, stronger, and more courageous. Fuck you, Wright. You're nothing."

Mal strode from the room as Wright shouted obscenities at him. He climbed into the backseat of Saint's truck. He didn't let go of Scarlett until they reached Riverstone and a nurse gently pried her from his arms.

Chapter Twenty-Six

PAIN AND FEAR. THAT'S ALL SCARLETT KNEW. SHE drifted in and out of consciousness. Soft hands touched her skin, did things to her despite her wish for them to leave her alone, and then retreated. Soft voices sounded in her ears.

She thought it was Justine's voice sometimes. Justine whispering, "Hey, honey. You're doing great. Just great. I need you to keep getting better so you can be in my wedding. You promised, remember? You're going to love the dress I picked out for you. It's baby blue, so pretty, and I think it's going to go perfectly with your eyes. Neil came to see you, by the way. He says you're a fighter. Keep fighting, pretty girl. Oh, and Ricky said hi…"

Ricky and Neil. Had she really heard those names in her ear? Maybe. Or maybe she was dreaming about everything. But, dreaming or not, where was

Mal? Why wasn't he there? Why wasn't his voice one of the ones she heard?

She wanted him to be there. She wanted Mal to chase the shadows away. He was the only one who could.

But the shadows tormented her without fail. Memories of Josh doing things to her. Cutting her. Was that real or a nightmare? Whenever her mind examined the memories too closely, she felt herself retreating, her soul pulling inward and down, diving deep into a place where she felt nothing.

Feeling nothing was divine. Maybe that's where she needed to stay.

But she didn't stay. Every day, she floated toward the surface again. And then she opened her eyes, blinking at the light. It wasn't a bright light. The sound of beeps and whirrs assaulted her ears. The sterile scents of cleaning solution and alcohol. It took her a moment, but she realized she was in a hospital.

Alive, at least.

Her skin felt tight in places. Stretched. She blinked, trying to focus. The ceiling was white, the walls a soothing gray, and the lights had been turned down so they didn't disturb her. She tried to move, but her body ached when she did.

Cuts.

"Hello?" she whispered, turning her head to blink at the wall. The door to her room was open, and she could hear nurses moving outside in the corridor. An unoccupied chair sat beside her bed, and the television wasn't on.

Scarlett started to cry, hot tears dripping down her cheeks, making her angry and frustrated at the same time. Why cry? She was here, alive, no matter what Josh had tried to do to her. So long as she was alive, she could do anything. Go somewhere else, start over. She didn't need anyone to do that. She knew how to be alone. She'd learned how to be alone years ago, and she could do it again.

Scarlett squeezed her eyes shut and worked to control her emotions. *Stop, damn you. Stop.*

She heard footsteps near her door, but she didn't open her eyes. Then she felt a presence in the room and her eyes shot open as fear spiked in her brain. What if it was Josh come to finish the job?

But it wasn't Josh. It was Mal, sinking down into the recliner as quietly as he could. He slid his leg in front of his body, which meant it was aching, and lowered himself softly. He was wearing jeans and a gray T-shirt that molded to his chest, and her heart soared at the sight of him.

"Mal?"

His head snapped up. He shot from the chair and came to her side, his hand taking hers gently as he stood over her. "Yeah, baby. It's me. You want some water?"

She nodded. Mal picked up the big, lidded cup with the straw and held it to her lips. She drank, the cold water soothing her dry throat. Someone had filled it with ice recently.

"How are you feeling?" he asked when she was done.

She sniffed. Her cheeks were still cool where the air touched her tears. He noticed the tracks and wiped them softly away with his thumb. She smiled at him, or tried to. "I don't know," she whispered. "What happened?"

"You don't remember?"

She frowned. She didn't want to remember, but she did. "Josh ran me off the road. And he took me to a motel, tied me up. Then he… he used a knife—"

"Shhh," Mal said, bending to press a kiss to her forehead. "We found you. I'm so sorry I didn't protect you, honey. I'm sorry he got to you. But he won't do it again, I swear it. He's in military custody and he's not getting away with anything this time. He'll find himself in Fort Leavenworth before this is all over, I promise you."

She hoped that was true. "How long has it been?"

"You've been here for two days. The cut on your back got infected, and they've been pumping you full of antibiotics. But you're going to recover. You'll be just fine."

She could feel the cut on her back aching. Josh had said he was going to carve a flag there, and he'd pressed deeper than before. She shuddered with the memory. "Is it bad? The cuts, I mean."

Mal was still holding her hand. He squeezed softly.

"Most are superficial and won't leave permanent scars."

Josh hadn't cared about scarring her because he hadn't intended for her to live. Just to suffer.

"And the flag?"

"Flag?"

"He said he was carving a flag on my back."

"Jesus." Mal closed his eyes for a second. "There's no flag, Scarlett. Just a deep slice that bled out a lot."

"I think I passed out when he started that one. He probably intended to wait for me to wake up again so he could keep going."

Mal's expression was thunderous. "Probably so. But we got there before he could."

She closed her eyes and thanked God for that. "How did you find us?"

"You had *Find my iPhone* turned on."

"But I didn't have my phone." She remembered it being locked up in Scott's office and deciding she'd be fine until the next day without it.

"No, but we did. Hacker got it from the hospital when we were trying to find you. Because of that, he was able to determine where your computer was."

The gravity of what he'd said sunk in. "If I'd had it with me, you wouldn't have found me, would you?"

Mal pushed her hair behind her ear with his other hand. The gesture was tender and sweet, and she wished with all her heart it meant something more. But Mal was in love with Haylee, and she was just a friend. A friend he cared about, but still a friend.

Her heart ached for all the things they couldn't have together because of that.

"We would have found you," he told her.

"But it might have been too late," she said past the tightness in her throat.

"Yes, it might have been. But it wasn't. You're here, Scarlett, and you're going to be fine. You hear me? *Fine.*"

Emotion clogged her throat. "I know."

But the truth was that she didn't know anything of the kind. She felt as scared, alone, and helpless as she ever had. At this point, she wasn't sure those feelings would ever go away. Maybe, once she was better, she'd move on again. Find a new place and start over where she had no memories.

Except she didn't want to leave. She wanted to stay here with Mal. She wanted him to love her the way she loved him. Because she *was* in love with him. It hadn't been a lightning bolt. More like a relentless wave of feeling that rolled over her and didn't stop. She hadn't meant it to happen, but he made it impossible not to fall for him. He was the funniest, kindest, sexiest, most thoughtful man she'd ever met.

She wanted to tell him. But she couldn't. If she told him what she felt, everything would change between them.

And that she couldn't bear. Not just yet. Maybe not ever.

WHEN SCARLETT WAS RELEASED from the hospital a couple of days later, Mal took her home and put her in his guest room while he took the couch downstairs. He wanted, more than anything, to lie in bed with her and hold her close, but she needed her space. She also needed to heal, and he didn't want to inadvertently cause her pain by brushing up against her during the night.

She'd argued with him, saying she'd be fine in her apartment, but he'd refused to contemplate it. No matter how furious she got with him.

And she did get furious, but in the end she'd agreed. He thought it might be because she took one look at the garage and remembered how Josh had been inside her place, stealing her laptop and going through her things. She didn't know what all he'd touched and she probably didn't want to think about it.

She'd had enough to deal with, especially once Mal told her that Jessica Saunders was dead. He'd done that before they left the hospital. She'd sobbed so miserably that it had broken his heart. There'd been nothing he could say to comfort her. Nothing he could say to fix it.

Bliss had gotten more information about Dr. Saunders' death. The police were investigating it as a homicide. She had died from blunt force trauma, but her car hadn't been going fast enough to cause the kind of damage that had been done to her. It was as if someone had staged the scene, steering the car into the tree at a lower speed and then slamming Dr. Saunders' head repeatedly against the steering wheel until her injuries were enough to kill her. The pills and alcohol in her system had been ingested in a very short amount of time—as if forced into her all at once.

The police couldn't tie Josh to the scene yet, but he was their primary suspect.

Mal had told Scarlett the details after they'd gotten home. She'd nodded, her lip trembling, and he'd wanted to hold her tightly and tell her how sorry he was. He'd watched her helplessly, though, not wanting to hurt her by touching her. When she digested the news and didn't cry, he'd told her that Josh had broken into his house, and what Josh had done. Mal wasn't going to hide anything from her. She'd only be angry if she found out later, and she wasn't so delicate he had to protect her from the things she deserved to know. Even if he hated piling more shit on her.

She hadn't seemed surprised. "I'm sorry," she'd said. "It's all my fault."

"It isn't," Mal had snapped back vehemently. "Don't ever blame yourself for the actions of someone else. We make our own decisions in this life, and he made his. The shit he does is because he's fucked up inside, not because you made him do it."

Scarlett had nodded, her eyes brimming with emotion. "Thank you."

Wolf had stripped the bed the same day he'd

found the damage, put the sheets into a garbage bag, and taken them outside. Mal had set fire to them after he'd come home from the hospital that night when the nurses had forced him to go. He'd found himself wandering around the house with furious tears in his eyes, wishing he'd broken Wright's jaw when he'd had the chance. Starting a bonfire was a poor substitute, but it'd needed to be done.

As for the mattress, Mal had put a protective cover on it when he'd bought it like the salesperson had told him to do. Nothing got through that cover, but it didn't matter that the mattress was untouched and damage free. He wasn't sleeping on that bed ever again. He called up a thrift store that picked up furniture and resold it to help homeless veterans, and then he went to buy a new mattress. While he was there, he bought a bed too. He'd never used a fancy headboard, hadn't cared, but he knew Scarlett liked pretty things. She'd told him when they were in his bed on Sunday morning, before all hell had broken loose, that an early American-style bed would look good in his house. He'd had no idea what she was talking about so she'd pulled up Pinterest and showed him.

And now he'd bought the damned thing. It hadn't been delivered yet, but it was coming next week—and he was wondering if he'd done something stupid. Buying a bed to please Scarlett when they weren't even a couple. Was he jinxing himself by doing so? God knew he'd fucked this whole thing up six ways to

Sunday, but he wanted to fix it. More than anything, he wanted to fix it.

But Scarlett wasn't ready yet. How could he tell her what he was feeling when she was still so withdrawn from him? From everyone?

Mal clenched his jaw as he stared out the kitchen window at the back yard. He'd had everything he'd ever wanted, but he hadn't known it. Typical of his life, really. He'd realized, when Haylee had been holding his hand once they knew Scarlett was missing and telling him she was sorry, that he didn't love her after all. Scarlett had been right about that. It'd been a lightning bolt moment in time that had affected him that day at the pool table, but it wasn't real. It'd never been real, except in his own mind.

He'd envied Wolf. Envied the companionship and sense of belonging that his friend had, and he'd wanted it too. He'd been so lonely and envious that he'd gotten it all wrong. It could just as easily have been Saint and Brooke, or Hacker and Bliss, but it hadn't been. It'd been pretty Haylee Jamison and her boldly teasing expression when she'd looked at the man she loved. Envy was a powerful emotion. It wound itself into your brain and made you think it was something else. Something more meaningful.

Mal shook himself and poured coffee into two cups. It was the first morning after he'd brought Scarlett home, and he was eager to see her. He carried them up the stairs, not knowing what kind of reception he'd get, but determined to be there anyway. He knocked softly.

"Come in," she said.

He opened the door and pasted on a broad smile. Scarlett was sitting up in bed. She put her phone down and looked at him warily. He hated that look, but he understood. It was going to take her time to trust anyone after what Josh had done to her.

"Brought you some coffee."

She ducked her head, her gaze dropping to the bed. "Thanks."

He set the cup on the nightstand and took a step backward. "I thought I'd sit with you. If you don't mind."

She looked up then, her eyes shining. "I don't mind."

Mal resisted pumping his fist in the air. First, the sudden move might scare her. Second, he didn't really know if it was anything to feel triumphant about. He sank into the chair he'd brought into the room before she'd arrived. It wasn't a very comfortable chair, but he didn't really care.

"How was the bed?" he asked.

"Fine." She sipped her coffee.

"Did you sleep okay?"

She shrugged. "Well enough. I'm still a bit tender."

Her cuts were healing, and the red rings around her wrists from the cuffs weren't as angry, but she was going to be sore for a while. She had to be so careful not to break any of the scabs open. For the wound on her back, the dressing would have to be changed regularly. He knew how to do it, and he intended to. Unless she insisted he take her back to Riverstone every time.

She might. Scarlett was stubborn when she made up her mind.

"It'll be that way for another week or so."

She nodded. "I know."

Mal scrubbed a hand through his hair and sighed. "I'm sorry, Scarlett." He didn't call her Scar anymore because he thought that might upset her. But damn, he missed teasing her like that. "I don't mean to annoy you."

"You aren't annoying me, Mal. God knows I've told you to be patient enough times that you deserve a chance to tell me the same."

Unease swirled inside. "I wasn't trying to tell you to be patient." He gripped the mug in both hands. "Hell, I don't know what I was trying to do. Just—I hate seeing you this way. You're strong. No nonsense. I'm the dickhead who can't get it in his head that it takes time for his leg to heal."

"How is your leg doing, by the way?" she asked.

He blinked at the change in subject. Or was it a change? Hell, he'd introduced the topic. She must think he wanted to talk about himself instead of her. Or maybe she wanted to talk about him instead of her. Maybe she needed to talk about something else.

He wouldn't force her to keep talking about things that made her uncomfortable. Or should he?

Fuck. He was out of his depth here.

"It aches sometimes, but it's stronger every day. The doctor figures I'll be cleared for full duty in another couple of months."

"That's good," she said brightly. "I know that will make you happy."

"It will."

But she made him happy too. Except he couldn't say the words. They sounded hollow. Fake. Like he only cared because of what she'd been through. It wasn't true, but he didn't know how to tell her without it sounding that way.

She studied the contents of her coffee cup. Mal's stomach twisted with nerves. His heart throbbed with feeling. *Tell her.*

But he couldn't. He didn't know that she wanted to hear it. Hell, the last thing Scarlett needed was to feel pressured by a man telling her that he adored her and wanted to be with her, especially when they hadn't known each other more than a few weeks now. She'd had enough of that with Wright, though that asshole had twisted it into something ugly and perverted.

"I think I'm still tired," she said softly.

Mal's feet were lead. His stomach was a solid lump of iron. He swallowed past the sick feeling and got to his feet. "Okay. I'll leave you alone for a while. Text me when you want more coffee, or breakfast."

"You don't have to serve me, Mal. I can make it downstairs. In fact, I think I'm supposed to move around a bit."

"Fine. But don't be stubborn about it. If you can't do it, then let me know. I'll be here. I'm not going anywhere."

"That's what friends are for," she said.

He stared at her, confused. She almost sounded bitter. But that couldn't be right. She was tired. Upset by her ordeal.

"Yes," he told her firmly. "It is."

Chapter Twenty-Seven

THE DAYS PASSED IN A BLUR, BUT SCARLETT WAS getting stronger all the time. Physically and mentally.

What Josh had done to her—what he'd taken away from her—were things she would be dealing with for a very long time. But she refused to let his evil define her life.

Refused.

Still, that was easier said than done. It was all well and good to say she wouldn't let him affect her life or her mind another moment, and another thing in reality to make that happen. She spent a lot of time pushing thoughts of Josh from her head. Pushing away fear and frustration and an animal instinct to run whenever she woke up from sleep.

And then there was Mal.

Her heart was a wounded thing in her chest when it came to him. Every time she laid eyes on him or heard him moving in another room, she swore it whimpered. He'd been so sweet and earnest to her, but everything he did was out of friendship. And a sense of responsibility, probably. It wasn't his fault that Josh had tracked her down and tortured her, but he acted like he was holding the blame for it deep inside—despite the fact he'd emphasized to her that Josh did what he did because he was fucked up inside.

She didn't know how to tell him it wasn't his fault that Josh had kidnapped her other than to just say it, which she had. He said he knew that, but she wasn't sure she believed him. Especially when he looked at her with worry in his eyes.

Well, no more.

Today, she was going to insist she move back to her apartment even if the thought of being alone scared her in some ways. But she had to go sometime and there was no longer any reason not to. She was getting around with very little pain, her wounds were healing, and the smaller ones had closed up and scabbed over. She'd been told not to pick at the scabs so they didn't scar, and though her skin sometimes itched where it was healing, she did not pick.

She shuddered as she stepped into the shower. It was horrific what Josh had done to her. She had nightmares about it sometimes, and there were nights when she woke up to find Mal knocking on her door because she'd been screaming. If she hadn't locked the door, maybe he would've entered. But she didn't want that. She didn't want his pity. She had to learn how to be alone again, because alone was her default setting in this world.

She washed carefully, her gaze lingering over the word MAL on her belly. She didn't know Josh's exact plan, but she knew he'd had some idea of blaming Mal for her torture and death—and then killing Mal too. If Mal knew what the plan was, he hadn't told her. Maybe she should ask, but she just hadn't had the guts yet.

There were other cuts on her arms and torso, her breasts. Josh had carved symbols, suns and moons and stars. Shallow cuts, the doctor had told her. Not enough to permanently scar, but the pain and blood had been frightening when it was happening. Now she was a patchwork of scabs and scratches. It almost looked like she'd gone ten rounds with an angry cat.

Her back was a different story. That wound had gone deep, but it was held together now with tiny staples and tape. It still stung sometimes, but it wasn't a source of constant pain anymore. Her wrists were ringed in healing scabs where the cuffs had cut into her, but those would fade with time as well.

If only her memories would fade as easily.

Scarlett got out of the shower and dressed in a loose maxi-dress for comfort. It was pale turquoise, with white and dark blue flowers on it. She slipped on a white long-sleeved shirt and tied it at the waist so her arms would be covered, then took a good look in the mirror. Her roots were red as the color began to come back. Maybe she should get some red hair color and go all in. Mal had said he wanted to see her as a redhead.

"It's not about what Mal wants," she grumbled to herself. "It's about what *you* want."

Except she didn't know what she wanted.

With a growl of frustration, she left the room and went downstairs to find Mal in the kitchen fixing breakfast. Pancakes this time. Her stomach growled.

"Hey, Scarlett," he said as he threw her a look over his shoulder. "You want some pancakes?"

"That would be great. Thanks." She went to pour herself some coffee, then resolutely turned and went to sit at the table. She didn't want to stand near Mal and feel his heat or smell the subtle scent of his soap even though she was using his shower upstairs and smelled it all the time. There was something different when it was on his body, though.

"Here you go," he said, plopping a plate piled high in front of her.

Scarlett started pouring syrup, forcing back the silly tears that wanted to come. She liked this little bit of domesticity with him, but it wasn't real. The only way to get over it was to cut herself off. Like ripping off a bandage, *har-de-har*.

"I think I should return to the apartment today," she said. "It's time I let you get back to living your own life."

Mal returned to the table with his own stack of pancakes. He sat down and reached for the syrup. "Okay. If that's what you want."

She wanted to scream that it wasn't what she wanted at all, but that would be a very bad idea. Sure, let Mal know that she'd gone and fallen for him when he was hung up on Haylee. Just what she wanted was to be pitied for yet another reason.

Poor thing, tortured by her ex and in love with a man she can't have because he doesn't want her.

Scarlett stabbed her pancakes viciously. "I think it's best, don't you?"

"If that's what you think."

Scarlett dropped the fork and dragged in a breath so she wouldn't explode.

"What's wrong, Scarlett?" he asked, eyeing her cautiously. As if he sensed the imminent meltdown.

"You!" she said. "You don't do anything but agree with me. If I say it's raining, you'd agree even if the sun was shining. You don't say anything contrary to what I've said, you don't argue with me, and you never call me Scar anymore."

Oh geez.

He blinked. "I didn't think you'd like that name."

She folded her arms and turned her head to look out the window. She was acting insane, but she couldn't seem to stop. "It's a nickname, Mal."

"Yeah, but…."

She swung around to glare at him. "You didn't want to remind me of what Josh did to me? Or the fact I'll likely have some scarring on my back and wrists?"

He nodded helplessly, and she wanted to get up

and throw her arms around his neck and ask for his forgiveness. She also wanted to shake him.

Instead, she swallowed. "I'm not likely to forget what he did, with or without the nickname."

He reached out and took her hand in his. Her body wanted to melt. Her brain refused to let it.

"I'm sorry. I'm trying not to upset you. That's all it is. If you want me to call you Scar, then I will."

She tipped her head back and looked at the ceiling. It was blurry, and she was a nut. "I just want you to talk to me like you did before. Stop treating me like I'm made of glass."

"I know you aren't made of glass. You're the strongest person I know."

She couldn't help but look at him, their gazes colliding in a tangle of heat and emotion. At least for her. "I don't know about that, but thank you."

He squeezed her hand. "You are. I know you aren't magically over what happened, but you fight against letting it run your life. I admire that. And it does make you strong, no matter what you think."

"Even when I have nightmares that bring you to my door?"

"Even then."

The sound of a large truck crunching its way into Mal's driveway broke into their conversation. "Expecting an elephant?" she asked, trying to dispel the swirl of hot emotion in the room.

He grinned. "It's my new bed. Wait until you see."

He got up and went to let the movers in. Scarlett

wandered into the front room to watch as they brought the furniture inside. First they brought the king-sized mattress in. Next was the bed and frame. Her heart started to pound as she looked at the bright American hickory wood as it went up the stairs.

Twenty minutes later, the movers were walking out the door and Mal shut it behind them. He turned to her, looking like an eager kid about to get a puppy or something. "Want to see?"

"Um, sure."

She'd known that he'd been sleeping on an air mattress in his room for the past several nights, after moving there from the couch. She'd wanted to tell him he could climb in with her, but she'd figured it wasn't a good idea if she ever had any hope of moving on with her life.

She went up the stairs behind him and followed him into the master bedroom. He stepped aside to let her look. Scarlett blinked. Her heart throbbed harder. It was the same bed she'd shown him on Pinterest when she'd been telling him how to make his room into more of a retreat and less of a sterile place to sleep. He'd teased her about decorating his room, but he'd kept asking questions. Apparently he'd been paying attention.

"Do you like it?"

It hurt to see that bed. To know it wasn't for her. Silly to feel that way, maybe, but she couldn't help it.

She wrapped her arms around her body.

Protecting herself. "It's beautiful, Mal. It looks great in here."

He frowned. Then he swore before gripping her shoulders and lowering his head to look into her eyes. "I thought you'd be happier about it."

"Why would I be happy?" she whispered, her soul hurting. "It's not for me. It's for you."

"I don't know how to do this anymore," he said, his voice sounding strangled. "I want to go back to the way we were before. I want you to be happy again."

"We can't go back, Mal. We never *had* anything. It was sex. You made it very clear that's all it was. But I don't want to do that anymore. I don't want to have sex with you while you love someone else. I want more than that. I *deserve* more than that."

Her eyes were blurry and she was busy cursing herself for it when Mal tugged her gently against him. She didn't resist, damn her weak heart. She curled her fingers into his T-shirt and closed her eyes, breathing deep so she could remember what he smelled like when he held her close.

He stroked her hair. "You do deserve more," he said, his chest rumbling beneath her ear.

"Why?" she cried out, undone by his soothing tone when what she would have preferred was for him to push her away and tell her she needed to snap out of it. "Why would you do that? Why would you get *that* bed?"

"Aw, hell, Scar. Because I want you to be happy, that's why. Because I want you to stay here with me."

He gently pushed her away and tipped her chin up with his fingers when she wouldn't look at him. Tears fell freely down her cheeks and she bit the inside of her cheek angrily, trying to make them stop.

"I'm not in love with Haylee," he said. "I'm in love with you."

Scarlett blinked. Then she blinked some more. "Wait… what? Did you just say…?"

She couldn't speak. Was she hearing what she wanted to hear? Dreaming again? If she was dreaming, at least this one was more pleasant than the others.

"You heard me, Scar. I love *you*. I didn't want to dump that on you right now with everything else, but I think maybe I made a mistake by keeping it to myself. Maybe you needed to hear it, even if you don't feel the same. You're worthy of more than being a fuck buddy, and you're damn sure worthy of more than the kind of twisted pretense at love that Josh showed you. And maybe you're thinking this is all too fast, and how the hell can I know it's love when I thought I loved someone else for the past few months, but I know it's love because I don't *feel* right without you. I don't just want you physically, though believe me I want that and it's been killing me not being with you, but I'd be happy just sleeping beside you again. Holding you. Waking up beside you in the morning, and going to bed with you at night. I love fishing with you. Hell, I love thrifting with you. I love how you snap and sparkle when challenged, and how bright your personality shines. You just—hell, you just blow me away. I don't want anyone else. I want you."

———

MAL'S HEART hammered so hard he thought it might beat right out of his chest. He'd just put everything on the line, and it was very possible he was about to get hurt. Scarlett stared up at him, blinking rapidly, her jaw hanging open.

"Say something," he whispered, his entire being on edge. Had he gone too far? Blown his chance? She'd said she deserved more, but what if she didn't mean love? What if she meant something different, like maybe she deserved a man who'd never been stupid enough to suggest a friends with benefits arrangement to her in the first place?

Of course she meant love!

What else was there?

"I-I-I…"

He waited for her to speak, but Scarlett burst into tears. She put her forehead against his shirt and held on, crying for all she was worth. He felt utterly helpless.

Mal teared up too, but he didn't cry. He just stroked her hair, held her gently, and took encouragement from the fact she wasn't running away. No, she was clinging to him. Clinging and crying like her heart was broken.

"Baby," he said softly, kissing the top of her head.

Aching with love for her. Wanting to fix this but not knowing how.

This was what his teammates had been telling him. The ones who were in love, anyway. This feeling you'd move mountains for her if she asked. This bone-deep desire to make everything better for her. When she hurt, you hurt with her. It was agony, and it was also the best thing he'd ever felt in his life.

She clutched his shirt. "I'm sorry. Sorry." She sniffed and lifted her head. Her eyes were shining. "I just—" She pulled in a breath and let it out again. "I never thought you'd say those words. To me. Are you sure, by the way? This isn't some guilt-trippy thing, right?"

He blinked. And then he realized what she was doing. Sweet, sassy Scarlett was having a hard time believing he was in love with her. She was looking for reasons he'd made a mistake, giving him a way out, and waiting for him to take it. Waiting for him to tell her he'd gotten carried away with the whole love thing and maybe it was just lust after all.

He knew why. Scarlett had been alone for so long that she didn't trust that someone could love her for herself. She'd risked her heart when she'd let Josh into her life, at least in the beginning when it was still new, and that hadn't turned out well at all. He hadn't loved her. He'd wanted to control her, and he'd worked hard to cut her off from everyone in her life.

She'd let someone in, and that jerk had been a douchebag. She didn't believe she was worthy of love.

And maybe she didn't love Mal in return, because she hadn't said so, but she *was* worthy of love. And he intended for her to know it.

Mal put his hands on her cheeks, cradled her face, and stared into her eyes. "I'm sure. From the first moment I met you, I knew you were special. Different than anyone I knew. You were the only person in that whole place who gave as good as you got. The others ignored me when I was a jerk, but not you. You threw it back at me, and rightfully so. I was fascinated with you, Scar. Yeah, I still thought I loved Haylee, but you were right about that, too. It was a single moment I built into more than it should have been, for reasons I'm not quite sure of, though I think envy was a big one. I envied Wolf—and Saint and Hacker, too. They're happy. I wasn't. But I am now—or I will be when you tell me you'll stay. You can still live over the garage if you want. I wouldn't push you to move in with me or anything. But please just stay close to me. You can sleep here sometimes, I'll sleep there, whatever. I don't care so long as we're together. I love you. I want to be with you. But if you don't want the same thing, I won't push. I promise."

Her smile wavered at the corners. "Silly man." She stood on tiptoe and pressed a soft kiss to his lips. "I want to be with you, too. I love you, Mal."

It was his turn to blink. "You do?"

She wrapped her arms around his neck suddenly and laughed. "Of course I do. Why did you think I was so bent out of shape about the bed? I couldn't bear the thought of you sleeping in it with someone else, once you were done with me. I picked it out—and I was right, by the way—and you were going to share it with someone else."

"Never," he growled.

Mal swept her up as she squeaked, then carried her over and laid her down on the mattress before settling in next to her. He wanted to make love to her, of course he did, but more than that he just wanted to be with her. He lay on his back, looping an arm around her as she cuddled into his side, her leg thrown over his.

"I only want to share this bed with you, Scar," he said softly as he stared up at the ceiling, happiness suffusing him with warmth. "And maybe our kids, if we decide to have any. Though they can only stay if they're having a nightmare or something. Otherwise I need you and your beaver to myself."

Scarlett giggled. "You're a goofball."

He pressed a kiss to her forehead. Her laughter lit him up inside. "Yeah, but you like goofballs."

"I do," she sighed. "I really do."

Epilogue

THREE MONTHS LATER...

SCARLETT WALKED into Buddy's still wearing her scrubs. She was late, but she'd had a last minute patient she'd taken on for another therapist who'd had a family emergency. She stopped just inside the door and let her eyes adjust as she scanned the tables, looking for her crew.

And there they were. Mal, Wolf, Saint, Hacker, Harley, Muffin, Easy, Gem, and Zany. She'd finally figured out the code names that went with each guy, and that's how she thought of them now. Bliss, Eva, Brooke, and Haylee—who'd just announced to them all last week that she was pregnant—were at a smaller high-top table. Bliss saw her first and waved.

Scarlett made her way over, slipping between

tables. A man at one of the tables nodded at her as she passed.

"Hey, Russ," she said. "How's work?"

"It's going. How about you?"

"Same."

"Liking the red hair," he told her. "Did I ever tell you that you've got a twin in Florida?"

Scarlett laughed at the joke they shared every time they met. "I've heard that before. Such a lame pickup line. You have to work on your game."

Russ snorted. "So you keep telling me. Take it easy, Scarlett."

"Thanks. You too."

The first time she'd met Russ, she'd been scared because he'd recognized her. Russ had been in Josh's unit, and he'd known him, but they hadn't been friends. After Josh's arrest for Jessica Saunders' murder, she'd seen Russ again at Buddy's. She'd dyed her hair red at that point so her natural color could return. He'd come over to talk to her, and she'd gotten the whole story. He'd known her from seeing her with Josh, and from his time in rehab at the orthopedic center where she worked. She hadn't been his therapist, but he'd seen her repeatedly while coming in for therapy. That's why he'd thought he recognized her that night.

He'd told her he was glad she'd gotten away from Josh. It'd taken her a second to realize he meant romantically since he couldn't know that Josh had held her prisoner and assaulted her. He'd told her that he'd always thought there was something off about Josh. Turned out he was right since not only had Josh been arrested for Dr. Saunders' murder, but the police were tying him to unsolved murders in two other states. And three other women had come forward with tales about abuse and stalking. The Air Force was involved, and the chain of command had some explaining to do about why they hadn't taken previous allegations seriously.

Scarlett had submitted written testimony about her ordeal, and she would testify in person when the time came. She wasn't afraid of Josh anymore, and she wanted him to pay for what he'd done. Florida, where he'd be tried for killing Jessica, had the death penalty. It was entirely possible that's what he'd get. Still, she didn't spend time thinking about it. Josh wasn't ever getting out of prison, regardless. His threat to her life—and to other women's lives in the future—was over.

Mal stood up when he saw her. He met her halfway and wrapped her in a hug. Then he kissed her like he was starved for her. She kissed him back, not caring what anyone thought. She loved this man. So much.

"Get a room," Easy called out.

Mal's arms tightened around her, but he broke the kiss and put his forehead against hers. "I missed you, Scar."

"I missed you too. But it's only been about ten hours since you saw me last."

"Precisely. I don't know what the hell I'm going to do when we go on a mission."

Scarlett's heart thumped at the idea of Mal being gone for weeks at a time, but she knew it was going to happen. Sooner rather than later since he'd been cleared to return to full duty. Brooke, Eva, Haylee, and Bliss had shared their strategies with her for getting through it. They spent a lot of time together, for one thing. They had sleepovers sometimes where they watched chick flicks and cooked or gossiped or whatever. They talked about hard things too, like their fears for their men, and they talked about fun things like weddings and future plans.

"We'll get through it," Scarlett said. "Besides, you wanted to be with your team again."

"I know," he grumbled. "That was before I had you."

He'd told her not too long ago that he'd thought HOT was his life—she'd learned all about the secretive Hostile Operations Team and what they stood for once she and Mal were together—but then he fell in love with her and realized that his life was so much more than HOT. He wasn't defined by his job any more than she was—though she'd also decided to return to school and get her certification to become a physical therapist instead of an assistant.

Mal was one-hundred percent behind her. She'd started looking at programs, but hadn't applied yet. She would, when there was time. Right now she was busy enjoying building a home with Mal. Thrifting, shopping, adding decor. Though they still hadn't hung those pictures she'd bought for the apartment.

Not that she was living there anymore. They'd decided to renovate it and rent, but they were still working on it. And she was trying to decide whether to hang the pictures there or put them in the farmhouse. She'd just about decided to put them in their bedroom, but she was wondering how Mal was going to take having a bunch of flower pictures in there. She'd already added a duvet with ruffles. He hadn't blinked, but there was always a line between cosy and too feminine.

Mal took her hand and led her the rest of the way to the table. She had a sip of his soda, stole a french fry, and then ordered her own club sandwich and fries before eventually joining the women at their table. They talked about life and work for an hour or so—until Haylee frowned.

"What is wrong with Mal?"

Scarlett shot him a look, her heart leaping into her throat—and then she laughed. Mal was making a duck face at her. She made one back, giggling, before turning back to the women.

"Sorry, that's his idea of a signal that he wants to go home."

Haylee snorted. "That idiot."

"He suggested it the first night I joined you guys here. Only he wanted me to do it if I wanted to leave. Needless to say, I told him there was no way in hell. But he's determined."

The women were laughing. "God, what a goof," Bliss said. "Sky would do something like that, I guarantee it. He's going to be sorry he didn't think of it."

Scarlett shouldered her purse and stood. "Sorry, but I think I'd better go. God only knows what he'll do next."

"I'd almost pay to see it," Haylee said. "Better take him home, Scarlett, before he embarrasses himself."

Scarlett laughed. She liked being Scarlett rather than Erin. Scarlett was strong, and Scarlett was loved by a goofy, strong protector, and by her new friends. "I think you're right."

She met Mal by the door and they walked out into the warm night air and over to her car. He pinched her ass as he held her door open for her. "Drive safe, baby," he said. "I'll be right behind you."

"I know." She reached for his package, just because, and caressed it.

He growled. "Dammit, Scar, that's not fair."

She liked the way he instantly grew hard beneath her hand. "Think of me on the way home. Because I want to suck this beautiful cock as soon as we're inside."

"Not happening, honey. I'm plowing you on the kitchen table as soon as we're in the door."

"Table's kinda hard," she said, her insides turning to liquid heat at the thought.

"Fine, then we'll do it on the couch."

"Oh, I didn't say no to the table. Just thinking how

it's going to work. Like, do you plan on bending me over it? Or should I lay on top and spread my legs?"

Mal pushed her against the side of the car and ravaged her mouth with a hot kiss. "Maybe we should drag those scrubs off and do it right here," he whispered in her ear. "Me, deep inside you. You, making those noises you make. Damn, that's hot."

"Better idea," she said, her body zipping with sparks. "Let's go home and do exactly that in the driveway."

He arched an eyebrow. "That could work. Nobody to see us there. And nobody to hear you when I make you come."

"Then let me go and let's get out of here."

He kissed her again, then stepped back and waited for her to get inside her car. "See you at home, Scar. I love you."

"I love you, too."

Mal pushed her door closed and waited for her to back out of her spot before he got into his truck and followed her home. And then he did everything he said he was going to do, until she was sated and drowsy. She fell asleep in their bed later that night with his arms around her and his breath in her ear.

"Beautiful girl," he whispered right before she dropped off. "I'll love you for the rest of our lives, and I'll protect you with my last breath."

She knew he would. They'd weathered the storm. They always would.

Together.

Bonus Epilogue

"Mal, I can't see a darned thing," Scarlett grumbled after he slipped the silk scarf over her eyes.

"I know, honey. Just hold onto me."

Scarlett hooked her arm into his, holding on tight. "No choice. Not that I mind, but it'd be easier if I could see."

"Patience, babe."

He led her slowly across the yard and into the woods. It was autumn and the leaves had started to fall. The crunch under her feet must have told her they'd entered the woods, but she didn't say anything. If she knew where they were going, she didn't let on.

Finally, they stopped. "Don't take it off yet."

"Okay."

"I have to do something. Don't move."

"Where would I go? I can't see."

He kissed her lips real quick. "That's my girl."

Mal walked over and pulled the double doors with

glass panes open, then lit the candles he'd placed inside. He hadn't wanted to leave any lit while he went to retrieve Scarlett, just in case. It wouldn't do to catch the woods on fire. Or to burn down the She-Shed when he'd been working so hard on it.

Joshua Wright had invaded the space once, leaving behind his soda can and potato chip bag when he'd been spying on Scarlett, but Mal had worked to change everything so it would never remind her of Josh again. Josh, who'd been sentenced to life in prison with no chance of parole. He hadn't gotten the death penalty because he'd cooperated with the police in other cases he was involved in. Evil bastard.

Mal finished lighting the candles and then returned to Scarlett's side. "Ready, gorgeous?" he whispered.

"Yes."

"Close your eyes."

"Mal, I'm already wearing a scarf. Is that necessary too?"

"Okay, fine. Then take the scarf off and tell me what you think."

Scarlett shoved the scarf up—and gasped. Her eyes widened as she walked toward the open She-Shed, handing him the scarf as she went. "You put double doors up. And built a patio. And there's electricity. How did you do that?"

He grinned. "I ran a cord. A very long cord. It's just a string of hanging lights."

But they looked perfect hanging inside the shed

and on the front patio where he'd put a table and chairs. Yes, he'd built a patio so they could sit outside and eat a meal. Like now.

He picked up the picnic basket he'd stashed earlier and set it on the table so he could take out the things he'd prepared. Scarlett was looking at everything around her with a stunned expression.

"I had no idea this is what you'd been doing when you asked me not to come out here."

"I wanted to surprise you."

"I'm surprised." She stepped inside, her jaw hanging open at the sight of the iron bed where they'd first made love. He'd painted the iron headboard, changed the mattress to something more comfortable, and added the frilly, girly linens she liked. Each time they'd gone to the thrift stores together, he'd found something. He'd had to buy it on the down low, then return and pick it up when Scarlett was at work, but he'd collected several things that he knew were her style and tried—God, how he'd tried—to create a room she would love out here in the woods.

"Do you like it?" He felt like a shy little boy asking for her approval.

Her eyes glittered as she turned to him. "It's amazing. You even hung pictures. Flowers, I see."

He shrugged. "Well, you do have a fondness for them."

She caressed the linens, studied the side table with the books and vase of flowers, the desk, the candles everywhere, and then hugged herself. "It's so pretty."

"I thought we'd have dinner on the patio, then maybe some dancing."

"Dancing?" She arched an eyebrow.

He tapped his phone and something slow and sensual started on the Bluetooth speaker he'd set on a side table. "You doubted my Derek Hough moves. Imma show you later."

Scarlett snorted. "Okay, whatever you say, twinkle toes."

"Just you wait. I'm gonna dip your ass to the floor. Then I'm gonna twirl you like a top."

Scarlett lost it then, giggling happily while Mal pulled out the wine and cheese, the chicken salad and crackers, and the chocolate cake. Which Scarlett had made because he'd been teaching her how to follow recipes and make meals. It turned out that she enjoyed cooking and baking. His mother had taught her how to make Texas chili the last time they'd visited Galveston, and she'd dutifully written down every step. She'd made it once since they got home, and it'd been almost as good as Mom's. Not that he'd tell her she needed more jalapeños. She'd get there on her own.

"Sit down, princess," he said. "Let me serve you."

"Oooh, I can do that."

He poured her a glass of wine, fixed her a plate, and set them both in front of her. Then he fixed his own. Scarlett ate slowly, mostly because she was so busy asking about everything he'd done, what gave him the idea, why he didn't let her help him, and a million other things.

Finally, it was time to dance. He stood and held out a hand. She took it and he swept her into his arms, twirling her across the patio to an instrumental version of a popular boy band song. As they swayed beneath the stars and the twinkling lights, Mal knew without a doubt that what he was about to do was the right thing. He reached into his pocket and took out the ring he'd placed there earlier—and had checked about a million times to make sure it was still there—then twirled Scarlett over to her chair and dropped to his knee.

"Scarlett Rose, I love you with the fire of a thousand suns."

She gasped.

"And I'd really, really love for you to be my wife. When I asked you to stay, you stayed. Now I want you to marry me and stay forever. You're in my life, my heart, my soul. I need you."

Mal felt himself coloring, mostly because his mouth had gotten away from him and muddled his romantic proposal with too many words. Maybe he'd been a little too influenced by Cade and Brooke's wedding a couple of months ago—but Scarlett's eyes were shining, and she was smiling.

"Yes, I want to marry you and stay with you forever."

"Oh thank God."

He slipped the ring on her finger and kissed her. She held up her hand and studied it.

"Is this the ring I liked in the antique store?"

"The very one."

"You spent too much," she said on a choked breath.

"No, I didn't. You loved it, and I love you."

"I wasn't hinting about getting engaged that day."

"I know. But I'm glad you were looking in that case. I mean if I'd been left to my own devices, God knows what I'd have picked out. I kinda liked that big yellow one, you know."

She laughed. "You mean the bumble bee ring."

It had been a bee. The body had been a big yellow stone. The wings and head were silver, with little jewels for eyes. It'd been gaudy as hell, truth be told. But he liked teasing her.

"Yeah, what was wrong with that one? But no, you had to like some dumb diamond ring."

Scarlett threw her head back and laughed. Then she flung her arms around his neck and kissed him. "I love you, goofball. Only and always you."

He pulled her to her feet and into his arms so they could sway to the music some more before he took her inside and made love to her on the frilly, feminine bed.

"Lucky, lucky me."

Book 4: HOT PACKAGE - Billy & Olivia

Book 5: HOT SHOT - Jack & Gina

Book 6: HOT REBEL - Nick & Victoria

Book 7: HOT ICE - Garrett & Grace

Book 8: HOT & BOTHERED - Ryan & Emily

Book 9: HOT PROTECTOR - Chase & Sophie

Book 10: HOT ADDICTION - Dex & Annabelle

Book 11: HOT VALOR - Mendez & Kat

Book 12: A HOT CHRISTMAS MIRACLE - Mendez & Kat

———

The HOT SEAL Team Books

Book 1: HOT SEAL - Dane & Ivy

Book 2: HOT SEAL Lover - Remy & Christina

Book 3: HOT SEAL Rescue - Cody & Miranda

Book 4: HOT SEAL BRIDE - Cash & Ella

Book 5: HOT SEAL REDEMPTION - Alex & Bailey

Book 6: HOT SEAL TARGET - Blade & Quinn

Book 7: HOT SEAL HERO - Ryan & Chloe

Book 8: HOT SEAL DEVOTION - Zach & Kayla

————

HOT Heroes for Hire: Mercenaries
Black's Bandits

Book 1: BLACK LIST - Jace & Maddy

Book 2: BLACK TIE - Brett & Tallie

Book 3: BLACK OUT - Colt & Angie

Book 4: BLACK KNIGHT - Jared & Libby

Book 5: BLACK HEART - Ian Black!

————

The HOT Novella in Liliana Hart's MacKenzie
Family Series

HOT WITNESS - Jake & Eva

———

7 Brides for 7 Brothers

MAX (Book 5) - Max & Ellie

7 Brides for 7 Soldiers

WYATT (Book 4) - Max & Ellie

7 Brides for 7 Blackthornes

ROSS (Book 3) - Ross & Holly

Filthy Rich Billionaires

Book 1: FILTHY RICH REVENGE

Book 2: FILTHY RICH PRINCE

———

Who's HOT?

Strike Team 1

Matt "Richie Rich" Girard (Book 0 & 1)
Sam "Knight Rider" McKnight (Book 2)
Kev "Big Mac" MacDonald (Book 3)
Billy "the Kid" Blake (Book 4)
Jack "Hawk" Hunter (Book 5)
Nick "Brandy" Brandon (Book 6)
Garrett "Iceman" Spencer (Book 7)
Ryan "Flash" Gordon (Book 8)
Chase "Fiddler" Daniels (Book 9)
Dex "Double Dee" Davidson (Book 10)

Commander
John "Viper" Mendez (Book 11 & 12)

Deputy Commander
Alex "Ghost" Bishop

Strike Team 2

Cade "Saint" Rodgers (Book 1)
Sky "Hacker" Kelley (Book 2)
Dean "Wolf" Garner (Book 3)
Malcom "Mal" McCoy (Book 4)
Noah "Easy" Cross (Book 5)
Ryder "Muffin" Hanson
Jax "Gem" Stone
Zane "Zany" Scott
Jake "Harley" Ryan (HOT WITNESS)

SEAL Team 1

Dane "Viking" Erikson (Book 1)
Remy "Cage" Marchand (Book 2)
Cody "Cowboy" McCormick (Book 3)
Cash "Money" McQuaid (Book 4)
Alexei "Camel" Kamarov (Book 5)
Adam "Blade" Garrison (Book 6)
Ryan "Dirty Harry" Callahan (Book 7)
Zach "Neo" Anderson (Book 8)
Corey "Shade" Vance

Black's Bandits

Jace Kaiser (Book 1)
Brett Wheeler (Book 2)
Colton Duchaine (Book 3)
Jared Fraser (Book 4)

Ian Black (Book 5)
Tyler Scott
Thomas "Rascal" Bradley
Dax Freed
Jamie Hayes
Mandy Parker (Airborne Ops)
Melanie (Reception)
? Unnamed Team Members

Freelance Contractors

Lucinda "Lucky" San Ramos, now MacDonald (Book 3)
Victoria "Vee" Royal, now Brandon (Book 6)
Emily Royal, now Gordon (Book 8)
Miranda Lockwood, now McCormick (SEAL Team Book 3)
Bliss Bennett, (Strike Team 2, Book 2)
Angelica "Angie" Turner (Black's Bandits, Book 3)

About the Author

Lynn Raye Harris is a Southern girl, military wife, wannabe cat lady, and horse lover. She's also the New York Times and USA Today bestselling author of the HOSTILE OPERATIONS TEAM ® SERIES of military romances, and 20 books about sexy billionaires for Harlequin.

A former finalist for the Romance Writers of America's Golden Heart Award and the National Readers Choice Award, Lynn lives in Alabama with her handsome former-military husband, one fluffy princess of a cat, and a very spoiled American Saddlebred horse who enjoys bucking at random in order to keep Lynn on her toes.

Lynn's books have been called "exceptional and emotional," "intense," and "sizzling" -- and have sold in excess of 4.5 million copies worldwide.

To connect with Lynn online:
www.LynnRayeHarris.com
Lynn@LynnRayeHarris.com